When the

Sky

Burned

A DAY TO REMEMBER

When the Sky Burned

LIZ TOLSMA

BARBOUR
PUBLISHING

When the Sky Burned ©2025 by Liz Tolsma

Print ISBN 979-8-89151-052-4
Adobe Digital Edition (.epub) 979-8-89151-053-1

This book is a work of fiction. Names, characters, places, and incidents are either products of the author's imagination or used fictitiously. Any similarity to actual people, organizations, and/or events is purely coincidental.

Published by Barbour Publishing, Inc., 1810 Barbour Drive, Uhrichsville, Ohio 44683, www.barbourbooks.com

Our mission is to inspire the world with the life-changing message of the Bible.

Printed in the United States of America.

DEDICATION

*To the memories of the unknown dead consumed
by the fire in Peshtigo on October 8, 1871.
The world may not know you, but God does.*

The half has not been told; the whole will never be known.
*Unknown newspaper reporter visiting
Peshtigo in the fire's aftermath*

*To you, O L*ORD*, I call.*
For fire has devoured
the pastures of the wilderness,
and flame has burned
all the trees of the field.
Even the beasts of the field pant for you
because the water brooks are dried up,
and fire has devoured
the pastures of the wilderness.

JOEL 1:19-20 ESV

Chapter One

PESHTIGO, WISCONSIN
TUESDAY, SEPTEMBER 12, 1871

On the easel in front of Mariah Randolph sat a blank canvas, as white and pristine as a snowy morning. Untouched. No beauty. No ugliness.

Just plain.

Her paints and brushes, the tools of her trade, sat in a wooden box beside her, but she had yet to pick them up and employ them. They were precious and difficult to secure in this off-the-beaten-track lumbering town tucked in the northeast corner of Wisconsin. Only when Papa made a trip to Milwaukee or Chicago could she replenish her stock.

So she had to take the time to imprint the scene unfolding in front of her on her mind, commit every shape and color to her memory before she dared dip the brush and commence creating. There was no room for error, no throwing out the canvas and beginning from scratch.

But this sky, she would never forget. In mere minutes, it had been seared onto her brain.

For a better view, she sat on the third-floor balcony Papa had built for her on the house they occupied on the edge of town, near the piney woods that ringed Peshtigo. What a sight she had today.

The sky in every direction was awash in shades of orange and scarlet and yellow, a dramatic backdrop for the red and jack pines in their varying shades of green. The smoke that had shrouded the sun, at times enough to call for lighting lamps in the middle of the day, had been blown westward by a stronger wind. Now it would be the Sugar Bush area and the farmers who labored to clear the land there suffering from the choking smoke.

She squeezed a few small dollops of color onto her pallet, touched her brush to them, and applied them to the canvas. Every now and then, she peered over the top of it to revive her memory of the view, but for the most part, she kept her focus on the work in front of her.

When Papa had brought back a book from Chicago on a new way of painting called *en plein air*, or outdoors, it spoke to Mariah. Much to Mama's consternation, she had spent a great deal of her childhood up a tree, observing the world from above, the blur of colors passing by on the streets of Green Bay.

Here in Peshtigo, where they had moved a few years ago, the lure of the outdoors increased, and en plein air allowed her to escape the stuffy confines of a studio with its headache-inducing paint and turpentine odors.

The noon whistle sounding from the woodenware factory startled her. Thankfully, she was wiping a brush at the time and didn't mar her piece. She stood and stretched. Time always flew when she was working. If Mama or Papa or the factory whistle didn't interrupt her, she could paint for hours on end without any effort.

Her rumbling stomach reminded her that she had such a strong drive to paint this morning she had skipped breakfast in favor of coffee. Overriding the smoky odor clinging to hair, clothing, and furniture, was the fragrance of chicken soup. Mama must have lunch just about ready.

Mariah set her brushes to the side. No need to clean up. She would hurry through the meal as much as Mama allowed and then return to continue working. If possible, the sky was redder than earlier in the day, the scene more spectacular than before. More breathtaking than the smoky haze that was blowing their way again.

She turned to go inside just as the balcony door opened, and her fiancé, Hollis Stanford, filled the entrance, his shoulders broad, his waist narrow.

"Oh, darling, I didn't know you were coming north." She swept toward him, and he planted a far-too-chaste kiss on her cheek.

"I wanted to surprise my favorite girl." He pulled out a bouquet of stunning pale pink hothouse roses, the tips of the petals white.

She took them and inhaled, the perfume of them almost heady. "You must have tiptoed in, because I didn't even hear you."

"Likely too engrossed in your work. Is that it there?" He pointed to the canvas.

She stepped in front of it. "It's not finished yet."

"No, but it's beautiful. Masterful, as always. Let me take a better look. Please?"

The way he had of gazing at her, his blue eyes intense, had him always getting his way. She moved to the side, and he inspected it more closely.

"Wonderful. You have captured the movement of the trees so well. And the colors are vibrant and true to life. Well done, my dear, as always. Soon you shall have that show in Chicago, as I promised."

Despite their earlier formality, she hugged him with all her might. "Thank you. You're so good to me, and what have I done for you?"

"Ah, you're my precious jewel, the beautiful woman always at my side. Someone I can be proud of."

She smoothed her hair. "What a dear you are."

"I believe your mother has luncheon ready. Shall we go in?"

The way he said it, as if they were about to partake of the finest meal in the grandest home in Chicago, teased a smile from her. This was, after all, only a small backwater town in the Wisconsin woods. The railroad connecting them to the rest of the world hadn't quite made it here, though there was a short line connecting the mouth of the Peshtigo River on Green Bay with the sawmill and the woodenware factory in town.

Always the gentleman, he allowed her down the stairs first, and she entered the dining room just as Mama was setting the soup tureen on the table covered with a pristine white cloth.

"Did you know Hollis was arriving today?" Mariah handed Mama the ladle.

"It was as much of a surprise to me as it was to you." Mama's words were tight, the disapproval in her tone crystal clear.

Why didn't Mama like Hollis? He was an upstanding man, and his father owned a railroad. Not only was Hollis wealthy, he was also doing a commendable job of raising his young daughter after his wife passed away two years ago.

He held out the dining room chair for her and, once she was seated, pushed her in. With Papa in Marinette for the day on business, it was just the three of them for the meal. Hollis spoke about his work on the railroad, how his father was handing over more and more control of the company to him, and the progress he was making on building their Chicago house.

"I only wish I could see it." She dipped her spoon into the herby soup. "Shouldn't a woman have some input into what her home will look like? I have so many decorating ideas."

"No need to worry yourself about that. I've hired the best interior designer in the city, and I guarantee you will love it. For you, nothing is too good. And I love surprising you."

That he did. She sighed and bit off a piece of yeasty buttered bread as he continued his soliloquy on the virtues of city life over town life.

"But we will spend time in Peshtigo as well, won't we?"

"Of course, darling, though I assure you that you will be quite busy with your artwork and charity gatherings and running the household."

Mama dabbed the corners of her mouth with her napkin. "We'll miss you and hope you will spend as much time as possible here."

"I wouldn't have it any other way." Mariah waved her spoon in small circles to cool the soup.

When the meal was finally over, Mariah helped Mama clear the dishes and went to get water to wash them.

"No, you go ahead and spend time with Hollis." Mama tied her apron around her waist.

Mariah reached for her own apron. "I'm sure he has work to do at the office."

He sauntered into the kitchen at that precise moment. "Nothing that can't wait. Why don't we take a stroll? There is something I want to show you."

"Another surprise?"

"A wonderful one."

Lady, her little, white powder puff of a dog, yipped at her heels.

"Aw, do you want to go too?" She scooped her up.

"No." The volume of Hollis' voice had Lady shaking.

"You frightened her." He was no fan of the poor little puppy.

"It's just that she can't come where I'm taking you."

Mariah kissed the top of the dog's head and set her on the floor again. "Next time, sweetie." She reached for her plate still sitting on the kitchen counter, swiped a bite of bread she hadn't finished, and fed it to Lady. "Maybe that makes up for it."

Hollis consulted his pocket watch. "It's time to go." He snapped it shut and moved toward the front door.

Mariah hurried to catch up with him. "I hope the wind hasn't picked up. This smoke is getting to be unbearable."

"You should return to Chicago with me. The air is clearer there, and the breezes off the lake are refreshing."

"I couldn't. There are still preparations to be made for the wedding and only until the New Year to complete them."

"I told you to hire someone to take care of that. You shouldn't have to be worried about it."

"I enjoy it."

They continued in the direction of the railroad office, her skirts sweeping the sawdust that covered the sidewalks, dust that was now also mixed with ash. The wind had indeed increased, and the smoke watered her eyes.

She pulled him to a halt. "I apologize, but I need to cover my mouth. It's difficult to breathe right now."

"I'm going to insist that you return to Chicago with me, at least until these fires are out. Our wedding isn't that far off, and you can meet with my staff, who will make sure that every one of your wishes will be met."

"That is sweet, but I will stay here." She covered her mouth with her monogrammed handkerchief, another of Hollis' gifts. "Tell me, how is Angelina getting along?"

"Quite well, from what the nanny tells me. She is bright and intelligent, though sometimes a handful. I truly don't know what I would do without her."

"You have your hands full, helping to run a company and take care of a child. Next time you come this way, bring her along. Since I'll be her stepmother, it would be nice to get to spend time with her. I truly adore her."

"I don't know. That's a long trip for a small child."

"She's not that young. Papa was taking me on the train by himself long before I was six. You have a private car and staff to assist you."

"I will see what I can do."

"Please?"

He huffed. "All right. I can't deny you anything, can I?"

"You are good to me." Though complaining wasn't in her nature, he

11

did refuse to allow her to be involved in the construction or decoration of her own home.

They arrived at the railroad office. Compared to the woodenware factory, it was small, but it was sure to grow in the coming years, especially once the lines reached the town. They were getting so close.

"What is it you have to show me?"

He led her inside. The windows were closed against the smoke, but the weather was warm and the building stuffy. At least she could put away her handkerchief.

He led her down the hall, past several other offices, and upstairs where his space occupied almost the entire floor. After he opened the door, she entered, the plush rug on the floor cushioning her footsteps.

"Oh, do you have new furniture in here?"

"Yes, that's my surprise."

She wound her way around the desk that was polished to a high sheen. The leather-upholstered chair was as soft as a baby's skin, and she sat in it. To the left was a sideboard holding gleaming cut-crystal glasses and decanters filled with amber liquid on a mirrored tray.

"I do feel sorry for you having to be stuck inside so much of the time dealing with paperwork."

"Not at all. And you need to take care when you're in the sun. I don't want my bride showing up at the altar nut-brown."

"I promise to wear a hat or a bonnet."

He came and drew her out of the seat and into his arms. "I can't wait until we are properly married." He bent down and kissed her, moving his hands farther down her back.

Before she could step out of his embrace, a knock came at the door, and someone cleared their throat.

She jumped back, her cheeks even hotter than the fires ringing the town.

Chapter Two

There was a saying about the ground opening up and swallowing a person whole. If only that could truly happen. How could Jay have entered his boss' office after knocking but before an invitation to come in?

The tips of his ears must surely be as red as the sky right now. His schoolmates had always teased him about his unfortunate reaction to embarrassing situations. Their cackles resonated in his head.

"I'm so sorry, Mr. Stanford. I didn't realize you were, um, engaged." What a bumbling fool he was. He turned and fled down the stairs, through the hall, and to the safety of his office.

Relative safety, that was. Once Hollis was finished with his business with Mariah... He couldn't even think without making a mess of his words.

Best to forget about what he witnessed and concentrate on the numbers in front of him. He sat behind his desk, the one that was a fraction of the size of Hollis Stanford's, opened his ledger, and set to work entering the figures from invoices and sales receipts.

The work slowed the pounding of his heart and the racing of his mind, and soon he was lost in the world of adding and subtracting. Using his neatest handwriting so there could be no mistaking the numbers, he labored over each computation to ensure accuracy.

Some time passed before a rustle of skirts drew him from his task.

Being that this was a railroad operations office, not many women stepped inside.

That was, except for Mariah Randolph. The tap of her boots sounded on the stairs, descending to the main level. Before she passed him, the scent of roses drifted inside his office. How anything could overpower the permeating odor of smoke was anyone's guess, but her perfume did.

And then the swishing skirts and tapping boots stopped. Right outside his open door.

"Good afternoon, Jay."

He stood, knocking over his chair. He fumbled to straighten it. By the time he set the room and himself to rights, she was sure to be gone.

But no, she remained in the doorway, her red hair and green dress glowing in the dim light. "Hello, Mariah. What brings you by?"

What an idiotic question. That hole had better appear, and quick.

Her cheeks pinked the tiniest of bits. "Hollis wanted to show me the new furniture for his office."

"Of course. It has been the talk of all the employees here. Quite grand, don't you think?" That was a little better conversation.

"It is lovely, but far too masculine for my tastes."

"That makes sense."

"I almost hate to go outside and into that smoke."

"Yes. Let's pray the good Lord sends the rains soon."

"It's been forever since we had even a drizzle."

"It has." Jay shuffled a few papers on his desk.

"I'm so sorry for keeping you from your work. Have a good afternoon." She turned to leave.

"Wait." The word shot from Jay's mouth like a bullet from a pistol. And just like a projectile, there was no way to take it back. His ears must be the reddest ever by now.

"Yes?" She gazed at him, the color of her eyes matching her dress.

He swallowed hard and wiped his sweating hands on his black pants. "May I walk you home?"

She tipped her head, then nodded. "That would be lovely."

"Mr. Stanford won't object?"

"Why would he be bothered by an old friend walking me home—especially when he didn't offer?"

Oh no. Maybe there were problems in their relationship. Still, Jay closed his ledger, set his curved-brimmed hat on his head, and led the way from the building into the smoky afternoon. Mariah covered her mouth and nose with her handkerchief, and he fished in his pocket until he found his and did the same.

With cloth covering their faces, conversing was almost impossible. They passed the saloon, the tinny piano music already seeping from underneath the doors. Hollis should never have left Mariah to walk this way unattended. He was supposed to be a big-city gentleman.

"Are you working on any more art?"

She nodded, not a hair out of place. "I started a new piece this morning. The fires are devastating, especially for the lumber industry, but the sky is spectacular. How could I not record it on canvas? Hollis has promised to take some of my paintings to Chicago. He has a gallery interested in displaying and selling my work."

"That's wonderful." That was why she was engaged to a man like Hollis instead of a lowly bookkeeper such as himself. Hollis could open the world for her. Jay could manage her finances. There was no comparison.

After a few turns, they arrived at the three-story white clapboard house teetering on the edge of town, a pair of dormers jutting from the wood-shingled roof. "Thank you so much for seeing me home. I appreciate it. May I offer you some refreshment for your efforts?"

"No, thank you. I must be getting back to the office." He tipped his hat.

"At least come up and see the painting I was describing. It's not completed, so you must give me that grace."

"I'm not an art critic."

She nodded, a small smile playing on her lips. "You're a friend, and that's even better. I would like your honest reaction. Don't spare my feelings."

With no other choice, he followed her inside.

"Mama's likely napping, so we must be quiet."

"Of course."

They made their way through the well-appointed sitting room dominated by a fireplace and a large portrait on the far wall, up the carpeted stairs, and through one of the dormer rooms cluttered with an easel, several canvases, and boxes filled with tubes of paint. At last they stepped into the darkening afternoon, and she motioned to the painting in front of him. "What do you think?"

Breathtaking. Amazing. She'd captured the scene spread in front of them, not with the exacting nature of a camera but with broad strokes that evoked the flames and the trees they consumed.

"It's nice." Ah, he should just cut off his tongue for all the good it did him. "I mean, it's. . . . There are no words for it." Would that cover his blunder?

"Thank you. Of course, it's not finished."

"I can see what you have in mind. If possible, what you have painted is even better than the scene out there."

The pink heightened in her cheeks. Probably because of the heat. Was the warmth from the fire tangible from this distance, or had he managed to fluster her? "Thank you. I appreciate it."

"I would hang that in my living room. If I had one, I mean. Mrs. Anderson would never—I mean—" There was no point in continuing.

"No, I don't think your landlady appreciates fine art. Her boarding-house is rather utilitarian."

"Exactly." He released a pent-up breath.

"But I'm glad you like it. I only hope the Chicago elite who will be the buyers are going to be impressed."

"How could they not be?"

"You're very kind." She smoothed a stray strand of hair from her perfect face.

"I should let you get back to work before your light changes too much."

"You know art better than you give yourself credit. You need to return to your books too, I'm sure. Didn't you knock on Hollis' door at the office about something?"

"Oh, that's right. I did. I had forgotten."

She gave him a soft smile that revealed a dimple in her right cheek.

"I need to get back to work before Mr. Stanford docks my pay."

"He wouldn't do that when you were merely helping me. If he does, let me know, and I'll make it right."

"Thank you. You're too kind. Enjoy your painting." He skedaddled before he could blunder any worse than he already had.

By the time he returned to the railroad office, he had cooled down and had his head back on his shoulders. He also remembered why he needed to speak to Hollis in the first place.

It wasn't going to be a fun conversation. As he climbed the stairs to the boss' office, the jitters returned. He knocked, and this time, he waited for a reply.

"Come in."

He entered a room that was much too extravagant for his tastes. The oversized furniture, the ornate Oriental rug, the crystal decanters of whiskey, were over the top. When Jay had work to do, it was best for him to have a space that would help him focus and do his job the right way.

"I would like to apologize for my earlier intrusion."

"From now on, Franklin, I would appreciate it if you waited until I gave you permission to enter."

"Yes, sir."

Hollis rose, and though an imposing figure behind his massive desk, he was far less threatening when the top of his head only came to Jay's chin.

"Do you mind if we sit?" Jay shifted the logbook he carried from under one arm to under the other.

"Not at all. But don't get too comfortable in those chairs." Hollis chuckled, but it came out like a monkey's laugh.

Jay settled into one of the seats. It was comfortable, but he perched on the edge, placed his ledger on his lap, and once more wiped his damp palms on his pants.

"What can I do for you?" Hollis eyed the whiskey bottles on his left.

"Well, sir, as you know, I keep very careful account of the money coming in and the bills going out. In addition, I retain all the incoming and outgoing invoices. I have double-checked my work and, well, have come across a small discrepancy."

Hollis leaned back, his hands clasped behind his head. "How much of one?"

"Just a hundred dollars or so. Compared to the money the railroad generates, it's a drop in the bucket. But it—it bothers me nonetheless."

"I'm sure it's nothing more than a math error on your part. No reason for concern. As you said, the overall company is worth vastly more than a hundred dollars. What you deal with here is only the line that extends from Green Bay and will eventually run near the town."

"I understand that, sir, but I must account for every penny. Nothing but complete accuracy, or your father, well, he will remove me from my position."

"He will do no such thing. You are his golden boy." A slight sneer tinged his boss' words.

"I beg your pardon?"

"You came from nothing, and thanks to Father's generosity in educating you and securing a position for you here, you have become marginally successful."

"And I appreciate everything he's done for me. That is why it is of vital importance to me to ensure that I handle the finances of this part of his company to the best of my ability."

Hollis stood once more and moved around his desk. Jay also came to his feet, the ledger book in his hand tumbling to the floor.

As he bent to pick it up, Hollis slapped him on the back. "Both my father and I appreciate your dedication. You are one of the most conscientious employees I have ever had the pleasure of knowing."

"Thank you, sir." Jay smoothed the pages that had wrinkled.

"Don't worry about this one little mistake. If you would like, I can take a note to our banker the next time I'm in Chicago and have him double-check everything."

"I would appreciate that. In the meantime, I will do just as you suggested and go over the numbers again. There is the possibility that I miscalculated."

"Good man. Thank you for stopping by and alerting me to this issue. Now back to work."

"Thank you, sir." Jay left the office and returned to his quarters. Several more times, he examined the figures, but he continued to achieve the same result.

They were his friends, these numbers. His constant, always either right or wrong. There were no gray areas, no shades of black and white. No in between.

In his crazy, unstable world, they were unchangeable. There was one way to understand them, and that was it.

Numbers always behaved. But something didn't fit here.

Perhaps the bank did make a mistake when they last sent him a record of the deposits and withdrawals. Or. . .

Jay didn't even dare think it.

Chapter Three

FRIDAY, SEPTEMBER 15, 1871

Another beautiful day dawned, but instead of the sky painted scarlet by the sun's rays, fires splattered it red and orange. While it gave Mariah an opportunity to continue painting the dramatic scene and perhaps improve upon what she had already recorded on the canvases, how long could these blazes continue to burn? At some point, they had to consume all their fuel and spend themselves.

Still, she climbed to the third floor and out to her balcony. Not too much longer and she would have enough paintings for Hollis to arrange a show for her in Chicago. How amazing it would be to see her pieces hanging on a wall, potential buyers perusing them and discussing them, taking them home and displaying them in their grand mansions.

Then again, they could hate everything she produced, and she would be an utter failure.

She wouldn't know until she tried. Jay had liked what he had seen, but he didn't know much about what constituted fine art. His approval, though, touched her, as did his kindness in seeing her home.

Hollis was a busy man, working on this railroad project that would link Peshtigo to the outside world. It had to be a huge undertaking and one that devoured his time. In the end, it would mean even more explosive growth for this Northwoods town.

She settled at her easel and readied her supplies, squeezing the colors onto her palette, appreciating the new metal tubes that brought paint already mixed. Then she stared at the panorama in front of her, absorbing all she saw, calculating the colors in her mind.

Within a few moments, she was once again lost in her work. She formed splashes of hot red and orange, bright yellow, and midnight black into a tableau of a great fire. Every now and again, ash floated on the slight breeze and stuck to the wet paint.

Because there was nothing she could do about it, she incorporated those bits into the work, giving it a degree of texture. She sat back, tapped the brush against her chin, and examined the piece. Yes. It was coming along. She had quite a way to go before it was complete, but it had the potential of being one of her best.

Much to Mama's consternation, Mariah sprinted through lunch and once again threw herself into the painting. The light was changed from the morning, but she adapted.

Just about the time her neck ached and screamed for her to take a break, Mama came onto the balcony. "Goodness, Mariah, are you still at it?"

"I want to get this just right. An hour from now, a day from now, it will have changed. If I don't capture it at this moment, I may never get it right."

"You didn't hear Lady yipping when the messenger knocked?"

Mariah turned toward Mama, who was slim enough for Papa to span her waist with his hands, not a gray hair on her head. "Someone was here?"

"Yes, and they brought this package for you." She handed Mariah an envelope. It hadn't come through the post, which was strange.

"Do you know the person who dropped it off?"

"No, I've never seen him before. There are enough transients in town that it's impossible to be acquainted with everyone."

Mariah accepted the proffered envelope, and Mama returned to her duties downstairs. There was no indication on the outside who the package was from, only her name in handwriting she didn't recognize. Very, very odd.

She lifted the wax seal and drew out several papers from inside.

Dear Miss Randolph,

It has come to my attention that the railroad company your fiancé, Hollis Stanford, runs has a history of irregularities with its financial books. My belief is that these irregularities stem from problems Mr. Stanford has managing his money. Please be aware of the kind of dishonest, disreputable man that you are about to join your life to. He is not the suave, charming man of good character that he appears to be on the outside.

There was no signature on the letter. To be sure, she turned it over, but there was nothing. The script matched the outside of the envelope, so there was no guessing who had sent it.

Also included were several pages that contained rows and columns of numbers that meant nothing to her. She had barely eked out a passing grade in arithmetic in school.

Had Jay sent this? He was the bookkeeper for the local branch of the company. If anyone would know about these so-called irregularities, he would. She had a fair mind to march to the office and tell him just what she thought of his tactics. He was jealous of Hollis and his position in the company, and this was how he sought to separate her from him.

That had to be it. Hollis would never steal from his own family's railroad. Why would he? He had more than enough money to support himself and a wife and children in a very comfortable way. He never lacked for anything, and if he did, his doting father happily supplied it for him.

Which brought her back to Jay. If it was he who had sent this, why hadn't he said anything yesterday when he escorted her home? Why have a letter delivered? He was a bit of a fumbler, awkward in a way, so perhaps that was it.

Then again, he had always been so nice to her, so kind. Oh, her brain was as tangled as the pile of ribbons in her dresser drawer.

There was only one solution to this. She untied her apron, laid it to the side, then cleaned up her paints. She tucked the papers into her beaded leather handbag and set off for her friend Lucy Christianson's home in the Sugar Bush. As she strode, she kicked up puffs of dust from the road. Among the hardwood trees that grew in this area were farms that the men and women labored to clear.

From the corner of her eye, she spied flames snaking along the ground, not climbing the tree trunks or lighting the leaves on fire but just winding their way around the oaks.

Strange. It was turning out to be an unusual day all around.

Lucy and her husband didn't live too far into the Bush, so soon Mariah turned up the drive to the log cabin Henry had built for his wife before their marriage.

When she moved to Chicago, life would be different for Mariah. She would be stuck in Hollis' social circles, attending teas in the afternoons and functions with him in the evenings. From her limited experience, she thought his friends were boring snobs, at least those she had met so far.

In a town like Peshtigo, with only a few churches, it was easy enough to get to know all the permanent residents. Other than Hollis, no one was very wealthy. Papa earned a comfortable living from owning two dry goods stores in their section of Wisconsin.

She hadn't made it to the door before Lucy hurried out and enveloped her in a hug. "What a pleasant surprise. I'm so glad you came to visit. It's great to be married, and my home keeps me busy, but I do miss the people in town."

"And I miss getting to see you as much too. It will be awful when I go to Chicago."

"Let's not even talk about that now. Come in. I just made an apple cake, and I can put the coffee on."

They linked arms and together entered the house. Even with the windows washed until they gleamed, the trees surrounding the home left the place ever in the shadows. At least in town, Mariah had light to paint by.

Lucy pulled the kettle forward on the stove.

"I'm happy the smoke isn't as bad out here as in town," Mariah said. "The trees must help to cut it down."

"The wind isn't blowing this way today, praise be. When it is smoky, the trees hold it in. There are days I don't dare go outside because it's too difficult to breathe."

"The rains have to come soon."

"We have been saying that all summer, and nothing. Henry says the crops haven't been as good as in other years. We have the stream nearby and a decent well, so I at least can tote water for the garden."

"I've heard Mama coughing more lately. This isn't good for her lungs."

"It isn't good for any of us. But let's not talk about that anymore. Goodness knows we live it every day. I want to hear all the details about your wedding."

So the topic shifted, and Mariah shared her plans with Lucy. "Hollis thinks I need help and wants me to hire someone to do it, but that takes away the fun."

"He just doesn't understand women."

"He had better hurry up and learn, since he'll soon be spending the rest of his life with one."

Lucy laughed, and it was good to think about things other than the drought and fires for a while.

After a time, Mariah had drained her cup to the dregs and picked up every crumb of cake with the back of her fork, and she could no longer put off the true reason for her visit. She reached into her bag and pulled out the mysterious envelope.

"What's that?" Lucy leaned forward in her chair.

"A note I received by courier this morning. I have no clue who sent it or what it could mean." She pushed it across the table. "Go ahead and read it. I don't mind. In fact, I hope you can help me answer some questions."

Lucy unfolded the paper. The longer she read, the deeper the lines in her brow grew. She shook her head. "What do you make of this?"

"Perhaps someone who is jealous of my relationship with Hollis and wants to separate us?"

"You don't sound convinced of that theory. And who might this culprit be?"

"Jay Franklin?"

"Jay? You can't be serious. He's one of the meekest, mildest men I know. I just can't see him inventing charges against Hollis. He doesn't have a mean bone in his body, and he's a little timid. Don't get me wrong, he's one of the sweetest men around."

"I think you're running off the rails, Lucy."

"Right. Sorry."

"You do make a good point. He saw me home yesterday when Hollis was too busy and never said anything about it. Then again, Jay might be too shy to open his mouth. You should have seen how red he got yesterday when he caught Hollis and me embracing."

"I believe we can rule Jay out as the one who sent that letter." She narrowed her eyes and shot Mariah a pointed gaze.

Mariah's best friend believed Hollis capable of stealing from the railroad? "No."

"Think about what the note said."

"Speculation and nothing more. That doesn't make sense. Hollis has no motive for theft. None. He is also polite and kind. Look at all he wants to do for me and my painting career."

"But he couldn't be bothered to make sure you arrived safely at home, with all the lumberjacks running around who have had one too many tipples."

"Not in broad daylight."

Lucy raised one of her blond eyebrows.

Mariah shot to her feet. "Please, I'm begging you not to besmirch Hollis' character the way Mama does. It would be too much coming from you."

"This letter is pretty clear."

"From an anonymous tipster. We have no idea who the person is who sent this. They may have a vendetta against Hollis or a grudge. This could be their revenge for some slight they've perceived."

"You could be right." Lucy shrugged. "Are you sure you don't recognize the handwriting?"

"I'm sure."

"So that's not a clue. What else do you have to go on?"

"Nothing. That's the problem."

"You're going to need help with this."

"That's why I came to you."

Lucy shook her head, a loose strand of hair swinging with the motion. "I'm afraid I can't help. It's the end of the season, and I have more canning than I can manage as it is. Henry wouldn't look too kindly on me gallivanting off on an adventure."

"He doesn't have to know."

Lucy held Mariah by the hand. "Whatever you do, don't lie to your husband. That will never end well."

"So what am I supposed to do?"

"I suggest you enlist Jay's help."

"But he's a suspect."

"He's not, and both you and I know it."

Lucy was right. But Jay? Lovable but fumbling Jay? How would he ever be able to help her solve this mystery?

Chapter Four

Lamplight broke the shadows that blanketed Jay's office. Everyone else had gone home long ago, leaving him alone with his numbers.

Numbers that swam before his bleary eyes, black marks on the page that blurred into a solid blob, now incomprehensible. Even when his strange ways and his clumsiness chased away potential friends, when his father left him and Ma, numbers were always there, steady and constant.

Not now. The columns didn't add and subtract the way they always had. They didn't follow the rules set out for them since the beginning of time. He wasn't going to leave without making them work, without making them behave. There had to be something he was missing. A transaction that wasn't there or. . .

He'd been at it all day, but still the numbers refused to obey, to line up in the orderly manner that put a smile on his face. Instead, they were a bunch of unruly children who refused to queue after recess.

He sighed and finger-combed his hair. If only he could find it. That elusive piece of this puzzle. He rubbed his aching temples.

Who was he kidding? It was late, and he was exhausted, and there was no answer to this question. At least, there wasn't a tidy answer to it. All the possibilities were messy. Very messy.

They all implicated someone in wrongdoing.

He stood and paced the small room, barely large enough for his desk and his ledgers, a few pens and inkwells stowed in the middle drawer. Wood, wood everywhere. On the walls. On the floor. On the sidewalks outside. Piles of cut boards, rough-hewn trees, and sawdust.

From his pocket, he withdrew a handkerchief and wiped his nose.

Time to go home and get some sleep before morning called again. He slipped his pocket watch from his waistcoat. Actually, it was already morning. How had it gotten so late? He set his books in neat piles on one corner of his desk, picked up a few papers to take with him, and made his way to the street.

Despite the hour—or maybe because of it—the plinking of piano keys and the shouts of men likely three sheets to the wind and cheated at poker by a swindler filled the air. Not the ideal time to be out and about, but he skirted the saloons as much as he could.

A few blocks down, he came to his own much quieter street and his room in the boardinghouse. Tucked away in a sock underneath his mattress was his life savings, the dimes and quarters he stashed away here and there in the hope of purchasing property, building a house, and finding a woman who would share his life with him. Not that one would, but he kept that flickering flame of hope alive, however small it was.

As he passed the Randolphs' beautiful clapboard home, he glanced at the third story, where a light danced in one of the two dormer windows.

That could be none other than Mariah, still at her own work. And what work it was. He could lose himself in her paintings, imagining himself in the scenes she created, though they were different than anything he'd ever seen, either on the walls of the Stanford mansion in Chicago or in the heavy leather-bound volumes in Mr. Stanford's huge library.

A rustling came from his left, likely a cat in the bushes, but when he turned, a shadowy figure stepped into the glowing orange light from the distant fire, her manner and walk graceful, even long after midnight. The movement of her hips was like the sway of leaves in a gentle breeze.

"Mariah."

She gasped and clutched her bodice. "Who is it? Who's there?"

Great, he had gone and done it again. Broken the beautiful mood. Blast his lack of social skills. "Just Jay."

"You gave me such a fright."

"Forgive me. I never meant to."

"I know. It's just that I didn't expect anyone to be out this late, at least not on this street." She released her grasp on her dress. Even with only the thin firelight bathing her, he managed to make out splotches of paint on her apron.

"I'm on my way home from the office."

"At this hour? Really, I must speak to Hollis and get him to reduce your workload."

"No, no, please don't do that." He shook his head so hard he'd likely end up with a headache. "It's just this one night. Sort of a special project. Nothing worth mentioning to him."

"Are you sure?"

"I am, though it is very kind of you to offer."

"Don't hesitate to let me know if I can be of any assistance."

He had to get the focus off himself. "And what are you doing out at this time of night?"

She gazed at the sky, and so he did too. The nearby flames illuminated the darkness, glowing orange and yellow. Smoke obscured the moon and the bevy of stars which usually sparkled against the dark drapery of the heavens.

"I wanted to see what it looked like now." She returned her gaze to him. "At different times of days, the appearance of the fires changes. Sometimes they are bright and hot and consuming. Right now, they have a softer glow, almost like that of charcoal in the stove. I love how it varies from hour to hour."

"And you mean to paint them all? I mean, all the different scenes?"

"Of course. Whenever have you encountered such a phenomenon? Whenever might this occur again?"

"Very good point. But it isn't safe for a woman to stand in the middle of the street alone. I could have been coming from one of the saloons and..." Propriety demanded that he leave the sentence unfinished, though his face heated.

"Thank you for your concern. I do appreciate it. Hollis gives me enough grief over my wanderings, but he is very close to getting me an exhibition at a Chicago studio, so I must finish this series. It needs to be ready to go when we have a definite date."

"Congratulations. That truly is fantastic news. You should be proud of yourself."

"Mama says that pride goeth before a fall."

"Well, yes, of course that's right. I only meant that. . ."

A playful smile worked her lips, and she touched his upper arm. Just a brush of her fingers, but enough to send a shiver through him. "I know what you mean. And yes, it is chilly out. I should return to my studio and my work, and you must get up for work soon."

"Yes, of course. I didn't mean to detain you so long." He went to tip his hat, but he had none. He must have left it at the office. What an idiot she must think him.

"It's always pleasant speaking to you." The hint of a smile played at her lips. "Have a good night's sleep."

"You too."

She took a few steps in the direction of her house, its dark outline stark against the glowing skies, then turned toward him. "Is there something troubling you?"

To be able to confide in someone, to work through his suspicions and arrive at a plausible conclusion, would lift such a weight off his shoulders. "Why do you ask?"

"Just how you've looked the past few days. Kind of worn and tired. I know that's not the most polite thing to say, but I count you my friend, and I'm concerned."

He toed the sawdust-covered dirt road. Anyone else. Anyone. But how could he tell her? "Is it improper for us to be standing in the middle of the street in the middle of the night unchaperoned?"

"And who is going to see us?"

"You never know about Mrs. Abbott."

Mariah let loose a high, tinkling laugh. "She's in her seventies if she's a day. It's more than likely that she's been in bed since eight o'clock."

He chuckled along with her. "You're right."

"I've been told I'm pretty good at keeping confidences."

His attempt to steer the conversation in a different direction had, apparently, been thwarted. "It's nothing to concern yourself over, though I appreciate your willingness to help. If I ever need it, I'll be sure to tell you."

She shot him a little wave, and he returned it. But in doing so, he dropped the papers in his arms, and they fluttered to the ground. "Drat and blast."

"Oh, dear." Mariah bent down. "Let me help." She scooped up a few sheets, but others skittered down the street, and he chased after them.

Each time he caught up to one, it scampered away, like a mischievous cat refusing to be caught.

Such things happened only to him. Here he was, in the middle of the night, alone with a young woman, a beautiful one at that, chasing papers down a street in the light of a forest fire.

At last he corralled all the stray pages and returned to Mariah. She held some of them in her trembling hands, her eyes squinted. The not-too-distant flames were enough to illuminate the notes he had scribbled.

"What does this mean?"

He ripped them from her grasp. "Nothing. Forget what you saw."

"You had several numbers circled with question marks next to them. Why?"

"It would mean nothing to you."

Now she drew herself up to her full height, almost as tall as his shoulders, back as straight as a pine. "Because I'm nothing more than a—"

"I didn't mean it that way."

She relaxed her shoulders a tiny bit. "You didn't even know what I was going to say."

"But I did, and that's not what I intended."

"Still, you have questions about the company's books. Am I right?"

How could he deny it when she was spot-on? Then again, her fiancé was the one he was questioning, so he couldn't tell her the entire truth. "That's my job, to check and double-check the numbers. I must have made a math error along the way, one that I need to find and correct. Nothing more."

"What if I share something with you?"

He scrunched his eyebrows together. "What might that be?"

"I received a note the other day."

"Yes?"

"Do you know anything about it?"

"Why would I?"

"So you didn't send it?"

"No. What is this about?"

She once again focused her attention on the sky before returning it to Jay. "I'm not sure what it means."

"Does it pertain to what we were just discussing?"

She nodded, her hair coming loose from its pins and tumbling about her shoulders. "I hesitate to tell you this, though I believe I can trust you. Lucy assured me I could."

"Of course. Always."

"Someone believes there to be irregularities with the company's books and that Hollis is somehow involved."

Jay held tight to the papers in his arms lest he drop them all again. "Who sent the letter?"

"That's just it. I don't know. But you suspect the same, do you not? That the numbers are wrong because someone has tampered with the books."

He heaved a sigh. "Yes."

"Please, don't tell me it's Hollis. He would never do such a thing. What reason would he have?"

For starters, Hollis wasn't the most upright and forthcoming man, but that news wouldn't sit well with Mariah. Jay may be bumbling, but he didn't lack tact. "You're right. And don't worry about any of this. You are too enmeshed with Hollis and the company to be involved."

"But this company will be my children's heritage, especially if I produce a son, so I do have a stake in what is happening."

Jay nodded. "There is that, but you have your painting and your upcoming nuptials to keep you busy. What Hollis is doing for you is wonderful, and you should take full advantage of that. There is no need for you to worry about the company."

"I will try not to. I had better get going before my candle burns the entire town to the ground. Good night, Jay."

"Good night, Mariah." He stood in the middle of the street until she extinguished the light in the third-story window. The soft crackle of the fire floated on the night air, along with plenty of ash.

There was too much to worry about in life.

Chapter Five

The air lay over Peshtigo like a thick, heavy blanket. With only a small breeze, the smoke didn't dissipate. Coughs became the norm for all residents, and they used handkerchiefs to cover their mouths and noses to protect them from the poison vapors.

The conditions left Mama weak and with a dry hack, so she chose to remain at home this Lord's Day morning. Instead, Papa gave Mariah his arm and escorted her the two blocks to Peshtigo's main thoroughfare. The sallow, jaundiced hue of the sky had various churchgoers gazing upward, pointing and mumbling.

They wove around a couple who had stopped in the middle of the slatted boardwalk. Instead of focusing her attention on the heavens, Mariah kept hers on the dusty toes of her black shoes popping in and out of her skirt's hem as she moved along.

Jay agreed with the anonymous note sender. There was more than a math error in the books. And he wasn't the one who had alerted her via the letter to the discrepancies. There had been a hesitancy on his part in releasing that information to her. Perhaps it had to do with the fact that she was engaged to the son and heir of the railroad, who was a tycoon himself.

But again, Hollis had no reason for doctoring the books. He had plenty of money for himself. Add that to a trust fund from his late wife's family to be used in raising his young daughter, and there was more than enough for both of them. A few months ago, he had taken her to Chicago to meet the child, and he doted on her. She had everything a little girl could wish for.

Except a mama. And that would be righted at New Year's when Hollis married Mariah.

No, it couldn't be him. Then who?

"Hello, dear."

Lucy's voice at her ear startled her from her thoughts.

Mariah released her arm from Papa's, and Lucy's husband strode to catch up to him. Then she caught her dear friend in a hug. "Good morning to you too." The handkerchief at her mouth muffled her words.

Lucy held a pretty pale-blue, hand-embroidered handkerchief to her own face. "Isn't this awful? I cannot wait for the autumn rains to start and all of this smoke to clear. The constant fall of ash is making it impossible for me to keep my house clean."

"And I'm worried about Mama's cough."

"This isn't good for any of us. But that's enough about that. We could drive ourselves crazy with dwelling on it. What have you been doing the past few days?"

Mariah slipped one hand from her white cotton gloves and wiggled her paint-stained fingers. "Guess."

"Why did I even bother to ask? I should have known. At least flour doesn't leave stains, or I might look just like you."

"Something interesting did happen a couple of nights ago." Mariah slowed her steps.

"Do tell."

"I went out to gaze at the night sky, hoping for a good angle from which to paint, and I ran into Jay returning from the office."

"You must speak to Hollis about reducing his workload. Poor man. No wonder he hasn't met a charming young woman with whom to share his life."

"I told him that, but he was evasive. It wasn't until I assisted him in retrieving the papers he dropped that I discovered the real reason for his late hours."

The men were far ahead of them by this point, but the two friends continued at their tortoise pace. "And what was it?"

Before answering, Mariah glanced in all directions. No one else was within hearing distance, but she still leaned closer to Lucy. "He has noticed discrepancies in the books and believes that someone is skimming money from the railroad."

"No. So he *is* the one who sent the note."

"On the contrary." Mariah adjusted the handkerchief at her mouth and brushed a few flakes of ash from the shoulder of her navy blue church dress. Little good that did. "He had no knowledge of it until I told him."

"Good. I'm glad that you put aside your misgivings and confided in him. What did he have to say?"

"Not much. He does believe that someone may well be tampering with the books, but he didn't share any suspicions with me as to who that might be. I did ask him not to even think about Hollis."

"Hollis does have the means and the opportunity."

"Not the motive though. He makes a healthy living."

"I can think. . ."

Mariah came to a complete halt. "What?"

"Nothing."

"Tell me."

"It's nothing. Of course you're right about Hollis."

The ringing of the church bells calling all worshippers to the sanctuary cut off any further inquiry Mariah might make. The clanging from the Protestant bell echoed that of the one on the Catholic church.

"We'd best hurry before we end up late for services." Mariah clutched her skirts and scurried along the boardwalk, kicking up a storm of sawdust as she did so.

Papa and Henry had saved seats for them, and the two women slid into the pew just as Pastor Beach took to the pulpit and issued the call to worship.

How could Lucy believe in Jay's innocence but doubt Hollis'? As they sang the opening hymn, Lucy squeezed Mariah's hand. Good. Even if she questioned Hollis' integrity, she would also stand beside Mariah. That was a true friend. She returned the squeeze.

Pastor Beach preached quite the fire-and-brimstone sermon, a common theme of his the past several weeks and rather appropriate. Though Mariah did her best to concentrate on his words, she found herself staring out the window on more than one occasion, the breeze having picked up, sometimes sending a shower of sparks bursting like fireworks in the sky. A scene she would have to paint tomorrow.

The last notes of the final hymn hadn't yet faded away before the shrill whistle from the woodenware factory pierced the Sunday morning peace, and Mariah startled. Before she could gather her wits, Papa and Henry pushed by and joined the stream of men on their way down the aisle and out the door. Bibles were left sitting scattered on the pews.

Jay stopped and leaned over, causing a bottleneck. "Hurry home. I have this foreboding in the pit of my stomach. The wind is blowing right toward town. Wet down as many blankets as you can and drape them over your roof. Lucy, do the same." Then the wave of people swept him away.

Mariah turned to Lucy, whose face was pale. Several times in the last few weeks the whistle had screeched out a warning for men to assemble to battle small fires around town, usually at either the sawmill or the woodenware factory.

But Jay's warning had goose pimples breaking out on Mariah's arms, and she rubbed them away.

Once all the men had exited, the women also made their way to the back door, albeit a bit slower and with a great deal more chatter.

Lucy pushed her way into the tide, and Mariah followed. "What do you make of Jay's warning? Is this the time they won't be able to save the town? And what about those of us who live in the Bush?"

The little cluster of three farming areas in the woods outside of Peshtigo was far more vulnerable, surrounded by trees on all four sides. At least in town, they had fewer pines to catch fire. Then again, when the streets were paved with sawdust... "I'm sure it's another flare-up like all the others."

"Still, I'm going to go home and see if there is anything I can do, if our house is in any danger."

"I would come, but with Mama not well, I must see to her and to our home."

"Of course." Lucy gave her a quick peck on the cheek. "The best any of us can do at the moment is pray."

"Without a doubt." They parted, and Mariah made her way toward Mama. There was no activity in that part of town, so the fire likely was at the factory or the sawmill. Perhaps even both. "Save us, Lord." She breathed the prayer into the hot, heavy air.

In a short time, Mariah arrived home and entered the front door.

"Is that you, dear?" Mama's voice was stronger than earlier that morning.

"It is." On her way into the sitting room, Mariah shed her hat and gloves. "Papa is off with the men to fight the fire. Jay thought it prudent for us to drape the house in wet blankets to keep it from catching."

Mama nodded while she coughed, holding her monogrammed handkerchief in front of her mouth, all while struggling to her feet.

Mariah shook her head. "Sit down. Exerting yourself won't be of any help. I can manage."

"How? Who will pump the water for you and help you carry the heavy blankets to the roof?"

"You may hold the ladder for me. That shouldn't tax you too much. Let me change and tie a bandana around my face so I can have my hands free."

"I'll gather all the blankets and quilts I can find."

Although Mama really should rest, she wouldn't be happy unless she helped, so Mariah nodded and made short work of changing. The entire time, Lady yipped around her feet. She reached down and scratched her fluffy white dog behind the ears. "You stay here and be a good girl, you hear? I can't risk having Mama trip on you."

Lady sat and stared at her with the saddest brown eyes.

"You can give me that look, but it won't change my mind. I'm sorry. Perhaps if we manage to save the town, the fires will be over soon and I can take you for a walk this week. Is that a fair compromise?"

Lady wagged her tail.

That brought a smile to Mariah's face but didn't ease the weight on her chest. What would happen if the men weren't able to extinguish the fire this time? Where would they go? They, like everyone else in town and in the Bush, stood to lose everything.

They most certainly would if she stood around with her arms crossed. At the very least, she could do her part and take care of their house.

When she returned downstairs, Mama stood in the entryway with a pile of white wool blankets and colorful patchwork quilts at her feet. A flash of pink caught Mariah's eye. "No, not Grandmother's quilt." She pulled it from the pile.

"If we have to use it, we have to use it."

"But it has been on your bed my entire life. It's so special to you."

Mama touched Mariah's cheek, her long, white fingers chilly. "What is more important than any material possession is that my home and family are safe and protected." Though Mama didn't admit to worry over Papa, her tight words conveyed that message anyway.

"The Lord will watch over him. And I'm here. We'd best get to work."

Mariah scooped up most of the bedding, leaving Mama one or two blankets to carry. Then she pumped water into the trough, fitting in as many of the blankets and quilts as she could. Mama held the base of the ladder, but it was soon clear that Mariah wouldn't be able to scale it while holding her skirts and the bedding.

Throwing convention to the wind, she tied up her skirts and climbed the ladder. By the time she reached the roof, she was already panting from the effort. It was going to be a long afternoon.

From her vantage point, she had a view of most of Peshtigo. On the other side of the river lay the woodenware factory where hardworking men and recent immigrants manufactured bowls and utensils and buckets and barrels. A group of men stretched in a line between the river and the factory. A similar line snaked between the river and the sawmill. Both businesses must be in danger.

Then a gust of wind blew several sparks onto the shingled roof of Mariah's home, and fire broke out in a couple of spots. She had to get to them and extinguish them.

But as she stood to do so, her foot slipped.

Chapter Six

A deep cough rattled in Jay's chest as he drew in lungs full of noxious fumes and relentless smoke with each breath. Sweat rolled down his cheeks, down his back, down his forehead and into his eyes, stinging them more than the smoke did. Though he wiped the rivulets away, it was in vain.

In order to gasp a lungful of clean air, many men, including himself, had taken to stopping from time to time to stick their faces into holes they had dug in the sand and so breathe clean air through this natural filter. Failure to do so might mean choking to death.

He was, though, out of his element. Chicago was his birthplace, a ledger and a pen the tools of his trade. With this much exertion, his muscles cried out for him to stop, to put down his bucket and let those stronger than he fight this blaze.

But he couldn't. He wouldn't.

If men dropped out of this bucket line because the work became too much, the flames would consume the entire town. No, he had to keep up this frantic pace. Each time one fire was extinguished, more sparks fell and new blazes roared to life. The dry lumber, the scads of woodenware items surrounding the factory, and the piles of sawdust everywhere were no match for the spark-laden wind.

If the middle-aged man beside him continued to feed him buckets at this pace, then he, younger than his neighbor by twenty years or so, must do his part.

"Keep it up, men. We can't stop. Can't give up." This came from the head of the line.

Another bucket. Another and another. They never stopped coming. He passed them along until blisters covered his bloodied hands, hands unused to such physical labor.

The wind blew an ember his direction, and it landed at his feet. While still passing along buckets, he stamped out the flame before it could take hold. What was this when fire fell like snowflakes from the sky?

For a moment, he glanced up, only to see a figure making its way toward them through the haze. From the shape, it was a woman. He squinted to better make out who it was.

She approached, and for a scant few seconds, the wind cleared the smoke. Thank goodness. He inhaled the somewhat fresher air. At the same time, his vision cleared enough for him to make out that it was Mrs. Randolph.

He waved. "Mrs. Randolph. Over here."

She paused for a moment then approached, her hair disheveled, her bodice damp. "Mr. Franklin, how good it is to find you. Do you know where my husband is?"

"I believe he's closer to the river."

She leaned over, gasping. Tears streamed from her eyes, possibly from the smoky air. "It's—it's Mariah."

A wave of cold washed over him. "What happened?"

"She climbed to the roof, foolish girl, to cover it in wet blankets, trying to save it from catching fire. She slipped and fell—not off but partway—and is now complaining of pain in her ankle. How is she ever going to get down?"

Though he glanced all along the line of men continuing to pass buckets, he couldn't make out Mr. Randolph's location. "I'll help. It may be that I'll have to carry her down, so I'm more suited for the job." Only in that he was younger. He was so tired that he might not even be able to lift one more pail of water.

"I hate to take you away from the line."

His aching back would thank him. "Once we have Miss Randolph put back to rights, I'll return." He stepped out of the line, and the remaining men filled his space.

She led him across the river to their home, now covered in colorful blankets and quilts. Mariah sat on the roof's edge, near a ladder, her knees bent, her head down.

"Mariah."

At his call, she gazed up. "Oh, Jay. My ankle. And I'm afraid. . ." She slapped an ember that alighted on a pink quilt.

"Don't fret. I'll come get you."

"How are you going to manage to return me to the ground?"

That was the question, but one he would answer as soon as he was beside her and could assess the situation.

"Never fear." Within a matter of moments, he'd scaled the ladder and was beside her. "How are you faring?"

She slapped out another spark. "The blankets are dry already. How am I ever to keep this up? We are going to lose our home along with all my paintings. Just when Hollis had the arrangements for a Chicago exhibition." A tear rolled down her cheek.

"Hold tight."

He reversed his way down the rungs, grabbed two buckets of water, and managed to ascend again without using his hands, Mrs. Randolph holding the ladder.

He poured the water over the roof and repeated the process a few times until everything was soaked. It wouldn't stay that way for long. The dry winds evaporated the water in short order, but it would buy him time to figure out a way to help Mariah down.

"How much weight can you put on the ankle?"

"I don't know. I'm afraid to stand in case I slip again."

"You must be very careful, but I'll hold you and steady you."

She gazed at him, her dark eyelashes brushing her pale cheeks. At last, she nodded and grasped him by the hand.

Though she wobbled, he kept his stance wide to hold them both upright. She tested her ankle and was able to support herself a bit with it.

"That's very good. Let me know when you're comfortable, and we'll begin our descent."

She nodded and after only a minute or two, nodded again. "I'm ready."

"I'll go first, a few rungs below you, so that I can help you. Take your time, go slowly, and stay calm."

Her look, eyes wide but shoulders and back straight, almost undid him. She trusted him. To keep himself from killing both of them, he swallowed and moved partway down the ladder.

She stepped off the roof with her twisted ankle, wincing, but managed to get both feet on the top rung. He held her by her waist, and so they made their way down.

As soon as she stepped foot on solid ground, she turned and hugged him. "This may be very inappropriate, but I owe you my life. Thank you so much for rescuing me. I feared I might be stuck on that roof forever."

"No thanks are needed. I was happy to be of assistance."

"How are things in town? I assume that's where Mama located you."

"It is. The bucket line is holding its own, though the struggle is difficult. All it's going to take is for the wind to pick up, and they won't be able to keep pace. With everything so tinder dry, an unnoticed spark will be enough to set the entire town ablaze."

Despite the heat, Mariah shivered. "Goodness. That's awfully dire."

"I won't sugarcoat it for you, even though you are women. The situation is grave. Our efforts might win the day today, but what about tomorrow or the day after or the day after that? I'm afraid that only several good soaking rains will alleviate the danger completely." He glanced at the roof, where sparks continued to fall. "I fear we must get back to work here. Do you think you'll be able to pump?"

"You're willing to help us?"

"Of course."

She limped toward the well. "I can lean against this from time to time as I need to. We all have our jobs that we must do."

He filled the first two buckets and once again ascended the ladder. Mrs. Randolph did a commendable job in steadying it so that he was able to climb without using his hands. By the time he got to the roof, several small embers threatened the structure. He doused those first then climbed down for more water.

A good couple of hours must have passed as they worked. If his muscles had been sore before, it was nothing in comparison to how much he ached now. Over and over, up and down and down and up. Mariah must be hurting as much or more than he was, though she didn't say a word but kept his buckets full, her dress sodden.

Each time he reached the roof, he took a single second to cast his gaze toward the woodenware factory and the sawmill. Both stood. No other structures burned. That was good. Perhaps, with God's help, they would save Peshtigo today.

The sun traversed its way across the sky until it touched the tops of the trees in the forest and became indistinguishable from the flames. Then, as suddenly as the wind had turned in Peshtigo's direction, it shifted and blew the sparks and embers away.

Across the river, shouts rose and men at the factory and sawmill dropped their buckets. The breeze cooled his hot cheeks, and he scrambled down the ladder for the last time. "Did you feel that?"

Mariah hobbled toward him, and Mrs. Randolph joined them. "Praise God. He turned the wind, and the town is saved."

"Yes, it is. Praise Him."

Mariah grinned. "I have never painted a person before, only landscapes, but I'm compelled to try to capture you on that ladder, helping to save our house. If not for you, it might have ignited, and I would never have been able to get down."

"You would have figured out a way. Please, though, don't paint me. I doubt anyone is going to want to stare at a picture of me working."

"Don't sell yourself short."

The temperature of his cheeks must have risen by another twenty degrees or so. "Well, thank you."

"No." Mrs. Randolph leaned against her daughter. "We must be the ones thanking you. We owe you a great debt. Why don't you come for Sunday dinner in two weeks?"

He turned to Mariah, who nodded. "Please do. By then, perhaps, I'll be able to show you my completed painting."

"That would be good. Thank you again. I should get back and see if there is anything else they need done at the factory."

"Wait, wait. Don't move." Mariah escorted her mother inside and returned a minute later, still limping, with a plate of cookies in her hands. "Oatmeal. Just a small token of our appreciation."

"As I said, it isn't necessary, but I will enjoy them."

"We'll plan on seeing you in two weeks, though I do hope to run into you before then."

Add another fifteen degrees to his heated cheeks. He had to get away before he burst into flames. "Until then." He turned and hustled down the street, only stopping to deposit the sweets at his place. No need to subject himself to the ribbing the other men would dish out if he returned with a plate of cookies to where they had been firefighting.

By the time he arrived at the factory, however, many of the men were already making their ways home. He met Mr. Randolph and relayed the story to him. Doubtless Mariah would embellish his role greatly.

Mr. Randolph clapped him on the back. "Well done, and thank you for what you did for my wife and daughter. Our entire family, really. I appreciate it and am relieved to learn that everything and everyone at home is well."

"Both your wife and daughter did more than their share. We are all sure to be quite gassed tonight and unable to move for our sore muscles come morning."

"You're likely right. Again, we owe you a great debt."

"Think nothing of it. I've been rewarded with a plate of oatmeal cookies and an invitation to dinner in two Sundays. That's more than sufficient payment."

They continued on their way, the breeze a welcome relief from the heat. Still, they kicked up sawdust with each step. More tinder awaiting a spark.

Mr. Randolph sighed. "I have to tell you, Jay, that I'm concerned for this town's future. We can't hold off the fire forever. I fear that one of these days, the outcome will not be as it was today."

"I hope you are wrong, sir."

"I do too."

But before he entered his home, Jay studied the still-glowing sky. They wouldn't be able to keep the blaze at bay much longer.

Chapter Seven

Shifting shapes danced in front of Mariah, the flames turning, twisting, changing, never still. They held her captive and left her unable to turn her gaze away. Once she had imprinted the scene in her mind, she dipped her brush into the paint and applied it to her blank canvas.

She had worn her lightest-weight dress, and still she was warm. A breeze to cool her perspiring brow would be most welcome, but it might also bring another haze of smoke and shower of dust and embers, so she pushed aside her discomfort and focused on her work.

Capturing the fire that played on the edge of town was not the easiest task. It never stood still but moved on a whim, once redder, then laced with yellow and orange. From time to time, the smoke almost obscured it, while at other times, it shrank back in the brilliance of the sun.

Perhaps that was why she was captivated, perhaps why she had filled so many canvases with pine trees and fire. Earlier in the week, she set in paint what she had witnessed on her way to visit Lucy. Mama and Papa hadn't wanted her to go, what with the Catholic priest and his hunting guide caught on all sides by fire the other day, only rescued when the boy failed to return home.

But she had been determined to see her friend. While making her way along the road, she'd observed the most fascinating phenomenon. Small flames licked along the ground, fueled by pine needles and leaves, though never jumping to the dry trees they wound their way through. After she completed this painting, she would set brush to canvas to capture that strange scene.

No one would believe that what she was painting was reality, the reality they had lived with for weeks now.

Every one of the townspeople was exhausted from the regular shrill of the factory's whistle calling all able-bodied men to stamp out yet another fire set by embers. Sometimes it sounded the alarm by day and other times at night. Sleep remained elusive for all the townspeople. So far, no major property damage had been reported.

Mariah lost herself in the ever-changing scene before her, the brush she grasped whirling and twirling over the canvas. Before long, the fire appeared, almost real enough to burn a hole in the fabric stretched on the wooden frame.

"Working hard again."

She turned and smiled at Hollis, who leaned on the doorframe as if he had nothing better to do in the world. From behind him, a golden-haired child peeked out.

Mariah rose from her stool. "Hollis, how good to see you." She approached him but didn't kiss him, and he made no move to bestow any measure of affection on her. "And who is this angel you've brought to visit me?"

A dimple appeared in the little girl's chin, and she gave a two-fingered wave.

Mariah squatted in front of her. "How good to see you, Angelina. You've come all the way from Chicago to visit me?"

She nodded. "I begged and begged Father to let me come. He said I couldn't, but I didn't give up. So Nanny and I came on the train too. Now I don't like it here because of the fire."

Hollis had asked her to go to Chicago with him to keep her out of harm's way, but now he'd brought his daughter here. Angelina was persuasive, and Hollis must believe that the town wasn't in danger. "Oh, there's nothing to fret about. The men are doing a very good job of keeping it away. I tell you what. You may stay with me while your father is at work, and if he has no objections, you may play with my paints."

At this pronouncement, she widened her piercing blue eyes, a characteristic she had inherited from her father. "Really? You would let me?"

Hollis scowled. "I don't think—"

"I have a large apron that would cover your entire dress, and you may have a canvas all your own. If you follow my instructions, you won't get a spot of paint anywhere on yourself."

Angelina gazed at her father, her eyes soft as she pleaded with him in the way girls universally used to get their way with their papas.

Hollis shook his head. "Of course, darling. You know I can't deny you anything."

Somehow, Angelina remained sweet in general, even though Hollis spoiled her in a ridiculous fashion. Because her mother had died in childbirth, Hollis used every opportunity to make it up to her. She never took advantage of it unless she really, truly, wanted something.

"Goody!" She jumped up and down until Hollis shot her a narrow-eyed glare that brought her to standing still and properly chastened.

He kissed the top of both Angelina's head and Mariah's. That scraped her nerves when he did that, as if she were no more than a child to him. Granted, she was almost a decade younger than he was, but she was to be his wife. In a moment, he disappeared down the stairs, leaving Angelina with her.

It would be one of her greatest joys to be the sprite's mother. Spending time with her was a passion almost equal to that of painting. A few moments later, she had Angelina set up with a small canvas, another pallet, and several brushes.

"What should I paint?"

"Whatever your heart tells you to. Are you happy or sad right now?"

"Happy that I get to be with you. Sad that Grandfather is home all alone. But happy that Father let me come with him on the train. But sad that I can't play with Polly because she lives in Chicago. But happy—"

"So you are feeling many different things. What is something pretty you've seen recently?"

"Lots of pretty hills from the train car."

"Yes. Wisconsin does have many beautiful hills."

"And fields."

"That too. So why don't you paint what you remember that looked like."

"All right." A few minutes later, she sat on the porch decking, stuck the tip of her tongue out of her mouth, and crinkled her forehead as she worked on her painting.

Mariah returned to her own piece, the paint now drying. After she squeezed a few fresh dollops from various tubes, she also set to work and once again lost herself in recreating the scene before her eyes, one which had changed a good deal in the short amount of time she had been away from it.

Sometime later, Angelina's cough broke the spell Mariah had been under. She coughed herself not too long afterward.

Angelina came to her side, her eyes red. "Can we go inside? I'm done painting."

"I am too, and all this smoke isn't good for us." The wind had changed direction and stolen the fresh air they had enjoyed. They cleaned up their supplies, and Mariah removed Angelina's apron. True to her word, she didn't have so much as a splatter of paint on her dress. Hollis would be pleased about that.

They went downstairs where Mama slept on the settee, pale and wan. The persistent poor air quality was draining the life from her. "How about we get some tea and cookies," Mariah suggested.

"All right. I know where the jar is."

While they waited for the water to boil before they could enjoy their afternoon tea, Mariah went to Mama and gave her a gentle shake.

Mama rubbed her eyes and sat up. "Oh, is it dinnertime already?"

"No. Angelina and I came in because the smoke is too thick, and I thought a cup of tea and a cookie would be good for you."

"The tea, yes, but I will decline the cookie."

"You must eat to keep up your strength. I'm worried about your health. You've lost so much weight."

"Once the rains come, I'll be my old self again. The air isn't healthy for anyone, man or beast. Let's pray that the Lord removes this plague soon."

"In the meantime, I'm going to put a treat on your plate. Even a few bites for Angelina would mean so much to her. She's busy putting the plate together now. I had better go supervise her." She kissed Mama's warm cheek, more sunken than ever.

Within a few minutes, Mariah and Angelina had the tea poured and the cookies set on a silver platter Mama had brought with her from

New York when she and Papa came to Wisconsin. Angelina insisted on carrying Mama's teacup and, to her credit, she moved at a snail's pace and without bouncing once. She delivered it to the polished coffee table without spilling a drop.

She gazed at Mariah. "See, I told you I could do it."

"And so you did. Well done. Shall we?"

Both of them sat on chairs that flanked the settee and sipped their tea like ladies of leisure. Once she and Hollis married, that was what she would be, her days filled with social calls. But she would insist to Hollis that Angelina didn't need a nanny. All the little girl required was a mother to love her.

"Do you want to see the picture I painted?" Angelina set her cup and empty plate on the table.

Mama nodded. "Of course. That would be lovely."

Angelina scampered away, sliding to a stop at the doorway and resuming at a more ladylike pace.

Mama coughed and took a moment to regain her breath. "You are going to be a wonderful stepmother to her."

"The only mother she has ever known. I am bothered by the way Hollis wants little to do with her."

Mama shrugged. "That's the way of men. Your father's attention to you is not the norm."

"But she longs for him to notice her, to spend time with her."

"I wouldn't fret about it. Once she is a bit more grown up and enters his sphere instead of being confined to the nursery, he will take more notice of her."

"I forget that you were raised among the upper classes. How did you manage to leave all that comfort behind to come to a small lumber town in the Midwest?"

"Love, dear. Love. Nothing was going to separate your father and me. I would have given almost anything to spend my life with him. Our hearts were connected, were one. He is a part of me."

Mariah fiddled with a loose string on the ribbon around her waist. She couldn't say she harbored such sentiments about Hollis, and he likely didn't have any such feelings for her. Then again, what Mama and Papa shared was unique.

Lucy and Henry did have that connection though. Perhaps it wasn't so uncommon. Was there something wrong in her relationship with Hollis? They were polite, and he was companionable, but that was all the further it went. He did take interest in her work, but so did Jay.

That thought brought her mind to a screeching halt. Where had it come from? Jay was a friend, a longtime friend, and nothing more. He understood the emotions behind her pictures, it was true, but he would never be able to arrange an exhibition for her in Chicago the way Hollis had.

She set her teacup on the platter and wiped her sweaty palms on her skirt. She felt too sleep deprived to make much sense of anything. That was all this discomfort was. When the fires subsided and the cooler weather arrived, her mind would clear, and her thoughts wouldn't meander into such dangerous territory.

Perhaps she had a slight case of cold feet as well. Her marriage to Hollis would change so much of her life. Of course he loved her, otherwise he would have had no reason to choose her to be his wife. There were plenty of eligible young women eager to marry into such a wealthy and prestigious family, ladies much more suitable than her. He had to love her.

She managed to still her racing thoughts and picked up her teacup again when a screech came from upstairs.

"Help me, help me! I'm on fire!"

Dear God, not Angelina.

Mariah raced up the two flights of stairs to the balcony where Angelina stood, smoke rising from her dress.

Chapter Eight

Without so much as a knock or a greeting, Hollis entered Jay's office, his blue eyes dark and stormy, though his light hair was slicked back without a strand out of place. He narrowed his gaze and directed it straight at Jay.

Though his mouth was dry, Jay stood. He wiped his hands on his pants then looked down to find smears of ink. "Mr. Stanford, what a delightful surprise." He almost choked on the words. "To what do I owe the pleasure of this visit?"

"Cut out all the niceties and save them for the ladies. Though I doubt you have much luck with them. Somehow, though, you have managed to cause Mariah to fall under your spell, and I'm not happy about my fiancée speaking to another man, no matter how awkward he may be."

Jay fiddled with the chain of his pocket watch. "You see, it's like this. I have known the Randolph family for several years, since I moved to Peshtigo. There is nothing more than that to it."

"I don't care if you have known Miss Randolph for a hundred years. Circumstances are now different, and there is not to be so much as a whiff of a scandal surrounding my future wife. Do I make myself clear?"

Mariah was the one person, other than Hollis' father, who understood Jay and was kind to him. Who didn't taunt him because of his lack of social graces. "Very clear, sir." Just because he understood didn't mean he had any intention of cutting ties with Mariah or her family. Soon enough, she would be living in the grand city of Chicago and would forget he even existed.

Hollis turned to leave then spun around once more. "And another thing, Franklin. No more late nights. If you cannot complete your assigned tasks within the workday, we will be forced to find a man better suited to the job."

Before Jay could formulate a reply, Hollis disappeared down the hall. Jay thumped into his chair and stared at the pile of bills to be paid. His first impulse was to question how Hollis knew he'd had conversations with Mariah, but that answer was obvious. Anyone who attended church or went anywhere in town was bound to know that. Word spread around Peshtigo faster than the wildfires in the Bush.

What left him scratching his head was Hollis' strange request to not work overtime. Could he possibly know about Jay's suspicions? The only person he had shared that privileged information with was Mariah. No, no. She would never share his secret with anyone.

Except maybe her fiancé? No. At that thought, he shook his head so hard his temples set to pounding, the ache greater than the one he already had.

Somehow, though, Hollis knew. Or at least suspected. His veiled threat only confirmed that Jay was right to question the man's ethics.

Jay resumed his work, finding comfort in the numbers that lined up and behaved the way they were supposed to behave. Except that these didn't. Instead of getting better, the problem only grew. The small amounts he had been off multiplied by the day. There was no more ignoring the fact that this was bigger than him making a mistake in his calculations.

After working a while longer, Jay threw his pen on the desk blotter and huffed out a breath. A break was in order, so he reached for his coat to step outside. Then again, the weather had warmed, and the beginning of October was more like the end of August.

Everything was strange and off.

Perhaps he should return to the boardinghouse and eat the fine chicken meal Mrs. Abbott had prepared there. With that plan made, he left the stuffy office and stepped into the acrid air. A yellow haze hung over the entire village, and it was impossible to inhale a deep breath without coughing.

A weight settled on his shoulders, and rather than the brisk walk he had intended, he settled for a slow stroll, though he was anything other than relaxed.

He turned down his street and gazed at the Randolph home. Come Sunday, he would be taking the noon meal with them. Since he had already accepted the invitation, there was no way he could back out now without injuring feelings.

Hollis had no choice but to accept that Jay would at least greet Mariah and make whatever small talk he could with her.

He hadn't gone far before screams came from the Randolph home. Two sets of screams, in fact. One a woman's cry, the other a young child's. Despite the poor air quality, he sprinted to the house. The calls of distress came from the rear of the building.

This time, he was the one who didn't bother to knock but instead raced inside, right past an openmouthed Mrs. Randolph, and took the stairs two at a time before bursting through the door onto the balcony.

Mariah had stopped yelling, but the golden-haired child continued to scream. And no wonder, with the way her full skirts smoked.

Jay pushed Mariah to the side, grabbed the girl, and laid her on the floor. Then he stripped off his suit jacket, wrapped it around the bottom of her skirts, and smothered the smoldering embers.

She wriggled and squirmed, but he held her fast. "Don't worry. I won't hurt you. I'm here to help."

A moment later, Mariah was at his side. "Mr. Franklin is putting out the fire." She squeezed his upper arm.

"Bring a bucket of water."

Mariah left to comply and returned a few moments later with what he had requested. Only then did he dare remove his jacket and douse the girl to ensure the fire was out. He turned to Mariah. "Watch her. I'm going to get another bucket in case it's not fully out."

She nodded, her green eyes wide and a slight tremble to her chin.

He hustled down the steps and to the pump in the kitchen. Mrs. Randolph stood beside the sink, wringing her hands. "What's happening? Angelina was playing upstairs, and we heard her screaming."

"An ember must have landed on her, and her skirts caught."

"Oh, no." Mrs. Randolph leaned against the counter.

"Not to worry. I'm fairly certain it's out, and I don't think it will start again. This is just in case." He lifted the wooden bucket from the sink and hurried up the stairs once more to find Mariah holding the weeping girl on her lap.

"Hush now, hush."

The yellow haze formed an aura around them, almost like the halos painters used to create around a Madonna and child. Mariah stroked the girl's hair and cocooned her. Already, she had a mother's heart.

As he approached, she withdrew a handkerchief from her apron pocket and dabbed the child's eyes. He stood for a moment more, absorbing the scene in front of him. Someone should record the sight on canvas. He had never seen Mariah more beautiful.

Then she glanced his way, and a smile formed on her lips. "Thank you for what you did. Your quick thinking is much appreciated. I have to confess to being rather shocked at the sight and not able to decide what I should do."

"That's understandable. The good Lord was watching out for you today and sent me home for lunch for a reason."

Mariah nodded, and Jay squatted to be at eye level with the girl. "And who is this?"

"This is Angelina, who is soon to be my stepdaughter."

He tightened the muscles in his jaw to keep his mouth from falling open. That explained why she was so maternal with the child. He set the unneeded bucket to the side.

"Angelina, this is Mr. Franklin. Mr. Franklin, may I present Angelina Stanford."

He shook her hand. "Pleased to meet you, miss. It's quite the honor. Your father is my boss at the railroad."

Angelina nodded then turned away into Mariah's embrace.

"She can be a bit shy."

"I understand. I'm quiet too, and that's not all bad."

Angelina took another look at him, fair lashes framing the bluest eyes he'd ever encountered. "I like you."

"And I like you. How about we go inside so that Mrs. Randolph can tend to you."

She slid from Mariah's lap but held to her hand as they made their way to the main floor. Mrs. Randolph fussed over the child and guided her to the kitchen to get a treat.

Mariah stuffed the handkerchief into her apron pocket. "I truly don't know how I can ever thank you, Jay. If anything happened to Angelina. . ."

"Say no more. Like I said, it was Providence."

A knock at the door drew Mariah's attention, and she went to answer it.

Great. There was every possibility it was Hollis, either come to collect his daughter or to have lunch with Mariah.

Sure enough, Hollis stepped inside and eyed Jay up and down. "Why are you here and not at the office?"

"Well, it's my lunch hour, sir, and I decided to have my meal at home, which led me right past this house. And then—"

"And then Jay was a gentleman and checked on us." Mariah stiffened her back.

Hollis narrowed his eyes. "Why on earth would he need to do that?"

"Father, Father." Angelina danced in from the kitchen, a cookie in her hand. "You will never guess what happened to me."

Mariah turned a shade of white purer than a fresh snowfall. Jay took one sidestep closer to her. If he needed to, he would throw himself between them.

"It was nothing, really, Hollis." Mariah clasped her hands in front of her. "She was playing on the balcony, and an ember drifted down and rested on her skirts. Jay heard me screaming and put it out before any harm was done."

"Well, I do have a black hole in my pinafore." Angelina showed her father her battle scar.

Whereas Mariah had gone white, red now built in Hollis' face. "Is this what happens when I leave you to watch my daughter? Weren't you with her?"

Mariah shook her head.

"And why not?"

"She went to get her painting to show Mama, that's all. I was downstairs, as we were in the middle of tea and cookies. Really, Hollis, she wasn't alone for long."

If possible, his face reddened further. He was a volcano about to erupt. "She shouldn't be alone at all. She is just a child. That's why I hired a nanny for her. This is unconscionable. What if she had died?" Hollis' voice rose in pitch and volume.

Angelina's blue eyes filled with tears. "Father, please don't yell. I don't like it when you do that."

"You should have been inside playing with your dolls. Something safe."

"I was painting a picture like Miss Mariah." Angelina sniffled.

"You are not to paint again. Do you understand me? That is fine for Miss Randolph, but not for you." He turned his attention and focused his fury on Mariah. "I have no objection to you pursuing this hobby, but you will not encourage my daughter to follow in your footsteps. From the first day you met her, I told you she is to be raised to be a lady. Is that clear?"

Jay fisted his hands, ready to land a punch on the side of Hollis' face if he dared speak to Mariah in such a tone again.

For her part, she stood, shoulders tense but unflinching. "I understand you perfectly, Mr. Stanford. Is there anything further?"

"I will be returning to the hotel with Angelina immediately and will leave her in the care of her nanny this afternoon. I had questioned bringing her to Peshtigo, but now I'm glad I did. It allowed me to ascertain more of your character."

Angelina pulled on Hollis' waistcoat. "But Father, I don't want to leave."

"If I say we're going, then we are going, and I will not tolerate any back talk. Is that understood?"

The girl nodded.

Hollis grabbed her by the hand and almost pushed her out the door. "We will discuss this later, Miss Randolph." The door banged shut behind him.

Mariah's shoulders slumped, and it was all Jay could do not to take her in his arms.

"I'm sorry you had to witness that." Mariah's words were little more than a whisper.

"And I'm sorry you had to experience that. Does he always act in such a manner with you?"

"No. I was careless and deserved that tongue-lashing."

"On the contrary. Children should be allowed to play. What happened, happened, and it had nothing to do with you. The ember would have fallen just the same if you had been there."

"I should have realized it was dangerous to leave her outside."

Jay shrugged. "Frankly, it's dangerous inside these days."

"Again, I thank you for coming to our rescue. You can't know how much I appreciate it."

"I would never stand by and watch someone come to harm. Please, don't be too hard on yourself. And let me know if there is anything I can do for you."

Like putting Hollis in his place.

Chapter Nine

The tinkling of a piano and blue smoke that didn't come from the fires outside greeted Hollis as he entered the saloon. In the middle of a weekday, the place was almost empty, save for the lone man with a long beard and a battered hat sitting at the end of the bar. He didn't bother to turn as Hollis made his way to the table in the far corner of the room.

Three others sat around the table stained by water rings from the bottoms of many hundreds of drinks which had sat on it over the course of the years. Hollis scraped back the remaining empty chair, removed his bowler hat, and sat down, the seat wobbling underneath his weight.

"Ah, Hollis, I was afraid you weren't going to show. It's not like you to be late." Mr. Randolph clapped Hollis on the back.

"A little matter arose that needed my attention, but I'm here now, so no more talking." He nodded in the direction of Mariah's father. "Deal the cards."

With the skill of a man who had performed the action on numerous occasions, Mr. Randolph shuffled the deck and doled out five cards to each of the men. Mr. Labrante, the hotel owner, and Mr. Sidley, the operator of a ship on Lake Michigan, each picked up their cards. Mr. Sidley raised one eyebrow. Both Mr. Labrante and Mr. Randolph kept their expressions neutral.

Hollis gazed at his own hand. Not much of anything useful. He tightened his jaw but worked to keep his facial expressions from showing his true feelings about his cards. He dropped some money into the center of the table.

"Glad you could make it to our game today." Play came around to Mr. Randolph, and he upped the ante.

Hollis slapped down three of his cards. "Of course. Wouldn't miss it." He resisted the urge to tell Mariah's father what he thought now of the deal they had struck over this very table some months ago.

Mr. Randolph slid three cards in Hollis' direction. "I didn't know if we would see you before the wedding. Have you stopped to see my beautiful daughter yet?"

"That was the reason for my delay. That and the fact that your daughter almost allowed mine to burn to death."

At this proclamation, all the men turned their attention from the game to Hollis. Mr. Randolph puffed on his cigar. "What do you mean?"

Hollis explained what happened. "From now on, I will insist that the nanny accompany Angelina at all times. Mariah is careless."

Mr. Randolph shrugged and replaced one of his cards with one from the deck. "She meant no harm. It's a wonder that none of us has been consumed by these flames yet, though I'm sure it was distressing for all involved."

Hollis folded. "I am concerned for my daughter's well-being and would never treat her the way you have treated yours."

"What?" Mr. Randolph shrugged. "You were all quite eager and more than a little drunk when you accepted the deal, all in an effort to keep your father from discovering your little vice. I saw an opportunity to ensure my daughter's security for the rest of her life. Don't tell me I don't look out for her welfare."

"Gentlemen, may we please return to the game?" Mr. Sidley stroked his large, waxed mustache.

"Of course." Hollis had to win today and win big. He couldn't keep taking money from his father's coffers. Sooner or later, someone was going to catch on, even though he had done his best to cover his tracks. Knowing his luck, it would be that fool his father had taken in and loved more than he had loved Hollis.

The cards, however, didn't fall in his favor. Mr. Sidley and Mr. Labrante won most of the hands. Mr. Randolph lost big. At least Hollis could cover his backside. Mr. Randolph didn't have a rich father who wouldn't notice a few missing dollars.

Once the whistle sounded at the woodenware factory marking the end of another day, all four men pushed away from the table and disbursed. Hollis grabbed Mr. Randolph by his bright white collar before he could scoot away. "I'd like to have a word with you."

"Of course." Mr. Randolph crossed his arms in front of him.

"Not here. Come to my office in a few minutes. No one will so much as blink at my future father-in-law paying me a call there."

"Fine. I'll see you then." Mr. Randolph picked up his suit coat. As he slid it on, Hollis made his escape from the saloon, a place he would be loath to be caught in, and headed to the railroad offices.

He passed Jay's first-floor room on his way to the stairs. The quick peek in afforded him a glance of the man hard at work, scribbling marks in that ledger of his.

Hollis had no reason to be jealous of him. Mariah could never be happy with a man of such low birth who could offer her nothing more than a simple home and a fool to keep her warm. While many would consider her to be far beneath Hollis' station, she had her beauty to recommend her as well as her general pleasing disposition and her taste in fashion and art.

He would wed her to please both her father and his. When she produced a boy who could be heir to the Stanford railroad empire, then he could resume his dalliances and leave her to be another ornament in his home.

He had hardly settled himself in his soft leather chair before Mr. Randolph knocked on the door and let himself in. "You said you wanted to talk to me about something?"

"Yes. I have already expressed my displeasure to your daughter with the way she handles mine. I appreciate her kindness and attention to Angelina, but she is far too familiar with the girl. That is not the way children are raised in my world. If you want me to keep my end of the bargain, speak to her and remind her of her place."

Mr. Randolph had the gall to chuckle. More than that, to outright laugh. "You are not in a position to tell me what to do. I know your dirty little secret, how you are taking money from your father to keep your creditors off your back. You don't want that information to become public."

"What about your creditors? I can make life easier for you and help you cover your debts if you keep your daughter in line. It would not look good for you for her name to be besmirched, even in this little backwater town." Hollis sat back and grinned.

He had Mr. Randolph over a barrel. Watching him squirm was entirely too much fun.

Chapter Ten

SUNDAY, OCTOBER 8, 1871

For about the hundredth time, Mariah checked the place settings on the snowy-linen-covered table. She adjusted the shiny silver forks, knives, and spoons beside the violet-sprigged bone china dishes.

Jay would never notice that she measured the ends of each piece of silverware to be in exact alignment with each other and the plates. On the other hand, it was what Hollis would expect. An expert chef prepared every meal at his home in Chicago, and well-trained servants laid out the table. He expected nothing short of perfection.

She pressed her stomach to halt its flip-flopping. In the dimness of the early morning, smoke hanging like a dark cloud over the town, the candlelight sparkled off the gleaming silverware, a bit of sun in the midst of the growing gloom.

Though unseasonable heat permeated the plastered walls, leaving the dining room as warm as the kitchen with the stove on full blast, when she attempted to crack a window to cool the air, a flurry of ash blew in with the strong wind. She had little choice but to slam it shut to keep the room pristine.

Of course, at that precise moment, Mama entered. "What on earth is all that racket?"

"I'm sorry. Like everyone else in town, I'm frustrated by these never-ending fires. It's impossible to keep the ash from settling on the dishes."

Mama sighed and nodded in solidarity. "What a blessing the fall rains will be."

"If they ever arrive."

"Why the pessimism?"

Could it be because of how Hollis had treated her? Thoughts of the other day when Angelina's skirts caught fire plagued her. Perhaps she was questioning her willingness to marry him. "Fatigue, nothing more."

Mama touched Mariah's face, her hand cool against her warm cheek. "Are you well?"

"I'm fine. As you said, nothing a good rainstorm won't cure, even though the temperature is more suited to August than October."

"In three months' time, you'll be complaining about the cold and longing for a day such as this."

Mariah chuckled. "Of course. That's what you do when you live in Wisconsin."

"If nothing else, we have a lovely dinner party awaiting us this afternoon after service."

Not anything Mariah was looking forward to. The thick, heavy atmosphere would be even worse with both Jay and Hollis at the table. At least Angelina remained in town and would come with her father. She brought a bit of sunshine with her wherever she went.

"You're right, Mama, as always. And speaking of the service, we had better get going to church. Are you ready to leave?"

"Let me grab my bonnet, and we can be on our way."

A short time later, they arrived at the church. One sign that Peshtigo was a thriving village was the fact that the schoolhouse was separate from the sanctuary. And they had multiple houses of worship, including the new Catholic church.

Mariah slid into the pew beside her parents and withdrew her hand-painted paper fan from her reticule. Even though she put it to work, it did little to stop a dribble of sweat from trickling down her spine and underneath her corset.

All the congregants sat in rapt attention to the sermon. The little children nestled on their parents' laps or sat beside them, hands folded.

No babies cried and needed to be taken from the building. Even Pastor Beach was less than his usual fiery self.

By the time she arrived at home, Hollis and Angelina already waiting outside the door, she was hot, tired, and rather cross. Every instinct in her cried out for her to berate him for not attending church. Instead, she raised one eyebrow and marched into the house.

She had gone three steps when contrition hit her hard. Hollis had never missed church before. Perhaps he or Angelina had been under the weather. That had to be it. She turned around to apologize, only to find Jay behind her instead of Hollis.

"What are you doing?"

He opened his mouth, but a split second passed before he found his voice. "Isn't this the Sunday that I was supposed to come for dinner?"

"Yes. That's not what I meant." She entered the living room and sank into the deep crimson sofa, pressing on her closed eyes.

The cushion sank beside her. "Is something troubling you?"

"Yes." Wait, what was she saying? "No. I mean, no. Everything is fine. It's just far too hot today, that's all. Fall can't come fast enough for me."

"If it's too awkward for me to be here at the same time as Hollis, I can leave."

"Is it too awkward for you?" She uncovered her eyes and stared at him.

He turned away and gazed at some point on the wall across the room for several moments. "No, it's fine." He returned his attention to her. "Unless you would like me to leave. Otherwise, I would prefer to be here."

She heard footsteps, and then, as if the house were on fire, he jumped to his feet and rubbed his hands up and down his pants. A moment later, Angelina burst into the room. "Guess what, Miss Mariah?"

She didn't have to work too hard to smile at the little girl. "What, sweetheart?"

"Father has promised to get me a kitten when we get back to Chicago, just like the black one that lives outside your door."

"Oh, is that so?"

"It is. And I know you like cats, so I'm sure that won't be a problem when you and Father get married and you're my new mother and you come to live with us."

Lady picked this moment to come in and yip and spin in circles, sending Angelina into a fit of the giggles.

"Will Lady be my dog too when you get married?"

"Of course she will. If we get a girl kitten, maybe I can sew a little bonnet for her to wear. I'll make a matching one for Lady."

Angelina laughed some more then scampered off to tell her father what Mariah had just said. He would brush it off as poppycock, but it would be fun. There was nothing better in the world than Angelina's cheerfulness.

Before Mariah could say any more to Jay, the rest of the family finished their climb up the steps and into the house, and she went to the kitchen with Mama to finish preparing the meal.

She mashed the potatoes while Papa carved the roast and Mama set a basket of piping hot, yeasty dinner rolls on the table. Who knew what Jay and Hollis might be saying to each other in the living room? While she would love to be a fly on the wall, it was probably best she not know.

Once they had prayed, and everyone tucked into their meals, the clinking of silverware against the fine china was the only sound in the room. Angelina couldn't leave the void unfilled, so she proceeded to tell her new favorite story, "The Three Billy Goats Gruff."

"Doesn't that frighten you?" Mariah stabbed a string bean with her fork.

"Oh, no. They are only made-up stories. That's what Father says. He told it to me, you know, and then I read it in a book with my nanny. She didn't think it was—what did she say, Father?"

"Appropriate."

"That's it. Appropriate for me, but it was fine. I never have nightmares."

"You know that children are to be seen and not heard at the table." Hollis cast a sidelong glance at his daughter before diving into his meal once more.

"How have things been at the office, Mr. Stanford?" Papa took a long swig of water.

"Fine."

"And when do you return to Chicago?" This question came from Jay.

If the air in the room hadn't been heavy already, it was now. Mariah held her breath.

"Tomorrow."

"No, Father, I want to stay with Miss Mariah." This outburst earned Angelina another frown from Hollis.

"This was meant to be a quick trip to check on railroad business here. I have already extended it too long. We leave tomorrow, and that is the end of it. Soon enough, Miss Mariah will come to live with us."

Angelina pouted but went back to eating.

No more was said about the railroad for the rest of the meal. Papa and the other two men chatted about the fires and the unusual nature of them. Angelina kept Mariah well enough engaged that she managed to tune out much of what the men said. It was enough to have to endure the blazes every day.

"Miss Mariah, aren't you listening to me?" Angelina tugged on the sleeve of Mariah's green Sunday dress.

Mariah smiled. "I'm sorry, sweetie. I got distracted for a moment. What were you saying?"

"Look. I ate all my beans. All six of them, one for each year old I am. I don't want to live to be a hundred and have to eat a hundred beans."

Now Mariah's grin was more genuine. "I would hate that too."

"You don't like beans?"

"I like them well enough, but not so much that I would want to eat that many."

"Angelina." Her father's voice was harsh.

"Don't worry about her, Hollis. You men are having your discussion. It's only right we do too."

"It will be good to return to the city where life is more civilized."

Mariah pushed back her chair. "How about some chocolate cake?" She picked up her plate and Angelina's.

"Let me help." Jay came to his feet.

"Absolutely not." Mama shook her head. "This is a job for the ladies."

"I insist." Jay was on his way to the kitchen before Mariah could even take a breath to object again. Once they had both set down their dishes, he pulled her to the side. "Since Hollis is leaving tomorrow, I want to get a look around his office this evening after the church service. I need you to keep him occupied."

"He will likely be making preparations to leave."

"He has staff to do that. Go spend time with Angelina or say a lingering goodbye to him. Just don't let him go to the office."

"I don't like this. What if he catches you?"

"If you do your job, he won't. I would go now, but it would be rude of me to run off so soon after the meal, and then it will be time for the service."

"What are you talking about?"

Angelina startled Mariah so much, she clutched her chest. "Nothing at all. Just that I am going to miss you something awful when you go back to Chicago."

"I'm going to miss you too. I want you to be my new mother right now. Can't you come with us? Nanny isn't nearly as nice as you are."

"Well then, how about I come to the hotel tonight and tuck you into bed and say goodbye?"

"Will you tell me the story about the billy goats?"

"I'm afraid I don't know that one."

"But if you're going to be my new mother, you'll have to learn it."

"I suppose I will."

After cake and coffee and more conversation, the guests left with just enough time for Mariah and Papa to get ready for the evening service. Mama was tired and decided to stay home. Papa had a meeting after church. As soon as the last notes of the final hymn faded away, Mariah made her way to the hotel to keep her promise to Angelina.

And Jay.

Hollis opened the door when Mariah knocked. "Good. I'm glad you're here. Nanny is busy packing Angelina's clothes so we can leave first thing in the morning. You can watch her while I go to the office to pick up a few things I forgot."

"No, do you really have to go right now? While I did come to see Angelina, who I really want to spend time with is you." Why did those words sour on her tongue?

"Then this is perfect. By the time I return, Angelina will be asleep, and you and I will be able to say a proper goodbye to each other." The gleam in his eyes sent a shiver down her arms, despite the rather warm evening.

"Please, won't you stay and tell her the story? I don't know it, and I'd like to hear it from you to be sure I'm telling it the right way." The excuse sounded flimsy, even to her, but she had to keep him from going to the office for at least an hour or so. Give Jay time to do whatever snooping he needed to do.

"She knows it well enough. If you'll excuse me."

As he passed her, she grabbed him by the arm. "Please, stay for a little while."

He scowled, thunder darkening his eyes. "You are behaving irrationally, and I don't like it one bit." He shook her off as if she were a pesky fly. "I will be back shortly. Make sure Angelina is asleep."

She could do nothing more than watch him leave.

And pray that Jay would be gone by the time he arrived.

Chapter Eleven

As soon as Pastor Beach pronounced the benediction over the congregation, Jay hustled out of church, nodding to members who greeted him but not stopping to hold conversations. Not that he enjoyed doing so anyway.

The air outside was thick and heavy, though there was no humidity. Not so much as a breeze stirred the browning leaves on the trees or the sawdust on the ground.

The calm before the storm? They could only pray, and had done so a few minutes earlier, that rain would come, even tonight.

Holding a handkerchief over his mouth because of the acrid, yellow haze, he hustled in the direction of the railroad office. The music of a tinkling piano spilled out of the saloon, packed with lumberjacks imbibing enough to hold them through the long week of work ahead.

"Good evening, my son." Father Pernin, the Catholic priest, waved a shovel in the air as Jay hurried by.

This brought him to a halt. "What are you doing, Father?"

"All day, I've felt in my soul that something is coming. I can't tell you what, but my spirit is troubled, so I'm burying some of the most valuable items from the church. Things we need for conducting mass."

"You feel our situation is that dire?" Though many of the town's residents had done the same, especially a couple of weeks ago when it appeared the fires would overtake them.

"Better to be wise and look foolish than to be proven a fool."

"Ah, yes, you may be right. Well, I need to be going."

"God bless you, my son." The priest returned to his work, though his shovel was so small, it might take him until morning to finish the hole he was digging.

At last, Jay came to the railroad office and slipped inside. Thanks to the persistent orange glow of the skies, he had no need of a lamp to light his way, and he knew well enough how to get to Hollis' office.

He opened the door and shut it behind himself, his heart racing like a runaway horse. All good so far. Get in and get out. His hands shook as he sorted through the papers on Hollis' desk.

All he needed was one piece of proof that it was the younger Mr. Stanford who was skimming the money from the accounts. It would also be nice to know where that cash went.

He sifted through the papers. Correspondence with government agencies. Not helpful. Drawings of the railroad route. Not what he wanted. Letters from the construction foreman about their progress. Not what he needed.

Then he froze.

Sucked in a breath.

Picked up the handful of mail.

Each missive from a creditor, demanding repayment of loans.

Loans made to Hollis to cover gambling debts.

So that was why he needed the cash. Going to his father to ask for it was impossible. The elder Mr. Stanford was an upright man and would have words for his wayward son. Judging by the astronomical numbers, the amount these letters demanded far exceeded what Hollis had the ability to pay.

The Stanfords were wealthy, but this was no pocket change. If paid in full, it may well cause both the family and their railroad empire great financial difficulty. This was much more than the missing money Jay had discovered. If Hollis was taking cash to keep his creditors at bay, he must also be taking it from the main Chicago accounts. The books here only covered the money from the Northwoods operations.

Jay had proof of Hollis' gambling debts. Close but not quite enough to prove that Hollis was skimming money from the company. What did he do with this information? Go to the elder Mr. Stanford? It would break his heart, which was in bad enough condition. Perhaps he needed to confront Hollis. No. That might get ugly fast.

He had to bide his time and come up with the smoking gun that would tie Hollis to the missing money without the shadow of a doubt.

Then came a creaking on the stairs. Jay held his breath. Probably just the settling of the building for the night. He stuffed the papers inside his suit coat, even though the ink might run because he was sweating so much.

The creaking continued, drawing closer. There was no doubt now that those were footsteps.

Mariah was supposed to keep Hollis occupied, away from the office as long as possible. She must not have been able to persuade him to stay with her.

Before Jay could formulate a reasonable explanation as to why he was in the office, Hollis entered, a candle in his hand, the circle of light around it illuminating Jay.

"Franklin. What the devil are you doing here?" Even the dim glow was enough to show Hollis' face reddening.

"I needed to get something." Not a falsehood.

"What could you possibly need in my office?"

"I thought something I was looking for was in here."

Hollis made a circuit of the room, holding the candle in front of him, surveying the papers on his desk. "These aren't how I left them."

"Maybe a mouse moved them."

"Aren't you a man?"

All Jay could do was stare at Hollis, whose eyes bulged.

"You are a bumbling, clumsy fool who fancies himself smarter than anyone. Wake up. You will never be anything more than the scrawny, dirty, sniveling child my father had the misfortune to rescue." Hollis sneered.

Jay fisted his hands and bit the inside of his cheek. "How dare you?"

"Yes, how dare you come into my office and mess with my private papers, some of which are now missing?"

The heat which had been building in Jay now turned icy cold.

"Do you deny going through my things and helping yourself to what isn't yours?"

"You are the one who is helping yourself to what isn't—"

Hollis landed a punch on Jay's left cheek, hard enough for him to stumble backward. Without a moment for him to prepare, Hollis punched him again, this time on the right cheek. Jay staggered and landed against the wall with a thud.

Hollis loomed over him, his shadow engulfing Jay, who fought to keep his mind clear. A moment later, Hollis lifted his fist again.

Then came the sound of a train, loud enough to rumble the ground underneath Jay's feet. What was going on? No cars would be running to the harbor on the Sabbath.

Hollis turned and raced from the room, leaving the candlestick sitting on his desk. Jay followed in hot pursuit. Within a few seconds, they both reached the front door.

A wall of fire greeted Jay, a great roiling ball of flame that careened down the street, throwing houses into the air. Seconds later, those buildings exploded.

His heart pounded, and his mouth went dry. In a few moments, they would be consumed. Jay burst through the door and tripped over Hollis' outstretched leg. He fell to the ground, pain radiating through his left arm.

Above him, all was fire.

———————— ◆•• ————————

Mariah did her best to follow along with the story of "The Three Billy Goats Gruff" that Angelina told her, but her mind strayed to Jay and what might be happening at the office. Perhaps she should go see. When Hollis was angry, he could be. . .

She shivered, then shook off the thought and turned her attention back to Angelina. "I'm sorry, darling, but I just remembered something I need to do. You'll have to finish the story when I come to see you in a few weeks."

The girl sat up in the bed and flung herself into Mariah's embrace. "Please, do you have to go already?"

"I'm afraid so."

"Can't I come?"

"It's time when little girls must go to sleep before they turn into old hags."

"That's not true."

"Oh, isn't it? Do you want to take the chance and find out?" Mariah softened her words with a half smile.

"No, I'll go to sleep."

Mariah kissed her cheek. "It won't be long, and then I'll be with you all the time. Before I go, I'll send Nanny in to say good night. I love you."

"I love you too."

Mariah hurried out the door, swiping away a tear. Angelina would be the best part of marrying Hollis. That and getting her paintings on exhibit around the world.

After letting Nanny know she was leaving, she scampered down the stairs and out the door. She hadn't taken even a single step before a horrendous roar filled the air and the ground trembled beneath her feet.

Screams split the Sunday silence. A man ran past, shouting. "Fire! Fire! We're done for!"

A whirlwind of flames raced like wild horses down the street. Toward their home. Toward Mama, alone.

Mariah spun on her heel, grabbed her skirts and sprinted up the stairs, then flung open the door. "Nanny! Nanny! Get out, now. Fire! A huge fire is coming this way."

Nanny appeared in the doorway, Angelina's coat in her hand. "I'll take care of her, miss."

"Get to the river. I have to warn my mother."

Another mad dash down the stairs carried her outside.

A stream of people, eyes wide, some screaming, headed toward the river that snaked through town, which now glowed orange. Mariah was caught up in the tide and surged forward with them. It took Herculean strength to break away and make it home.

By now, the fire nipped at her heels. Up the front steps and into the living room.

Mama stood in the middle of the room in her robe, clutching the silver chest.

"Leave that." Mariah had to scream to be heard over the fire's roar and Lady's wild barking. Mariah yanked the chest from Mama and threw it to the side, forks and knives and spoons clattering to the floor. Then she scooped up the dog, grasped Mama by the hand, then pulled her down the stairs and back into the sea of humanity fleeing the encroaching blaze.

Oppressive heat seared Mariah's lungs as soon as she stepped outside. She barreled her way through the mob, half dragging her mother behind her. The tornado of fire raced toward them, and the roar of the firestorm filled her ears. Outside, she sweated so much that she almost lost her hold on Mama. Inside, she was icy cold. What would happen to them? Was the world coming to an end?

Lady wriggled from her arms. "No! Come back!" Within seconds, Lady disappeared into the surging throng.

Embers fell from the sky like rain, igniting everything around them. The swirling winds lifted one house from its foundation, and it exploded into flames in midair.

Wheels of fire broke off from the main whirlwind and jumped ahead, setting buildings ablaze.

In front of them, a man struggled to control his horse that pulled a wagon with his family inside. A ball of fire fell into the wagon's bed and set it ablaze. The man dropped to his knees, the inferno consuming him as well.

Mariah bit the side of her hand to keep from vomiting. She gasped for breath as they sprinted ever forward. Excruciating pain ripped through her lungs each time she inhaled, the intense heat scorching them.

Her arms ached, and Mama dragged behind her. Ahead of them, a woman fell into a heap on the ground. Mariah turned. The fire continued to gain on them. Behind them a boy kneeled on the road, as if in prayer, and the flames swallowed him.

She gagged.

On they stumbled, Mariah praying they would make it to the river in time, before the inferno reached them. They had to keep moving. She pushed and pulled through the press of people. If only she could take a deep breath.

Mama worked to free herself from Mariah's grasp. "I'm slowing you down. Go! Go!"

"No! I won't leave you." She tightened her grip on Mama and continued forward. They reached the edge of the water. Bodies choked the river, some alive, some still and unmoving.

"Where's your papa?" Mama halted her steps once more.

They were wasting precious time. "At the river. We'll see him there." The lie slid off Mariah's tongue. Anything to prevent Mama from stalling.

A second could cost them their lives.

Many of Peshtigo's residents had fled here. Already the river was crowded. People clogged the bridge, some going in one direction, others heading the opposite way.

Out of nowhere, the bridge, like everything else, burst into flames and was flung into the water.

"Mama! We have to get in."

"Frank! Frank! Frank!" Mama wouldn't budge.

Nothing Mariah did got her moving. She had planted herself on the bank and wouldn't go a step farther.

The flames approached, the hot air singeing Mariah's face and eyes. Her heart pounded. The entire world was a roaring whirlwind of heat and flame.

They would die. She couldn't get Mama into the water, so they would die.

As many around her plunged into the river, she remained on the bank, still grasping Mama by the hand.

She stared her own death in the face.

Lord, don't let it hurt.

She'd barely finished the prayer when something, someone, swept her off her feet, carried her down the riverbank, and tossed her into the water.

She came up spluttering. Because she was unable to swim, it was good she was still near the shore, where the water wasn't deep. "Mama!"

A moment later, another splash came. "Get under!"

Jay. She fought him as he dunked her, almost out of breath before he let her go. "What are you doing?"

"The air is hot. Stay wet." On his other side was Mama, whom he now dunked.

Mariah obeyed, alternating being below and above the water. Over their heads, fire raced in flaming balls. On the bank stood a little girl clutching a rag doll.

Angelina?

Weighed down by her heavy skirts, Mariah scrambled for the bank to pull her into the water. She didn't make it far before flames surrounded the child.

"No!"

Chapter Twelve

Forever would the images from that awful night be seared into Mariah's brain. She had no need of canvas and oils to bring the scenes to mind. Burning logs floating by. How could they burn in water? Bloated cows—that was what she chose to think of them as—littered the water. And men and women who exited the water too soon after the worst of the maelstrom, flaming like lit candles.

"It's the end of the world." Mama cried these words each time she emerged from under the water. "It's the end of the world. Prepare to meet Jesus. He's coming soon. This is His righteous judgment on this wicked town."

At first, screams rent the night. As the minutes and hours ticked by, there were fewer voices. Some silenced by overuse. Some silenced by the burning hot air.

Some silenced forever.

In the course of one long nightmare, Mariah must have dunked her head in the water hundreds of times. Jay stayed by her side, Mama next to him.

"I'm so tired, Jay." Mariah shivered. How could she be cold when the air was super-heated? "When will this be over?"

"Don't give up. Keep going. Up and down. The movement will keep you warm. If you stop, you'll drown or die of hypothermia. I'm not going to let either of those happen. Not to you, not to me, not to your mother."

Mariah dunked herself again. Coming to the surface required more effort each time. Her skirts were weights against her legs, pulling her down, working to keep her under.

Perhaps she should give up. If it was the end of the world, she would soon be in the Lord's presence anyway. He would come and catch her into the air with Him.

Her lungs were burning when someone grabbed her by the neck of her dress and pulled her to the surface.

She spluttered. "Please, let me go. I can't keep on like this anymore. Let me die."

Even in the dim light of the smoldering fires, she didn't miss the scowl Jay threw her way. "Both of you, listen to me." He shot narrow-eyed glances at her and Mama. "We are going to survive. We will not give up, no matter how tired or cold we are. We will live to see the morning."

"It's the end of the world. It's the end of the world." Mama sobbed.

"No, it's not." Jay's voice was raspy, but his words were firm. "Don't give in to despair. The Lord will deliver us."

"It's the end of the world." Mama wouldn't be consoled, so Mariah slogged her way to her side.

"Jay is right. We can't give up. Don't ever give up. I need you, Mama, I need you. Fight this. I promise to fight if you do."

Mama nodded, and Mariah took her by the shoulders and pulled her under, Jay remaining beside them.

The smoke abated and allowed some of the light from the half-moon through. By this point, they were able to stay above water for longer periods of time, and a while after that, they didn't have to dive under at all. One man, possibly Father Pernin, climbed the bank and didn't burst into flames.

Beside her, Mama shivered. "So cold. So, so, so cold." Her teeth chattered.

Here and there, more people emerged from the water. Mariah pointed them out to Jay. "We have to get Mama warm, and by all indications, the danger is past."

"I'll help you take her up."

Jay supported Mama on one side while Mariah supported her on the other. Together, the three of them slipped and slid their way up the bank and onto dry ground.

Where grass had once grown along the river, it was no more. Only sand was left. That and smoldering piles of. . .well. . .something else Mariah refused to allow her mind to entertain. They found a place to sit in the sand, enough heat emanating from the debris that it would warm and dry them.

As they lowered Mama to the ground, Jay winced.

Mariah arranged Mama's half-burned skirts over her legs, her attention on Jay. "Are you injured?"

"Just a little pain in my arm."

"When did that start?"

"Before the fire."

She sucked in a breath. "Why didn't you say anything?"

"What could be done about it? We were in a fight for our lives. No doctor could examine it, and there was no time for a sling."

"Was it—?"

"I'll tell you later. Sit beside your mother. I'm going to assess the situation."

Mama reached out and grabbed Jay by his hole-dotted trousers. "Find Frank. Please, I have to know where my husband is." She coughed, a deep, unsettling rattle in her chest.

"I'll do my best. Stay here, and I'll return as soon as I can." He moved away, zigzagging among the survivors warming themselves along the riverbank.

Mariah drew Mama to herself, working to infuse her with what little warmth she had. "The worst is over now. Jay will find Papa, and we'll be reunited."

"What about Lydia? How did they fare?" Mama shivered once more.

Mariah's older sister, Lydia, lived a few miles away in Marinette with her husband. "I'm sure they're fine. Nothing to worry about." Except that there was. If the fire had continued on its trajectory, it would have consumed Marinette like it did Peshtigo. There was no saying how Lydia and John were.

Daylight broke across the horizon, and the scene that unfolded in front of them was one the likes of which no one had ever experienced.

There was nothing.

Just one stone chimney jutted from the ruins. That was it. The houses were gone. The saloons had been consumed. Even the churches had succumbed to the inferno.

Roads, trees, animals—the fire had destroyed them all.

Mariah surveyed the scene before her through eyes that had swollen to small slits. With her free hand, she touched her face, her eyelids puffy. As time went on, they ballooned more until she couldn't open them.

Her breathing increased. What was going on? What was happening to her? When she'd come out of the water, she had been fine. And now this? Why?

"Do you see Jay or Papa?" Mama leaned against Mariah's chest, and Mariah stroked her damp hair, loose from its pins.

How should she answer? Mama shouldn't worry. She was weak enough from the ordeal. "No, I don't." It was the truth. But the full truth was that she couldn't see a thing, and her burned throat was threatening to close.

Where was Jay? And Papa? How about Hollis and Angelina? If Mariah was this frightened, the poor little girl must be doubly or triply so. Had she even survived, or was that little girl who burned to death on the riverbank precious Angelina?

There were too many topics that were off limits for her thoughts right now.

If only she knew. If only someone could tell her what was going on.

Mama's weight against her chest increased. She must be getting weaker. "How are you doing?"

Mama didn't respond.

Mariah shook her, but still no answer.

"Mama! Mama!" Mariah shook her harder. "Mama!"

At last, a little moan. Just barely a whisper.

"Please, don't die. Don't leave me. Think about when the time comes for Lydia and John to start a family. You want to see your grandchildren, and I want you there for my wedding to Hollis. Please, wake up, Mama, please."

Another soft moan.

Where were the men? Jay couldn't have, wouldn't have gone too far. "Jay! Papa! Hollis! Help! We need you!" She screamed as loudly as her tender throat would allow.

A gentle touch on her shoulder relaxed her. Ceased her yelling.

"Who is that? I can't see."

"It's me. It's Jay."

"Praise God. It's Mama. She isn't waking up. She's so heavy in my arms. And I can't see. My eyes are so swollen, I can't see a thing. Help us." She reached out for him and grabbed him by the arm. He tensed, and she released her grasp. "Please, tell me what's going on."

"Take a deep breath. Don't faint. I wouldn't advise it."

"I need to know about my family."

"There are crowds of people. Most of them are bedraggled and don't look like themselves, so it's difficult to pick out anyone. I had a hard time making my way back here."

"But Angelina shouldn't be hard to find. She's just a little girl."

"That's just it. She's little. Just a small child in this ragtag bunch of survivors. I'll search again later. Right now, we have to tend to your mother."

"I told you I can't see. My eyes are burning, burning so."

"I've pulled a blanket from the water. It's damp, but at least we can roll it up as a pillow for under your mother's head. With my arm in a bad way, I need your help to lay her back. Straight back. Can you do that for her?"

She tamped down the bile rising in her throat and nodded.

"Good. Just support her head, and we'll get her on the ground."

She followed Jay's instructions, and soon they had Mama settled.

"I would get you some water to wash your eyes, but it's not clean, so I would advise against it. I did hear someone say that a few of the younger men have gone to Marinette to see what they can find out there and get supplies—if they have any. A few others headed south toward Green Bay."

"I suppose they had to do that with the telegraph lines burned through." That had happened a couple of weeks ago, so Peshtigo had been an island for a while.

"Help should be here soon."

"How is Mama?"

"She's pale and weak. Let's pray for the quick arrival of supplies."

Mariah stroked Mama's still-smooth cheek. "She's so cold." Where was the heat from yesterday? Likely burned up, the same as everything else.

"I gave my jacket to a woman who had no clothes at all."

"What?"

"The fire burned them right off her body."

"And she was. . .?" Mariah couldn't even bring herself to say the word.

"She isn't the only one in such a state. There are many others who have nothing, not even the clothes on their backs. We should be thankful for what we do have. Perhaps if you lie beside your mother, that will help warm her up. I'll do the same."

"That would be improper for you. I won't allow it."

"Mariah."

That one word snapped her attention to him.

"There is no proper or improper now. There is no rich or poor. There is nothing but survive or die."

Pain radiated in her chest. She gave a stiff nod.

"Good. Lie down as close to her as you can. The ground is warm."

Mariah did his bidding, and he was right. The fire that had burned away the grass had left the sand summer-like warm. Oh, how good to have a bit of the chill released.

Jay moved. "Take off your mother's shoes. We can bury her feet in the sand to warm them. I'm going to do the same, but I'll turn my back so I don't catch so much as a glimpse of her ankles, if that makes you feel better."

"It would." Even though she had no way of verifying that Jay kept his word, other than his general trustworthiness.

She got to work and soon had Mama's feet buried in the sand. After she brushed her hands on her still-damp skirts, she lay back down. "I'm finished, Jay."

He lay on Mama's other side, and they cocooned her. Little by little, her shivering ceased, and she warmed quite a bit. Mariah dozed, exhausted by the ordeal and the long night.

Sometime later, it was impossible to tell how long, the jingling of harnesses reached her ears. Mariah woke and sat straight up. "The wagons are arriving, aren't they?"

"Yes." Jay's voice came from above her. "That means Marinette must have been spared, because wagons from Green Bay wouldn't be here that fast. Truly a miracle. If I go to meet them, will you be all right without me here?"

"Yes, but please hurry back. While you're gone, see if you can find Papa or Hollis or Angelina."

"I will." Just like that, he was gone, leaving her alone with Mama.

And the darkness.

Chapter Thirteen

As he left the women on the sand near the riverbank, Jay couldn't help but glance over his shoulder at them. Mariah's beautiful face, still as lovely as ever to him, was red and swollen, no slits at all for her eyes. She must be terrified, but she kept up a brave front.

What an incredible woman she was.

Mrs. Randolph was in much worse shape. By the heat radiating from her when he left, he would say she had developed a fever, not a good thing in her already weakened state. Both of them needed to be tended to as soon as possible.

He met the wagon train. The older man with a leathery face who climbed from the seat of one of the wagons shook his head. "The men who came to Marinette told us about what happened here, but I wouldn't have believed it unless I saw it with my own eyes. Lord, have mercy."

"I have two injured women who need medical treatment as soon as possible."

"And by the looks of your arm, you do too."

"I'm not worried about myself. What supplies have you brought?"

"Not enough. Not nearly enough."

By now, others had gathered, all clamoring for water or food or blankets. The wagon driver directed a few of the men. "Get these supplies offloaded. Then go back and gather whatever else you can."

Between the contingent from Marinette and a few hearty survivors from Peshtigo, they made quick work of setting up a few tents. With his one good arm, Jay helped as much as he could. There were barrels of water and piles of blankets, but these were a pitiful amount against the scope of the need.

A man with a scar running down the side of his face stepped forward. "Bring the injured to the tent, and we'll get them tended to as soon as possible."

"This little girl is hurt." An older, heavyset woman stepped forward, carrying a child with golden locks.

Angelina.

Angry red blisters covered both her forearms, and her pink nightgown hung about her in tatters. Tears tracked down her dirty cheeks.

Jay hurried to her. "Angelina."

She shrank from his touch, burying her head in her nanny's shoulder. "I want Father. I want Miss Mariah." Hysteria tinged her words.

No matter what he thought of Hollis, it would be horrible for the girl to lose her only parent. He spoke to her in the softest, calmest tone he could muster. "Your father must be here somewhere, looking for you. Miss Mariah isn't far away. I'm going to bring her to see you. How would that be?"

Though her cries continued, she lifted her head and nodded.

"You go with Nanny to the tent where the doctor can help you, and I'll be back soon."

"O-okay." She sank back against Nanny's shoulder.

Jay directed his attention to the woman holding Angelina, her hair hanging in dirty clumps about her face. "Take care of her."

The nanny nodded, then leaned in to whisper in Jay's ear. "You haven't seen Mr. Stanford, have you?"

He shook his head, and her shoulders slumped before she headed for the tent. When someone approached to help them, he returned to Mariah and her mother, both of whom had fallen asleep. He knelt beside Mariah, brushing a lock of hair, long undone from its pins, from her face.

"Papa?"

"No. It's only me." How wonderful it would be if he could bring her father to her.

"Jay, you're back." She sat up. "I wish we had news of him."

"You will, soon enough, but I do bring a good word. I found Angelina."

"You did? Oh, Jay, thank you so much. Where is she? Are you hiding behind Mr. Franklin, sweetheart?"

"No." He touched her shoulder to settle her. "The wagons brought some tents, water, and food. There's a doctor as well. Angelina is there."

"Why? What happened to her?"

"Her arms are burned. She was happy to hear about you. I didn't see Hollis, and the nanny didn't know where he is."

"No." Mariah covered her mouth.

"That doesn't mean anything, just that he hasn't been reunited with Angelina. I'm sure he's searching for her."

"Yes, yes, of course." She flashed a brief, small smile.

"Let me help you to the tent, and I'll send a couple of men to take your mother. With my injured arm, I'm afraid I can't carry her myself."

She nodded, and his heart broke for her. For everyone. He pushed aside his rising emotions so he wouldn't be swamped by them, took Mariah by the hand, and guided her to the medical tent where a paunchy older man with receding hair assessed Angelina. Jay led Mariah in the girl's direction.

Angelina glanced up, and even though she winced as the doctor examined her wounds, her tears stopped. "Miss Mariah, Miss Mariah."

"I'm here, darling," Mariah said gently. "I had to make sure nothing happened to you."

Jay helped Mariah to sit beside Angelina, who sniffled and said, "What's wrong with your eyes?"

Mariah's mouth drooped. "It's nothing that the doctors won't be able to care for as soon as they can. Right now, though, I can't see anything. It's like walking around with my eyes closed."

"Can't you open them?"

"No, I'm afraid not."

"Not even if you think about it real hard?"

Jay stifled a laugh. Sweet, innocent dove.

"Not even if I think about it real hard. But Mr. Franklin told me you have some burns on your arms."

"They hurt." Her tears came again then, and while the doctor left to gather more supplies, Mariah took the wounded little girl into her lap and cradled and rocked her.

While they continued their conversation, Jay flagged down two young men and took them to where Mrs. Randolph lay. He reached down and touched her shoulder to wake her. Though she had been so warm not long ago, she was now cold.

Deathly cold.

◆ ● ◆

Mariah kissed the top of Angelina's head. "I wish I could kiss your burns and make them go away."

"That would be nice. They hurt." A shudder passed through her small body.

The doctor had returned, and now he leaned over, his bones creaking. "I will have to ask for a few chairs from Marinette in the next shipment of supplies. You, young lady, are just a mite short for me. Now, let me put some salve on those arms and get you bandaged."

"Will it hurt?"

Mariah rubbed Angelina's back. "It might sting a little, right?"

"That's right." The doctor was sedate and reassuring. Both Mariah and Angelina needed that. "The medicine will make your burns heal nicely, and the bandages will keep away an infection."

"Will you hold me, Miss Mariah?"

"I will do just that." She tightened her grip on Angelina.

"I'm ready."

The doctor chuckled. A few times, Angelina whimpered, so Mariah sang to her, and she settled down. The salve stunk like rancid fat. Likely, that wasn't far off from what it was.

The volume of speaking around her increased, so the tent must be filling. "Are there many injured, Doctor?"

"The injured are the fortunate few."

"My mother should be here soon. She wasn't well before the fire and had a rough night. By the time we came out of the river, she had taken quite a chill. She's an older woman and was wearing nothing but a night dress. All white."

"As I make my rounds, I will be sure to keep an eye out for her, and I'll be back soon to see to you."

"Thank you so much. For everything."

"Nanny and I went in the water." Angelina sniffled.

"That was good thinking on Nanny's part. Is she still here?" If only the swelling around Mariah's eyes would go down so she could see.

"I'm right here, ma'am."

Mariah directed her attention in the area of the nanny's voice. "Thank you for taking such wonderful care of her."

"I could do no less for the sprite. When you told us to go to the river, that's just what I did. Did what everyone else was doing."

"Bless you. You saved her life."

"And my own. I take no credit other than that."

"I'm sure you wish you had stayed in Chicago, far away from the raging blaze."

"That's for sure, but we were meant to be here for a reason. I guess I was supposed to take care of my girl and rescue her."

Mariah ran her fingers through Angelina's matted hair, working out some of the tangles. "What a mess we must be."

"No one looks like a fashion plate, that's for sure." Nanny chuckled. "At least we have clothes, burned and drenched as they be."

"Mariah?"

She turned to the sound of Jay's voice. "Oh, I'm so glad you're back. The doctor said he will watch out for Mama and will take care of her as soon as possible. He's expecting her arrival."

"Mariah." Jay sighed.

Something was wrong. She clamped her lips to keep from asking the question. Then she wouldn't need to hear the answer.

"Mariah, it's about your mother."

"No." She shook her head. "I don't want to know."

"I'm so sorry."

Tears and screams battled for release, but she bottled both inside. Instead, she sat with her back straight and her arms clasped around Angelina.

"Are you all right?" Jay's voice was soft.

"How can I be?" She swallowed several times, nearly unable to breathe. "Perhaps those who are better off are those who didn't survive."

"Miss Mariah?" Angelina's sweet voice pierced the fog of grief surrounding her.

"Yes."

"Don't be sad, even though it's hard not to be. Nanny says that Jesus is always with us. Like even when Papa has to go away. When Mama died. Sometimes I get afraid, but then I remember Jesus is next to me. I like that."

All Mariah could do was nod. Oh, to possess such a childlike faith. But nothing was right in the world at this moment. Not a single thing. All of her paintings were destroyed. Papa was missing. She couldn't see.

And the one thing she fought against accepting—Mama was gone.

The woman who had nurtured her, who had guided her, who had supported her, was gone. Yes, taken home to a far superior place than this, but her leaving ripped open a gaping wound in Mariah's heart.

Her swollen eyes wouldn't allow the release tears would afford. God refused her even that small comfort.

Angelina snuggled closer, her body warm against Mariah's chill. Together they sat that way for an untold amount of time. Voices were far off, as if Mariah were still underwater. Jay might have come and gone, but she paid little attention to him.

"Mariah?"

Jay again, his voice scratchy but sure. How was he managing to keep the panic at bay? If this swelling in her eyes didn't subside soon, she would go crazy. Would go crazy if she didn't wake up and discover this all to be the worst nightmare of her life.

"Mariah?" His question was more insistent and pulled her from the deep, dark place where she had retreated.

"Jay?"

He gathered her and Angelina close, just with one arm, and she responded in kind. She shook from head to toe. "I miss her so incredibly much already."

"I'm terribly sorry. I tried, but I couldn't save her."

"Don't blame yourself." As she said the words, the weight of the blame fell on her own shoulders. She should have done more to keep Mama warm, should have taken better care of her so she wasn't so weak in the first place. Spent less time on painting and more time helping in the kitchen and around the house to lessen the strain on her.

"I wish I could have done more." He continued to hold her, however awkward it might be, until her own shivering subsided. Then he released her. Angelina slid from her lap, and Mariah came to her feet.

"I have more news."

At Jay's ominous tone, her stomach clenched. "It can't get worse than it already is."

Behind them, a woman wailed and a child cried. Was there no solace in the world? Everyone in the village must have lost a family member. No one was spared this calamity. But it did nothing to ease the pain of losing Mama.

"I met someone here, one of the saloon keepers."

She shook her head, as if that would be enough to ward off the words that were coming. "Don't say anymore."

"Your father stumbled as he was trying to escape the flames."

"No, no. I beg you to stop." She clenched her fists so hard that her fingernails dug into her tender palms.

"The flames overtook him. He's—he's gone."

"That man has to be wrong." With her hands still fisted, she beat Jay's chest. "He's wrong! Just wrong!" Seered though her throat was, she was helpless against the screams that ripped her apart, at the wails that tore through her.

Jay caught her by her wrist, and then her knees went weak, and she collapsed to the ground.

Mariah's chest ached. "What am I going to do without them? Only yesterday they were alive, here with me. How can they be gone? Both of them. How? How did this happen?"

Jay didn't answer her questions, probably because there was no answer to them.

She lay in the sand underneath the tent and cried tearless sobs. One large hand and one small hand stroked her back and her hair. She couldn't allow Angelina to get upset from seeing her in such a state. For the girl's sake, she had to compose herself.

She drew in several deep breaths and swallowed the large lump in her throat. Later, in private, she could mourn. For now, she would have to muddle through until she figured out life again.

What a daunting task lay in front of her.

"Don't be sad, Miss Mariah." Angelina slipped her hand into Mariah's. "I'm lonely too."

Mariah sniffled. "I'm sure you are."

"I don't know where Father is." Angelina clung to Mariah's leg.

All she could do was stroke the child's hair. After a few minutes, Jay brought a chair, and Mariah sat once more.

The din around them intensified. People coming and going jostled Mariah. Remaining in utter darkness, she trembled.

Jay touched her shoulder. "The doctor is coming."

"Miss Randolph, please allow me to convey my deepest sympathies to you. So many have lost so much." The doctor's rich voice did nothing to soothe her soul-deep wounds.

Thankfully, Jay steered the conversation in another direction before she broke down once more. "Do you have news?"

"Yes. More supplies have arrived from Marinette. They're going to set up a hospital at Dunlap House, so we should get Miss Randolph and Miss Stanford ready to go."

"Any word?" Mariah didn't want to ask Jay or the doctor a direct question about Hollis. Bringing him up would only distress Angelina.

"None, I'm afraid." The doctor must be exhausted. "But don't lose heart. There are people everywhere. Many are milling about, calling after their loved ones."

Angelina sat up, and Mariah shook her head so no one would say anymore.

Neither did. Jay and the doctor helped her and Angelina to stand. The world swirled around Mariah, her head buzzing as she came to her feet. Jay steadied her, and the group headed toward what he said were the waiting wagons.

Each step Mariah took was hesitant. What if she stumbled on a rock or turned her ankle in a hole? What if she bumped into someone and either knocked them over or fell herself?

"Don't worry." Jay's voice was right in her ear. "I'm here, and I won't let anything happen to you. Do you trust me?"

Did she? "Yes, with my life."

"Then lean on me, and I will take care of you."

They arrived at the wagons, and Jay assisted her in climbing aboard then helped Angelina in too. They packed the injured and dying together, fitting as many in the wagon bed as possible.

Stuffed into the wagon, her heart aching, her eyes darkened, she fought to keep from allowing herself to drown in the ocean of sorrow and fear lapping at her feet.

Could this day get any worse?

At the first turn of the wagon wheel, the heavens above opened, and a heavy rain began to fall.

Chapter Fourteen

The kind doctor motioned for Jay to ride in the wagon headed for Dunlap House in Marinette.

He waved him away. "No. I'm fine. There are those who are much more seriously injured than I am. I can walk the few miles."

"Your arm is broken though. Have the doctor there take a look at it and set it. It would be a shame for that to heal wrong."

It throbbed worse than anything he had experienced before, but it was nothing compared to the pain others were enduring. Little Angelina snuggled against Mariah and didn't whimper, though by the way she twisted her face from time to time, it was clear she was in pain.

Jay clapped the doctor on the back. "How are you doing?"

"I'm holding up. Seeing others suffer is never easy, but on this scale..."

Jay nodded. It was a good thing Mariah couldn't see. What he had witnessed today, including people burned black, was something no one should have to lay eyes on. "Thank you for everything."

"Don't exalt me too much. I can do so little for so few."

The wagon wheels creaked as the drivers cracked the whips over the horses' backs. Jay stepped out with many other weary, bedraggled survivors with no place to go and followed the wagon.

The rain furthered their misery. It fell twenty-four hours too late. The best rain that showered in the area in many, many months, perhaps as much as a year. If only it had come sooner, the town might have been saved.

Untold lives would have been saved.

Why, God, why?

The Lord was surely being bombarded with that question on every side. Too many wondering why this awful disaster befell them. Was it punishment for the wickedness of the city, much like Sodom and Gomorrah? Not enough righteous found within her boundaries to save the town?

Peshtigo was not a paragon of virtue. Too much drink, too many loose women and unfaithful husbands, too many gambling tables. They might have four churches, but perhaps the remnant had not been enough for God to spare her.

Or had this calamity come to test the people's faith? Was *why* even an acceptable question to ask? All this pondering had Jay's head throbbing as much as his arm.

He patted the inside of his coat, which Mariah had returned to him when she received a blanket. The papers he had secreted away from Hollis' office were still there. A lack of privacy had prevented him from taking them out to discover if they were still legible after spending the night in the water.

If Hollis had met his fate in the fire, then Jay would have no use of them. Not that he wished the man ill, even after his stunt during the conflagration that resulted in Jay's broken arm. Angelina needed her father.

But if he had survived, the papers remained important. Despite all that had transpired, Hollis would have to be held accountable.

His thoughts wandered so far and wide that they arrived at Dunlap House before he knew it. Men from the community turned out and aided in carrying the patients from the wagon inside to the second floor, the one that had been a ballroom, a wide-open space now sporting numerous cots and pallets.

Jay followed Mariah and Angelina and ensured they were placed beside each other. A pale young woman came along and assessed them. "A doctor will need to see to the girl's injuries. I can get a basin of cool water for the woman's eyes. Would you be willing to bathe them?" She stared right at Jay.

"Of course."

She was gone just a matter of minutes before she returned with the promised water and a clean cloth. "I'm sure the lady's eyes will return to normal soon. The coolness of the water will help with the swelling."

Jay cocked his head. This slight young girl couldn't be more than sixteen.

The young woman gave a slight laugh. "I'm the daughter of the town's doctor, in case you were wondering how I know these things. I've worked with him since I was small."

Jay accepted the white porcelain basin and clean towel from her. "Thank you so much. We're grateful for what all the people here are doing."

She gazed at his arm. "It appears that you are in need of medical attention as well. You may have to wait, but you need to be examined. My father and I are tending to the survivors as fast as possible."

"But—"

"Go on." The nurse took the supplies from him, though he dropped the towel on the floor as he passed them to her. "It's good for you to get that set before you have real problems with it."

Just what the doctor in Peshtigo had said.

"On the first floor, you'll find some chairs set up. Wait there. It may be a while, but I'll make sure my father gets down there as soon as possible. I will keep the lady's eyes bathed." The doctor's daughter nodded to him, picked up the towel and wetted it before placing the cloth on Mariah's eyes, then turned and swished away to another patient.

Having been dismissed, Jay followed instructions and made his way through the swirling chaos toward the stairs. Fire victims were brought in on pallets or carried in by family members or others.

A strapping young man, so much Jay's opposite, carried in a featherlight elderly woman, her lower extremities angry with blisters. She coughed, and struggled to catch her breath.

A man not much older than Jay himself held a young boy in his arms, the child's upper chest and hands almost black with burns.

Would either of these victims survive? Of those who had made it out of the water alive, how many would be able to cling to life in the coming days? The death toll was sure to rise.

He found the chairs just as he had been told and settled himself. The back was straight and the seat hard. It would not be a comfortable wait, but at least he didn't have the life-threatening injuries so many had sustained.

"Jay." A fellow towered over him, his dark hair singed, his blue shirt hanging in tatters on his body.

They worked together at the railroad office. Shawn Atkinson drew plans and maps and the like. Burns marred the back of his hands.

Jay stood and reached out to shake Shawn's hand, cradling his own broken arm close to his body. "How did you fare?"

"You can see well enough for yourself. I imagine I look much like you. Just thankful to be alive." Shawn seated himself beside Jay.

"I keep praying that I will awaken and discover this to be nothing more than an awful nightmare."

"You and everyone else. I'm afraid it isn't."

"No. Who would have believed those forest fires would wreak such havoc, and in a few minutes' time?"

"Not even the most creative novelist could craft this plot. I heard tell that the Bush was hit hard too. Many, many are dead there. Entire families wiped out. Someone estimated about three or four hundred have died."

Jay sucked in his breath. "That's staggering. Looking at those brought here, that number is sure to rise."

"And what will happen to us?" Shawn shrugged. "Our jobs are gone, aren't they?"

That was a thought that hadn't even crossed Jay's mind. "Surely they'll rebuild any part of the railroad that was destroyed. That ensures we'll have work for quite a while. And it will be easier." Jay gave a wry smile. "No trees to cut down."

Shawn blew out a breath. "What a way to go about it though."

Jay leaned back, his head against the wall. He and Shawn and the others who hadn't sustained serious injuries were sure to be waiting for some time to come.

The casualties streamed through the door.

———— ◆◆ ————

Swishing of skirts and creaking of boots filled the air. The din of voices and the anguished cries of the injured vied for prominence. The weeping and wailing of utter misery prevailed.

Unable to listen to any more, Mariah covered her ears, but the sounds refused to be shut out. They played through her head, and she begged them to leave her alone. Leave her in peace and quiet. In dark solitude.

She needed to grieve, to mourn all she had lost. A mother. A father. A home. A blossoming career.

Possibly a fiancé.

And for the time being, her sight.

The doctor had stopped by to examine her and Angelina hours ago. He was confident she would regain her vision as soon as the swelling went down. She was not the only one suffering the same condition. In the intervening time, however, it was terrifying.

Exhausted, Jay had left to inform Lydia about their parents' deaths. Poor, sweet man to take on that task. Lydia was a fine hostess, well trained by Mama, and would be sure to offer him food and a place to sleep.

Angelina had fallen asleep soon after. Hollis had not come to find his daughter. With each passing hour, the likelihood of his demise increased.

If he could, he would be here with her. He wouldn't leave his only child, the beloved daughter of his first wife, to suffer on her own. Perhaps he was even a patient here. Mariah wouldn't be able to tell.

It was the darkness that was the worst. The utter depths of blackness. Not even a sliver of light pierced through her swollen lids. Nothing.

Beside her, Angelina stirred and grasped her hand.

"What is it, sweetheart? Are you all right?"

"Are you scared of the dark?"

What an appropriate question. Right now, she fought to keep the panic at bay, to remember that nothing was going to hurt her. Then again, she would have said the same two days ago, and disaster struck.

"Miss Mariah?"

"I'm here. Sometimes, yes, I am afraid of the dark."

"Are you afraid because you can't see now?"

What should she share with the child? Enough to be honest but not enough to frighten her. "I'm remembering what you told me the other day. Something my Mama also used to tell me whenever I was afraid." Mariah swallowed away the lump in her throat. "Jesus is always with us. He never leaves us alone."

"Sometimes I forget that and get scared. Right now, I'm thinking about the fire. That was the most frightfulest thing ever. Ghouls and goblins danced in the flames last night, and there was no hero to rescue us."

"What stories your father tells you. There are no such things as ghouls and goblins. Nothing like that at all. Now we are safe here where the doctor is going to take good care of us, and we are going to get better very soon."

"But I don't think I'll ever forget what happened last night."

Likely none of them would, not unless old age stole the memory. What a blessing that would be. "It will fade in time."

"Where is Father? I miss him."

"He is looking for you right now. It's hard to find people with so many of them hurt, so it may take a bit of time until he comes. But he will, that is for sure. He will never leave you here by yourself. Why don't you close your eyes and try to sleep? When you wake up, maybe he will be here."

"That would be nice. Will you tell me a story?"

Perhaps that would help Mariah get her mind off her own troubles. "Of course. This one will not feature ghouls or goblins though."

"That's good. I don't think I want to hear about them."

"I don't either. So this one is going to be about beautiful things like princesses in huge castles with many fancy gowns of all colors."

"Like pink. That's my favorite."

"Yes. Pink is this princess' favorite color too."

Together they spun the story, and after a few minutes, Angelina was yawning. Mariah brought the tale to a close, and soon the child's breathing was soft and even.

The pallet on the floor wasn't the most comfortable of all beds, and despite not sleeping at all the night before, Mariah couldn't settle down. Though she turned from side to side and repeated the princess story in her head, painting all the glittering scenes with her mind's brush, sleep refused to claim her.

"Is there anything I can get you?" The voice belonged to the doctor's daughter, and from how close it came, she must be leaning over Mariah.

"You need your rest."

"I'm fine. We were on the *Union* out in Green Bay last night. With the ferocity of the flames, we imagined there might be injured that needed tending today, so Pa and I made sure to get some sleep. What's your name?"

"Mariah Randolph. And yours?"

"Penelope Henderson. It's nice to make your acquaintance."

"And yours."

"Is the little girl your daughter?"

"Soon to be my stepdaughter. Her father is Hollis Stanford."

"Really? I didn't realize you were rich. Doesn't he live in a mansion in Chicago?"

There wasn't a better word to describe the large Italianate-style home that the Stanfords occupied, a sweeping staircase leading to the three-story square residence. "Yes, he does."

"Then why is his daughter here?"

"He often comes for business. They were to travel home today, but as you see, that isn't possible."

"Wow. Imagine what a wonderful life you're going to have. Servants waiting on you hand and foot. You're a very lucky lady. I like helping Pa, but to have the finest carriages and a cook to prepare meals would be wonderful."

"And there is love."

"Ah, yes."

Though, did she truly love Hollis? She doubted him and his honesty. She did have great affection for him, and especially for Angelina. If nothing else, she would give the little girl a mother, a true mother, for the first time in her life.

"Why isn't he with his daughter?" Penelope interrupted Mariah's thoughts.

"He's missing."

"No, he's not, ma'am." Another woman nearby piped up.

"What do you mean?"

"He was downstairs when I was brought in. Someone told him his daughter was alive and expected to recover. He said he had to get back to Chicago as soon as possible."

Chicago? What could be there that was more important than his little girl?

Chapter Fifteen

TUESDAY, OCTOBER 10, 1871

A new start. A new beginning. That was what this was. The old was destroyed, but the rebuilding process was underway.

Jay stepped into the building on the lumber company's property in Marinette, ready to begin anew. There were several such enterprises along the Menominee River. The fire had consumed some on the outskirts of town, but since this one sat near the mouth of the river at Green Bay, the flames hadn't reached it.

Mr. Stanford had arranged for the railroad to lease a small, unused office here until a new one was constructed in Peshtigo. Inside the single room, there were several desks scattered about. Cobwebs covered the corners, and grit hazed the windows.

No need for a larger space, because there weren't as many employees as before. Some lay in the hospital where Mariah and Angelina were patients. Because of overcrowding, a number of the injured had been taken to Green Bay.

And a good number were no more.

Shawn was busy at the desk in the corner, drawing new plans for the railroad line. But what was there for Jay and his one good arm? Peshtigo's ledgers had burned along with everything else inside the railroad's former headquarters.

The chair squeaked in protest as he lowered himself into it behind the worn desk. From the pocket of his coat, he attempted to pull the papers he had taken just before the disaster. Nothing was left of them. The water had proved too much, and they had disintegrated. Now he had nothing to prove that Hollis was deep in gambling debts, much less that he was skimming from the company.

Hollis, who was on his way to Chicago without so much as visiting his daughter and checking on her condition. He took the nanny's word that Angelina would be fine and hightailed it out of town. How could a loving father do such a thing?

There was no guarantee she would be fine. Infection could always set in. Many had developed bronchitis because of inhaling so much smoke. Lord willing, because Angelina's burns weren't deep, she would make a full recovery. Hollis leaving so fast, though, was beyond comprehension.

Jay glanced at the pile of pulp, some of it smudged black. Of course. That explained Hollis' rapid departure. He knew Jay had discovered the discrepancies. He was also aware that another copy of the railroad's finances was kept in Chicago. Once a month, Jay sent them out to the senior Mr. Stanford, who then passed them to employees at the Chicago office.

Since the fire occurred early in the month, what was in Chicago was the most up-to-date record.

Hollis wanted to get his hands on those books and doctor them before anyone else examined them. That weasel. Saving his own hide was more important than attending to his daughter.

There was precious little Jay could do to keep Hollis from covering his tracks, so he withdrew a sheet of paper from the desk drawer, dipped his pen into the inkpot, and composed a letter to Hollis' father. The letter wouldn't arrive in the city before Hollis, but this was the only course of action before Jay.

Without exposing Hollis' misdeeds, Jay communicated all that transpired in Peshtigo on that fateful night and the great need he had for a new copy of the financial records. Once he had them in his hands, he might be able to discern if the numbers had been tampered with or not.

He finished the letter, allowed the ink to dry, then placed it in an envelope and addressed it to Mr. Stanford. With nothing else to do, he made his way to the post office then headed for Dunlap House. At least he could visit Angelina and Mariah.

Thank goodness God had spared Marinette. This two-story brick building with turrets on either side was a haven in the midst of the storm. A place for rejoicing, mourning, and healing. In the few days since the fire, some order had been restored. People with minor injuries like Jay's had been treated and were convalescing at the homes of family, friends, or kind strangers, so the first floor was quiet.

He climbed the stairs to the second floor. Even here, it was more peaceful. The doctor and his daughter and a few other women who had volunteered to care for the patients had administered laudanum to the suffering and eased their pain.

He made his way down the rows of cots and pallets. There was a man with black burns up and down his arms. Farther on was a woman who coughed and coughed, likely from the amount of smoke she inhaled. Next to her was a tiny infant, its little face reddened by the flames.

Not able to stomach the sights any longer, Jay concentrated on the aisle in front of him, a straight space that only days ago had been the ballroom floor. How much had changed in the course of a few hours, a few days. Lives had been uprooted and irreparably changed. Death tore families apart. The flames stole almost every possession of the fire's victims.

Nothing would ever be the same. Five minutes was all it took for the bustling village of Peshtigo to be reduced to ashes. Would it rise again? Without the lumber industry, would it ever be what it once was? *Why, God?*

He ceased his musings when he came to where Angelina was standing near Mariah's pallet. A smile crossed Angelina's face when he neared. "Hi, Mr. Franklin. You came to visit me."

Yes, her, but mostly Mariah. But there was no cheery reception from her. Miss Henderson was bathing her with cool cloths, but this time, it was over more of her body than just her eyes. Jay knelt beside her. "What's wrong?"

Miss Henderson shook her head. "I'm afraid that, like with so many who were exposed to the elements for an extended period of time, Miss Randolph has contracted a fever. Quite a high one."

"She was fine when I stopped by last evening."

"Early this morning, she took a turn for the worse." Miss Henderson wrung out the cloth and dipped it in the water before placing it on Mariah's brow. Mariah's cheeks flamed bright red.

"Oh, Mariah." He touched her burning face. "You have to fight. Your sister couldn't stand to lose all of her family. I couldn't stand to lose you." He whispered the last sentence.

"Miss Mariah is real sick, isn't she?" Angelina piped up behind Jay.

He'd almost forgotten about her. So that he didn't upset her, he had to watch what he said. "Yes, she appears to be ill."

"She has a fever. That's what Miss Penelope told me."

"Yes. Sometimes when we get sick, that's what happens. But Miss Penelope and her father and the other doctors who are here are going to do their best and take very good care of her."

"I don't want her to die too. Lots of people have died. Then men come and take them away."

He turned all the way around to face Angelina. This was the point where she needed her father the most, but he had gone to Chicago to protect his backside. Selfish, egotistical man. Poor little girl. "What do you think we can do to help Miss Mariah?"

"I don't know." She frowned, and her chin quivered.

"It's going to be all right. Why don't we pray to Jesus?" Jay sure needed to.

"That's a good idea." Angelina bowed her head. "Dear Jesus, I miss Father and Grandfather. I miss Nanny. Please make Miss Mariah better. And me too. Amen."

"That was perfect." He gave her a smile then returned his attention to Miss Henderson. "You must have other patients to attend to. Why don't you allow me to take care of Miss Randolph?"

The nurse brushed a strand of blond hair from her eyes. Either she needed a strong cup of coffee or a long nap. "That would be wonderful. Thank you. Are you a friend of the family?"

"Yes. I have known Miss Randolph for a good number of years."

"She is fortunate to have such a good friend. Let me know if you need anything."

He took over the duties, but no matter how much he sponged Mariah's face, no matter how often he got another bowl of cool water, she continued to rage with fever.

A short time after his arrival, her sister stopped by to visit. Even before she got to Mariah's pallet, Lydia Stuart's eyes widened, and in a swirl of black skirts, she rushed to Mariah's side. "Please don't tell me she's caught a fever."

"I'm afraid so. Exposure is what the nurse said. The fever is stubborn and refusing to break."

Lydia's face turned as white as the cotton sheets, and she dropped to her knees beside her sister's pallet. She leaned over and whispered into her ear, though Jay didn't hear what she said. What agony the woman must be in.

Lydia dabbed her eyes with a handkerchief from her reticule.

A moment later, Angelina rose from her bed to stand beside Jay. "Is Miss Mariah going to heaven with Mama?"

Lydia glanced at the little girl and pursed her lips.

"I'll pray to Jesus that she gets to stay here and be my new mama. I don't even care that she can't see me, because then she won't be able to see my arms."

Lydia let out a strangled cry and crouched to the child's level. "Oh, my dear, you are so sweet. We don't know what God has planned for Miss Mariah, but you're right, we can pray."

And that was what they did, all through the long night. At some point, Angelina lay down and fell asleep, but the adults kept vigil, taking turns bathing Mariah's hot face, even as she moaned and thrashed. A deep cough settled in her chest.

When he wasn't caring for Mariah or praying for her, Jay paced the aisle down the middle of the ward.

There would be nothing worse than to lose one of his dearest friends, one of his few allies.

The train station in Milwaukee bustled with passengers coming and going, businessmen headed to meetings in Chicago or Minneapolis or St. Louis. Women dressed in traveling suits, hats on their heads, held their children's hands as they were off to visit relatives or some other leisure activity.

Hollis sat on a bench along the side of the room as the world hurried by. Usually, he didn't mix with the masses in such a way. Most of the time he stretched his legs on the platform and then returned to the comfort of his private car where a world-class chef prepared his hot, delicious meal.

Thank goodness Father had need of the private car so it had returned to Chicago soon after Hollis' arrival in Peshtigo, otherwise it would be nothing but melted metal wheels now. It may have been on its way back to Peshtigo when the fire struck, but though he inquired along the way, no one had seen it.

Hollis closed his eyes and leaned against the smooth marble wall of the station. He could relax because the incriminating papers were no more, no longer in Jay's hands. They would never have survived the night in the water, at least not without the ink running down the page and dissolving any figures it contained.

That was what he was banking on. If the papers from Peshtigo were indeed destroyed as he believed they were, that left only the copies in Chicago to worry about. He needed to rid himself of them to cover his tracks. That was his first order of business as soon as he returned home. Protecting his family from shame and ruin was his top priority.

His family. His little girl. Margaret would have scolded him up and down for leaving Angelina alone in a makeshift hospital in a rough lumbering town without so much as seeing her, but her mother was no longer present. She had been good for him and helped him keep to the straight and narrow. Her loss had brought his entire world crashing down. Gambling and drinking helped him forget her.

Angelina had the care of Nanny. He didn't trust Mariah, not after that incident on the balcony. With Mariah's father deceased, no one but the other two men at the gambling table that night knew about the bargain he had struck to marry Mariah. He would be able to break off the engagement and turn his attention to one of the very beautiful and vivacious society ladies who much better fitted his way of life.

And he wouldn't be forced to peddle his wife's artwork to the world. What a relief.

The train to Chicago wouldn't leave for a while yet, and he had seen the countryside between the two cities many times over, so he wandered to the newsstand to purchase a paper. Nothing could have prepared him for the headline.

CHICAGO BURNED. LIKELY AS MANY AS 300 DEAD. COMPLETE DEVASTATION. WILLIAM OGDEN'S HOUSE DESTROYED.

What was this? He squinted, as if that could help him make sense of the words printed on the page. William Ogden lived not far from them. If the fire had consumed his residence, what about their own?

Was Father alive, or had he met the same fate as so many in Peshtigo? What about their wealth? Their empire?

"Is everything all right, sir?" The newspaper man pushed his flat cap away from his eyes. "Can I help you in any way?"

Hollis pointed at the headline. "Is this true?"

"From all I've heard it is. Someone said a cow kicked over a lamp and that's what started it."

Whoever's cow that was should be hanged. All the grief he had seen in Peshtigo, all he had experienced in his own life, left him raw. No one should have to endure everything he had. If he lost his home and his wealth, he would have nothing.

Except for Angelina, his daughter whom he didn't dare open his heart to. She was the exact likeness of his late wife. If he allowed himself to feel for his daughter, it would break that dam of grief again, overwhelming him.

He returned to the present and the newspaper seller staring at him. "Do you know what was destroyed? How bad is it?"

"I have no idea other than what I read in the papers. What I have heard is there was a much worse fire in Peshtigo, way up north. All on the same night, can you believe it?"

He could, unfortunately. He reached into his pocket, pulled out a quarter, and handed it to the young man in exchange for the paper. "Thank you."

"Thanks, mister. Have a great trip."

Hollis tipped his hat and made his way to the platform where the train waited. All the way south, though he held the newspaper on his lap, he stared out the window; and as they entered the city, the landscape transformed from gold-tinged woods and just-harvested fields to homes and businesses to fire devastation. Where humble working-class residences had been, there was nothing. The interiors of the stone churches were burned, and the stained-glass windows blown out. Elegant tree-lined streets were reduced to ash.

The train arrived. With his mouth dry and his hands damp, he hired a carriage that drove him by burned-out industrial buildings, now nothing more than piles of rocks, and past the elegant homes of the Old Settlers, now mere smoldering piles of rubble. His stomach tightened with every turn of the wheels.

When they rounded the corner and the Italianate residence he had always called home rose in front of him, he blew out a breath. So far so good. They had fared far better than many of their friends and acquaintances. He tipped the driver and made his way inside.

The butler, Wilson, met him in the foyer. "Mr. Hollis, so good to see you. Your father has been waiting for you rather anxiously."

"Yes, it was impossible to get a telegram through. I suppose I could have sent one once I was on my way, but that would have been a waste."

"Where are Miss Angelina and Nanny?" The graying man with an English accent peered around Hollis.

He explained to Wilson.

The man paled. "My goodness. We, of course, had heard word of it but couldn't believe it was as bad as the press was reporting."

"It was worse. Anyway, I will go see Father now, if you don't mind."

"Of course. Let me take you to his office."

But Father entered the hall before they had gone two steps. "Oh, my boy, how good it is to see you." Father, always calm and collected, was rather undone, his eyes shimmering. He embraced Hollis and clapped him on the back. "Where is my sweet granddaughter?"

Hollis explained once again. They should have collected the staff, and he could have made the presentation a single time.

"What?" Father furrowed his brows, the creases not fully leaving when he relaxed his muscles. "You left her there alone?"

"She's not alone. She has Nanny and Mariah. They will look after her. I'm already late in getting home, and there must be a great deal of work to be done in rebuilding the railroad." He wouldn't mention the main reason for his return.

Father frowned and shook his head. "I can't believe you would leave that precious child there without you. What kind of man are you?" He spun on his heel and marched back to his office, slamming the door with a little more force than necessary. Once again, Father viewed him as a failure.

Then again, what kind of example had Father been?

<hr />

Thursday, October 12, 1871

A wave of consciousness washed over Mariah, but she struggled to open her eyes. She blinked a few times, but no light pierced the darkness. It must be the middle of a moonless, starless night.

Voices swirled around her. Soft, anguished words that she couldn't understand.

"At last her fever has broken. Now all we can do is wait for her to wake up." Jay's words broke through the haze.

Then images of the fire consumed her. Flames. Bodies. Total destruction.

And she was in the hospital. She couldn't see. "Hello." She croaked out the word from her parched throat.

"Oh, Mariah. Praise God you're awake. We thought you were going to die. And then what would become of me?"

"Lydia?"

"Yes, dear, I'm right here. Can't you see me? The swelling in your eyes is almost all gone."

What? That had to be wrong. This darkness consumed her because of the aftereffects of the fire. She would see again. With great care, she touched her lids.

Lydia was correct. Almost no puffiness remained. "I can't see. What's going on? Why can't I see?"

"Stay calm, my dear." Lydia, the sweet odor of lilies of the valley clinging to her, was beside Mariah. "Getting upset won't change anything. When the doctor comes by next time, we'll ask him to examine you. This is only temporary. I have no doubt that you'll soon regain your sight."

"But you can't be sure." Mariah fought to keep her breathing regular. "How long have I been sick?"

"Three days." Jay's voice came from the opposite side of the pallet as Lydia's.

"That long? Couldn't the fever have damaged my sight even more?"

"Don't worry about that now." Jay was being strong for her sake, but he was no physician. What did he know? "We'll wait to see what the doctor has to say and take it one step at a time from there."

Jay's tone was soft and smooth, meant to reassure her. This total darkness, though, was not anything she was familiar with. Not anything she ever wanted to be familiar with.

She tucked her hands underneath her to keep from clawing at her eyes, to tear the black veil away from her face. Her mind told her that wouldn't help.

A soft hand, Lydia's, stroked her cheek. "Don't get yourself worked up.

You'll only bring the fever on again, and you would set back your recovery."

"Have you ever had the darkness stifle you? Cling to you like a robe you can't throw off? There is nothing in front of my eyes. Only because of your voices do I know who is here. Or maybe I don't. Perhaps there's someone who hasn't spoken yet."

A little voice piped up. "I'm here, Miss Mariah."

Angelina. How could Mariah have forgotten about her? "Of course you are." Pitying herself for her condition wouldn't help Angelina, and it might send her into a fit of despair as well. "How are you feeling?"

"My arms hurt a lot, but I can see, and I didn't get sick."

"That's very good. I'm glad to hear it."

"Ah, my two favorite patients." That must be Dr. Henderson. His voice was familiar. "I'm glad to see you're awake, Miss Randolph."

"Just tell me one thing, Doctor. Will I ever see again?"

Chapter Sixteen

MARINETTE, WISCONSIN
FRIDAY, OCTOBER 13, 1871

Jay led a sorrel mare from the livery, the leather lead soft in his hand, the odor of hay clinging to the docile animal. Because so many had lost their livestock in the fire, it was difficult to secure a horse, but he and Shawn had each managed to get one. Beside him, the bridle of Shawn's dusty white quarter horse jangled as the animal tossed his head. Now on the street, they worked to hitch them to the borrowed wagon. In order for Shawn to draw new plans for the railroad, he had to see where the fire damage ended. Without the financial books, Jay had nothing else to do, so he went along to keep Shawn company.

"You ready for this?" Shawn slapped the rear of the sturdy horse.

Jay surveyed the sky that pinked like an embarrassed young woman. They had a long day in front of them and needed to get an early start. "Are you talking to me or to the stallion?"

Shawn chuckled. "Either one of you, I suppose."

Jay answered by climbing into the wagon, Shawn following suit. "I'm not sure any of us is ready for what we're going to find when we get to Peshtigo. Or where the town used to be."

Shawn clicked his tongue and slapped the reins, and the horses moved forward, the wagon wheels creaking. "At some point, I'm going to have to return. I suppose today is as good as any day. Not to mention that with winter not far off, I need to know what I'm dealing with and get survey crews out here as soon as possible."

"I understand. It's just not going to be easy, knowing how many people lost their lives there."

"And the toll continues to rise. Every day, new names are published in the paper."

Jay sighed. "I've been following that too. Yesterday, I discovered that Mariah Randolph's friend Lucy and her husband Henry were killed on their farm in the Lower Sugar Bush."

"What a shame. I remember them from church. Such a nice young couple."

"It's going to be very difficult on Mariah."

"You do know you keep talking about her, don't you?"

"I don't think so." Some of the trees along the way had been singed by the fire, and Jay kept his gaze aimed in front of him.

"You do. Best keep in mind that she's engaged to the most powerful man in Peshtigo. Maybe even the most powerful man in Chicago."

"A fact I'm all too well aware of."

"Careful, my friend. That smacks a little too much of distaste."

Jay sighed and turned his attention to the changing landscape. The trees around Marinette, by God's grace, remained alive, the hardwoods scattered among the pines now painted with vivid yellows and reds. As they left Marinette farther and farther behind, however, they saw that the tongues of fire had licked up the magnificent trees that had populated the area since creation.

A few more turns of the wagon's wheels, and the landscape changed again. Now there was nothing. A void. No trees. The fierce inferno had burned them completely, including the roots, leaving only holes in the ground.

Where farmhouses and barns had once stood, there was ash. Now and then they passed the rocky remains of a well, the only way to tell that a plot of land had been a home.

They rolled into Peshtigo, the town no longer comprised of stores, churches, and saloons. It was now a field of tents, cooking fires sending eerie curls of smoke into the clear sky. From the tents came the pitiful cries of children and the raised voices of their weary parents.

Jay's throat burned. When would life return to normal? Probably never. The town was irrevocably changed. Fire would taint it from this time forward.

The supplies brought from Marinette were inadequate to take care of the hundreds, maybe even thousands, of people without homes, food, or clothing. Last night, frost had covered the roofs of the houses. Before long, the northern wind would blow in snow to cover the ground.

As they rolled farther into the encampment, men and women appeared in the tents' openings. He and Shawn should have thought to bring supplies along, whatever they could find to distribute to the people here. The two of them had warm, dry places to sleep at night, enough food, and clothes on their backs.

These people didn't possess those most basic necessities.

To keep from reliving that dreadful night, Jay focused on his hands. By the time his mother was his age, hers were dry, cracked, and wrinkled from all the hard work she did, the washing and ironing she took in to sustain herself and a growing boy after Pa died. If not for Mr. Stanford, Jay's hands would resemble Ma's by now.

How could a father and son be so different? Yes, he and his father, from what he understood, were not very similar. From what Ma said, Pa loved laboring with his hands, even when it meant the job was in a factory, with long hours and backbreaking labor the staples of his life.

Hollis and the elder Mr. Stanford were like winter and summer. The older man, while one of the shrewdest businessmen in the Midwest, had a heart and reached out to the less fortunate. Hollis, on the other hand—

"What has you so deep in thought? Miss Randolph again?"

"In a way."

"Oh, the inconvenient fact that she is engaged to Hollis Stanford."

"You read me too easily, Shawn. I didn't think I was that transparent."

They rolled on, destruction still marring the landscape. Mile after mile it continued, bare and desolate. Was Marinette the only spot on earth that the blaze hadn't touched?

"What do you think about Hollis?"

"As a boss?" Shawn lifted his hat and scratched his head. "Fine, because he's almost never here. I dread when he's in town, but thankfully, it's not that often. I suppose once he and Miss Randolph are wed, he'll have even less of a reason to show up."

"There is still the matter of the business. Mr. Stanford has entrusted him with getting this section of the line built. Or rebuilt, as is the case."

"I suppose you're right."

"Do you find him to be a bit shady?" Jay was treading on very thin ice in an attempt to feel out what Shawn knew or didn't know.

"He's slimy, that's for sure. When he isn't at the office or at Miss Randolph's, he's at the card table in the saloon. Word about town is that he's not that good of a poker player."

"That's the word."

"His daddy must get awful mad when he loses so much. Good thing they have plenty of money. They'd better keep making it with the way Hollis loses it."

So Shawn didn't know where Hollis got his gambling money from. The fewer who had that information, the better. Any day, Hollis might return from Chicago and finish Jay off, just as he was about to when the fire roared through town.

Imagine being saved by such a conflagration, the same one that snuffed out countless lives.

Many more miles passed before blades of grass peeked up from the sand and trees again blotted out the horizon. That was one big fire, that was for sure. Jay relaxed against the back of the buckboard. "How do you know which direction to drive without any landmarks?"

"It's tough." Shawn pointed to the sky. "I'm using the sun to guide me. The North Star would be better, but I think this is working. Time will tell. At least we ended up on a road. If nothing else, someone can point us in the right direction. It would be something if we found ourselves in Michigan."

Jay chuckled. "It sure would be."

In the end, they didn't need assistance from anyone. They picked out where the railroad line had been, now nothing more than melted rails and wheels. Here and there, especially in and around Oconto, it was intact, but not enough to get a train through. Shawn pushed the horses, and they arrived in Fort Howard as darkness fell. On the tracks sat a long train, many boxcars trailing the steaming black engine.

Shawn pulled up to the station, tied up the horses, and they meandered to the locomotive. The engineer tipped his striped cap at them. "What can I do for you fellas?"

Shawn stepped closer to the engineer. "Why such a long train with only boxcars?"

"Where have you been? Haven't you heard about the tragedy in Peshtigo?"

Jay removed his hat and shuffled his feet. "Survived it, sir."

"I'll be. That must have been something. These supplies here are for the fire victims. Food, clothes, tents, blankets, all the necessities, courtesy of our own governor's wife."

Shawn swept his gaze up and down the snaking line of boxcars. "His wife? What about the governor himself?"

"He's in Chicago."

Jay stepped even with Shawn. "I think you had better tell us the story from beginning to end."

"Chicago got burned too. A few hundred dead there. Right in the middle of the city. Story has it that a woman's cow kicked over her lantern in the barn and that's what started the blaze. Not sure I believe it myself, but that's what people are saying.

"Anyway, when the governor heard about the fire there, he went to investigate and asked his wife to gather supplies for the victims. She was just about to send this train off when someone came with news about Peshtigo. I guess all the telegraph lines got burned, so you all couldn't get word out. When she heard about what happened in her own state, she ordered the train here. Now we need enough wagons to take this the rest of the way."

"Chicago was burned too?" Jay couldn't believe what the engineer said.

"Yep. Real bad, but I guess not anything like what you folks lived through."

Shawn blew out a breath. "There's nothing left. Just a brick chimney and the melted straps from the barrels at the woodenware factory."

"That must be a sight."

All Jay could do was nod.

"Are you headed back that way?"

Shawn took the lead, and Jay was happy to allow him to be the spokesman. "In the morning, we will be. We've been out inspecting the rail lines."

"Think you could take some of this back? A few of the townsmen here are preparing to leave at first light. It's going to take a few trips to get everything there."

"When we return, we can tell the men of Marinette to bring their wagons." Shawn stared at the long train in front of them. "They were spared."

"First bit of good news in a while." The engineer motioned to a couple of scruffy men who were lounging about the station. "You there. Put your muscles to work and load up this wagon. Won't hurt you none to do some work. These poor people need a bit of kindness."

For a good while, they hoisted tents, blankets, medicine, clothing, and other supplies into the wagon bed. Jay directed them and arranged everything to maximize what they could take with them. At last, he called off the loaders. "That's all the room we have. Thanks for the help."

The two men wandered off, and the engineer tipped his cap at them once again. "Let the people in Peshtigo know they have our prayers and that more supplies are on the way. Wisconsin hasn't forgotten them."

"God bless the governor's wife."

Jay and Shawn found accommodations at the local hotel. First thing the next morning, Jay climbed into the wagon beside Shawn. They and a good number of other wagons headed back toward Peshtigo.

Shawn guided the horses. "I guess I'll have to come another day to survey the line. We need to get these supplies to the people as soon as possible."

"I'm thankful that Miss Randolph's sister has room for me at her home in Marinette."

"And I'm able to stay at the hotel in town. Mr. Stanford must have pulled some strings to get me and some of the other railroad employees rooms there." Shawn shrugged. "Just make sure you don't get on Hollis' bad side when he discovers that you're staying at his fiancée's sister's house. That will be sure to set him off, and I've seen his temper. It can be fierce, especially when he's been drinking. What do you suppose Miss Randolph sees in him?"

"He does a good job of hiding his true colors from her." Although she was learning the kind of man he was. Actually, she had learned it and hadn't broken the engagement. What was she clinging to? "Plus he has a silver tongue with her." He'd sweet-talked his way into her heart and charmed her with his daughter.

Jay couldn't believe that her interest in Hollis had anything to do with his vast fortune and the opportunities his connections provided her to get her artwork displayed. She wasn't that shallow, that materialistic. Her heart was too good and pure. Wasn't it?

"When he finds out your living arrangements, you'd better keep your head low."

Exactly what Jay planned to do. Maybe an even better plan would be to hotfoot it out of northeast Wisconsin altogether.

Chapter Seventeen

Mariah sat on a rocking chair in the corner of one of Lydia's upstairs bedrooms, the back-and-forth motion settling her shaky hands. She had been there before, so she knew where everything was. She had a picture of it in her head. The bed with its pretty blue quilt was in front of her and to her left. Beside it was a washstand, a chip out of the handle of the porcelain pitcher. To her left was a large cherry dresser.

And this rocking chair. That was all the room possessed, but it was enough.

"Are you ready for me to read it?" By the creaking of the bed, Lydia must have had a seat.

"Telegrams almost never bring good news. I'm frightened of what Hollis has to say." Had he learned that she knew his secret? Or that Jay knew? Or had something else gone wrong in Chicago? Since he had never come to claim his daughter, Angelina remained at Dunlap House. Mariah had convalesced well enough that she could come to her sister's house, freeing up her pallet at the hospital for someone else.

"You'll have to hear it at some point, so I'm going to go ahead and get it over with."

Mariah ceased her rocking and clasped her hands together.

Dearest,

You have heard about the fire here. The house and company are safe. Many need help. Will be some time before I return. Take care of Angelina.

Yours,

H

"He's not coming for his daughter? Or sending her and Nanny home?" Mariah resumed her rocking.

"That's what he's saying."

"It doesn't make sense."

"Perhaps there is a great deal of devastation there as well, and he doesn't want to subject her to that and bring back the awful memories she must have."

Maybe what Lydia said was true. Maybe. Those little doubts that had plagued Mariah for weeks now resurfaced. He wasn't coming to be with his injured daughter or fiancée. There were other matters more important to him.

Was that the kind of marriage she wanted to enter into? Could it bring her joy and fulfillment? Perhaps being busy with Angelina and whatever children God blessed them with would be enough.

If he would even have a blind woman as a wife. He likely wouldn't want to take her out in polite society.

Mariah closed her eyes, though that made little difference in what she saw. "Then, if it's not too much of an imposition on you, we'll have Angelina as a houseguest."

"Our home is rather full."

"She can sleep with me. I've heard that most of the survivors are under tents. It's not going to get any warmer. What are they going to do come winter? I won't complain about sleeping with her, because at least I have a bed and walls."

Lydia blew out a soft breath. "That's a good attitude to have."

In honesty, having Angelina beside her would be good. Perhaps she would sleep better. Not be tormented with nightmares about the fire or wake up in the middle of the night confused because all was blackness.

No matter Hollis' reason for leaving Angelina here, it was nothing but a blessing to Mariah.

"All right." The bed creaked as Lydia must have stood. Her floral perfume wafted as she moved toward the door. "I will let Dunlap House know that Angelina will be coming here."

Lydia's footsteps stopped at the door, which hadn't squeaked shut. "How are you really doing? We've always shared everything. You were the first person I told when I realized I was in love with John. So talk to me."

Yes, they had always been close, but this was different, and it was nothing that Lydia would understand. The cloying, eternal night that sent Mariah's heart racing and her hands sweating.

So what could she tell her sister? "I want to see again so I can paint. What good will I be this way? Without my vision, I can't create, and if I can't create, I will shrivel up inside and lose who I am."

"If only there was something I could do. You shouldn't have to suffer like this."

"There's only one thing that can make this better, and the doctor can't give it to me."

"Then you wait on the Lord for it."

"But what if I never regain my sight?" That would be worse than death.

———◆•◆———

Before the fire, whenever Angelina would come to visit Mariah in Peshtigo, or on the one occasion that Mariah had traveled to Chicago, Angelina would almost burst with excitement at seeing Mariah.

The little girl who stepped into Mariah's room was a different child. No boisterous laughter, no tight hugs, no fits of giggles.

Subdued.

Mariah rose from the rocking chair where she had occupied most of her time since arriving the day before, found her way to Angelina, and wrapped her in a hug. "I'm glad you've come to stay for a while. This will be fun."

"I like you, Miss Mariah, but I'd rather go home. I miss my room with the pink roses on the walls and the piles of pillows and all my toys."

Of course, what an awful omission. She had nothing here. How boring to sit in a house all day with not a single thing to do. "I'm sure you would like to be where your things are, but we all have to make do right now. Maybe Miss Lydia will get you something."

"That's okay." Angelina's voice was so soft, Mariah almost had to strain to pick up what she was saying. "My arms hurt so much." Angelina sniffled.

"Come here, sweetheart." Mariah held out her hand, and Angelina took it then led her to the rocking chair. Amazing how the girl knew where Mariah wanted to go.

They sat together, Angelina on Mariah's lap, weeping. Mariah rocked and sang a hymn even though she'd forgotten many of the words. It was enough that they were together.

All this poor mite had been through would be enough to shatter anyone. The adults struggled with the blaze's aftermath. How much worse it must be for an innocent child.

On and on Angelina's tears came, Mariah rocking and singing the entire time. After a while, her crying slowed, then ceased. She hiccupped a few times, and her body went limp. She must have fallen asleep.

After Mariah kissed Angelina's temple, she closed her eyes, and fiery red dragons, their breath hot, surrounded her on all sides. There was no escape from their fury. The flames they emitted consumed everything in their path.

"Mariah."

Lydia's call jolted her from the dream and in turn startled Angelina. Mariah rocked a few times, and the girl returned to sleep.

Soft footsteps crossed the room, and then Lydia lifted Angelina from Mariah's lap. She laid the child on the bed then returned and helped Mariah up. "Why don't you come to the kitchen and work with me to make dinner? I'm not used to feeding all these mouths, and you'll know best what Angelina likes."

Mariah allowed Lydia to lead her into the hallway before halting. "What good am I going to be to you? I can't use a knife for fear of cutting off my fingers."

"We'll find a task for you, don't worry. You can start by setting the table. It's not Sunday, but in honor of Angelina's arrival, I have a chicken roasting."

"I'll drop the dishes and break them. You don't want me to touch them."

Lydia tugged her farther down the hall and to the stairs. "What's wrong with you?"

"You don't have to pity me or try to get me out of my chair."

"Yes, I do feel sorry for you, but I don't pity you. You would truly be helpful to me, and it would be good for you to learn to manage a few tasks. Since you were little, you've been setting the table. You've probably done it thousands of times, so I don't see the problem."

"That's what's wrong. No one understands what this is like. It's awful. Horrible. I can't see anything. The darkness presses on my eyes, on my shoulders, on my chest. The light never goes on. No one strikes a match to light a lamp strong enough to pierce this night. I've never been so scared in my entire life."

Again came that whiff of sweet perfume as Lydia wrapped Mariah in a hug. The human contact relaxed her, and for a few minutes, the choking fear left.

All too soon, her sister broke contact, and Mariah was once again left on her own and in the dark.

"If you come down and eat with us, it will ease your loneliness. Please, for me, try. Angelina, if she wakes up in time, will be happy if you do."

Her sister knew just which tactic to take to convince Mariah. "For Angelina's sake, I will try."

With Lydia once again guiding her, Mariah made her way downstairs and into the kitchen. The air, heady with the odors of roasting chicken, was warm and welcoming. There was almost a hum about the place. Life being lived.

Lydia got out the plates and put them on the table for Mariah to distribute. It took much longer than it would have with her sight, but she managed to get them all placed in a manner which Lydia declared to be perfect. She then got to work on the napkins and silverware. Each movement, each correct placement, was more sure than the last.

Perhaps she could do this.

There was one question which plagued her. For a moment, she stopped her task. "Lydia, what about a funeral for Mama and Papa?"

Sniffles came from the other side of the room, near the stove. "Mama was buried here." Lydia's voice was broken, her words halting. "Papa—" She gave out a soft, strangled sob.

Mariah followed the sound and went to her sister, wrapping her in an embrace. Together they stood and wept and wept, just the two of them, no parents to guide them or share their joys and sorrows with them. No grandparents for their children.

At last, Mariah stepped back, drew a handkerchief from her apron's pocket, and wiped away her tears. The blessing of crying had been restored to her. "So they haven't found Papa's body yet?"

"No." Lydia drew in such a deep breath that Mariah heard it. "They are discovering more bodies every day. Those who attempted to escape by hiding in wells. Those who died from the fumes but were miraculously untouched by the flames. No explanation for it. The reality is, though, that someone saw the fire overtake Papa."

Lydia need say no more.

In all likelihood, they would never recover Papa's body.

A short time later, John came in from his job at one of the stores in town, one Papa had owned and left his son-in-law to manage. He and Lydia smacked lips as they kissed.

"How was your day, darling?"

John huffed. "When I wasn't busy with customer orders, I was calculating what it will cost to build and supply another store in the revived Peshtigo. Having your father's financial records would be helpful, but I fear they've been lost. All in all, it was a bit frustrating."

The mention of Papa, and by extension Mama, swelled Mariah's throat. How she missed them every minute of every day. *Lord, when will this suffering end? You took so much from me. Too much. Why?*

It was the unanswerable question. One thing she did know for sure was that she would never return to Peshtigo. Not if she could help it. There was nothing but suffering there.

Mariah set down the last spoon. "We're only waiting for Jay, and I don't know how long until he will be here or if he will be. Yesterday, he went to survey how much of the rail line was burned. Because he didn't return last night, I fear that they must have had to travel a good distance to discover the end of the line."

"Seems like a job Hollis should be undertaking." Though John muttered the words under his breath, Mariah caught them.

She couldn't disagree. "Wash up, and if Jay hasn't arrived by then, I suppose we'll have to eat. What do you think, Lydia?"

"Why don't you mash the potatoes while I check on Angelina. But yes, I don't want her special dinner to get cold. I'll leave some to the side for him if he's not here when everything is ready."

Mariah, now alone in the kitchen, worked on the potatoes. Nothing sharp with which to cut herself, so that was good. And by concentrating, she could gauge the consistency and decide when there were no more lumps.

Just as she finished the task, a blast of chilly air filled the room, and the door slammed shut.

"Is that you, Jay?"

"Yes. Lydia put you to work already, I see."

"She's not going to allow me to sit and wallow in self-pity. She prepared a special meal tonight because Angelina is coming to stay for a while. I got a telegram from Hollis yesterday saying that he won't be here for a while and asking me to take care of his daughter. Someone brought it all the way from Green Bay."

"Where is Angelina?"

"Lydia just went up to check on her. She was napping, exhausted by all she's been through the past several days."

"I can imagine. Looks like I'm not too late for dinner."

"Just in the nick of time, as I would expect."

He chuckled, his laughter warming the room even more. "I had better go make myself presentable then."

A squeal came from near the stairs. Angelina must be up and must have run into Jay. More squeals and low laughter followed. Perhaps Lydia was right. Perhaps being with the family was good for her.

A tug on her skirts withdrew her from her thoughts.

"Miss Mariah, I heard we're having chicken. It's my favorite." Angelina was bouncy and boisterous again. Perhaps that cry had been good for her.

"I know. And guess what?"

"What?"

"I'm hungry."

"Me too."

Lydia took the pot of mashed potatoes from Mariah. "Then I guess we had better get everything on the table." As if called by a siren's song, the two men flocked to the dining room, and soon dinner was served.

The clinking of silverware on the china, the light conversation around the table, was all so...well...normal. The first bit of normal in a while.

"So, Jay, Mariah tells us that you went to survey the railroad, and I heard tell that there's a large shipment of supplies come by train." John's proclamation stopped all other conversation.

"That's true." He filled them in on the story of the governor's wife.

"Wow, that's amazing." Mariah set her fork on the edge of her plate. "You didn't happen to run into Lucy and Henry while you were in Peshtigo or hear anything about them, did you?"

"I did, but that's news for later. Right now, Angelina is the star of the show, and this celebration is for her."

Jay's words sent a shot of ice through Mariah's veins. He could only mean one thing.

It wasn't good news.

Chapter Eighteen

MARINETTE, WISCONSIN
TUESDAY, OCTOBER 24, 1871

For over a week, Mariah had sat alone in the upstairs room she now occupied with Angelina. She couldn't crochet or do needlework; she couldn't read a book; she couldn't do anything.

Nor did she have any desire to do so.

Mama and Papa were dead. Lucy and Henry were dead. Far, far too many had perished.

Why had she survived, only to live in this black prison? Why had God allowed this to happen? A stream of sun warmed her cheek, but she pushed the rocking chair out of its path. The sun had no reason to shine.

If only the world had truly ended that horrific night.

Even Angelina had learned that Mariah didn't want to be disturbed. She was spending her days with Lydia, cooking, cleaning, and visiting friends. When nighttime came, she crawled in bed without a word, though often she snuggled against Mariah, likely seeking comfort that Mariah didn't have the ability to give.

Her heart had turned to stone. It was the only way to prevent it from breaking into a million pieces. If she couldn't feel, she wouldn't hurt.

Lydia brought her a tray each morning, noon, and night, not pressuring her to come downstairs again. She managed to pick at the food but didn't eat much. What a shame to waste it when so many in Peshtigo had so little, but she had no appetite. It would be better if Lydia just gave her portion to the people remaining in the devastated town.

A tap sounded at the door, but she remained silent. As it opened, it squeaked on its hinges. "Mariah?" Jay's boots clunked across the floor as he came closer.

"I didn't give you permission to enter."

"That's what I hear. You've been shutting everyone out, so I took my chances. I had to persuade Lydia I had no ill intentions toward you and had to promise to leave the door open at all times so your reputation won't be smudged. You'll still be free to marry Hollis."

She swallowed the bitterness that rose in her throat. Since the telegram, there had been nary a word from Hollis. Not a peep from Chicago. While it was awful for her, it was far worse for his lonely daughter. "Why did you come in here?"

"I miss you at the dinner table. I miss your smile."

"It's nothing compared to losing your mother, your father, and your best friend."

His clothing rustled, and she conjured an image of him crossing his arms. "I never would have pegged you for being one to wallow in pity."

"Life surprises you."

"This isn't like you. Not at all. Yes, we each grieve in our own way, and yes, you have lost a great deal. There isn't a person who was in Peshtigo on October eighth who hasn't."

"You don't understand, nor would I expect you to."

"Then enlighten me."

She gave a wry laugh. "Was that an intentional play on words, Mr. Franklin?"

Outside, rain slashed at the windows. Plenty had fallen since that fateful night.

A chain rattled. He must be fiddling with his pocket watch. "I didn't mean to be disrespectful, but I did mean the sentiment behind what I said. Tell me what your world is like."

"Dark and frightening. Humans rely on their sight. Without it, I have lost my freedom, my independence, and my art. That's the worst. Before this, I was a keen observer of all around me. Vivid pictures danced from my mind onto my canvases. Now those images have nowhere to go."

"I always admired the way you saw the world in such a different way than I did. Now you're experiencing it from a unique perspective yet again."

"Filling canvases with black paint isn't going to net me an exhibit at any gallery or museum."

"Well, what I came to tell you is that I have to go to Chicago. All the company's financial records burned, of course, and I need to get the copies so I can continue my work. I wrote to Mr. Stanford, but I haven't received a reply. It's likely the letter got lost. Since I would have to go some distance to get a telegram out, I might as well travel all the way to Chicago."

"Will you be staying there indefinitely?"

"No. I'll be gone for as short a time as possible. Perhaps no longer than a few days."

"What happened the night of the fire? Did you get any information on Hollis?"

"I did, but I fear that being in the water overnight rendered the papers a sodden, illegible mess. While I'm in the city, I hope to comb the records and see if there is anything there that might implicate him."

"Are you so fixated on nailing him to the wall?"

"No, but if there is justice to be served, I aim to see that it is." The floorboards groaned as he made his way to the door. "I'll see you soon, Mariah. Take care of yourself." He left and shut the door behind him.

"Goodbye, Jay."

Wednesday, October 25, 1871

All the world was abuzz with news about the great fire in Chicago, especially on the train south from Milwaukee. As Jay made his way through the streets from the station to the Stanford residence, he could see the devastation. Rubble littered the roads. Charred skeletons of trees stood out against the blue sky. If not for the sunshine, the city would be nothing but gray.

Here, there had been great destruction. Lives had been lost. Lives had been upended.

It was nothing, though, compared with what had happened in Peshtigo. Not the level of devastation. Not the level of loss.

The very proper English butler ushered him inside the grand house and brought him into the parlor. Two horsehair sofas were turned toward the marble-faced fireplace, and light streamed in through tall windows covered with heavy velvet drapes. "Mr. Stanford will be with you shortly, sir." The slight man nodded and closed the door as he left the room.

Not more than two seconds passed before the door opened again. Jay stood, but instead of finding Mr. Stanford, he discovered himself standing nose to nose with Hollis.

The younger Mr. Stanford sneered. "Well, well. I assumed you would show up here one of these days. How is your arm?"

Jay glanced at the splint on his wrist. "Healing well, thank you. Or no thanks to you."

Hollis decanted a bottle and poured himself a glass of amber liquid. Jay had no idea what it was and was just as happy that he didn't. "Well, it's a shame that you survived."

Everything inside of Jay screamed to reply in kind, but he dug his fingernails into his palms and resisted the urge. "Your daughter is doing well. She sent you a note and a picture that she drew."

"You can leave it with Wilson. He'll make sure I get it." Hollis downed the drink in a single swig. "How can I help you?"

"I'm not here to see you but your father."

"He is out at the moment. I'm surprised Wilson didn't explain that to you. Why don't you come again tomorrow. Maybe you'll have more luck then."

"I don't plan on leaving until I speak to your father. He's expecting me about this time. I telegraphed him along my route here, so I know he hasn't gone too far afield. Thank you though. If you would rather, I'd be happy to wait in his office."

Hollis poured himself another drink, downed it, and thunked the glass on the sideboard. "Here is fine. But don't think you've come to tattle on me. Whatever evidence you believe you may have had, if you had any at all, you no longer do." Hollis strode from the room.

What he said was too true. Unfortunately. Mariah's words about nailing Hollis to the wall echoed in his head. Was that what he had been after all along? Why?

Jealousy.

The thought sent him dropping to the sofa.

No, this wasn't a vendetta against Hollis because he wanted Mariah for himself. They were friends, nothing more. He couldn't give her what she deserved. Hollis could.

It did sting, no doubt about it. Long ago, though, he had come to accept that he was a poor kid from Chicago who was where he was in life only because of the kindness of Mr. Stanford. The elder Mr. Stanford.

While he waited, Jay remembered what the numbers were on the letters from the creditors, or most of them, but if he took a pen and ink and put them to paper now, Hollis would claim he was setting him up.

He would be incorrect, but it would appear that way.

Perhaps tomorrow he could go to the company's main headquarters and speak to the bookkeeper there and see what he could glean. It was worth a shot. At this point, he had nothing to lose.

Mr. Stanford entered the room just as Jay flipped open his pocket watch. "Jay, my boy, always good to see you, though I do wish it were under better circumstances. Except for your arm, you look hale and hearty."

"Thank you, sir." Jay shook his hand. "I feel well. And you?"

"Oh, fine, just fine. I do miss my granddaughter, but Hollis tells me that she is still healing and having a grand time with Miss Randolph, so I'm thankful for that." Mr. Stanford scrubbed his face. He had aged a good deal in the few months since Jay had seen him last. "I'm thankful that she survived such a terrible ordeal with nothing more than some light burns on her arms and bad memories."

"Yes, sir." Hollis was up to his old tricks again, lying to his father. Yes, she was enjoying being with Lydia and Mariah, but she longed for her own family. Or perhaps Hollis didn't even think about how much his daughter was missing him and her home.

"How is Miss Randolph faring?"

"Holding up the best she can. Losing her sight hasn't been easy on her."

"No, I suppose it hasn't. And the death of her parents has to have been another difficult blow."

"It was."

"Come into my office, and let's have a chat. There are several items I want to speak with you about in regard to where the railroad goes from here after the disaster."

"You have been more than generous in paying everyone's salaries during this time. It's keeping many from going under."

"Well, what else can I do? My conscience wouldn't allow me to see anyone starve. In the next day or two, a train will leave here and head to Peshtigo, loaded with supplies. Everyone has called me crazy for taking items from the people of Chicago, but we have more here than we know what to do with. Outside of the state of Wisconsin, no one has heard anything about the calamity at Peshtigo."

"Whatever you can send, no matter whether it's great or small, it's all appreciated."

They retired to Mr. Stanford's study and spent the next several hours speaking about the company's finances and Mr. Stanford's vision for the future of the railroad. How Jay's tongue burned with warning about Hollis and his ways, but since he had no proof, there was no point in saying anything.

When they emerged from their conference, the housekeeper announced that dinner was ready. Mrs. Miller, Mr. Stanford's widowed sister who often acted as hostess, kissed Jay on both cheeks. "My dear, how very good to have you with us." She nodded, her pearl earrings bobbing with the motion.

"Thank you for accommodating me."

"Of course. I had Cook prepare all your favorites tonight."

Hollis marched into the room. "What is this, the homecoming of the prodigal?"

Mrs. Miller laughed. "Of course not. Cook makes your favorite dinner at least once a week, though when you bring your bride here, I daresay that she will be the one getting her requests. You gentlemen will finally be outnumbered, and I can't be more pleased. It will be good to have Angelina home as well, which I hope will be sooner rather than later."

"Yes, Auntie." Hollis seated himself and placed the linen napkin on his lap, his manners impeccable. "As soon as she is finished convalescing, I will bring her back."

"I do hope that you will include Miss Randolph in your plans as well. I have missed her a great deal, and we must finish the wedding plans, though I understand that it will need to be postponed, as she is in mourning."

"We will see how she is faring."

How could everyone be so cheerful when Mariah had survived such a dreadful fate? No one even mentioned that she was blind. Perhaps they were avoiding the unpleasant subject altogether. Such topics weren't to be broached in polite society.

It was enough to choke the life out of Jay.

The arrival of the soup course cut off more conversation, and dinner proceeded without mention of either Angelina or Mariah. Somehow, Jay managed to make it through all five dinner courses and cigars with Hollis and his father before retiring to his room.

He might not be wealthy, especially after what the fire stole from him, and he might not have the clout or prestige the Stanfords had, but give him a small town and a simple life over the big city.

If only he could give Mariah everything she desired, maybe then she would turn her attentions on him and away from Hollis.

Chapter Nineteen

The sun had risen over Lake Michigan, illuminating the sky and the destruction the fire had wreaked on the city of Chicago, by the time Jay made his way to the railroad offices. This was nothing like the simple two-story headquarters in Peshtigo. If it had been constructed from brick, marble, and granite like this structure, it might have survived.

He took the curving staircase to the second floor to the bookkeeping department where he had learned the trade and earned Mr. Stanford's trust. The office was abuzz with activity, men dressed in neat suits with pocket squares and ties bending over ledgers.

The aging Lawrence Williams got up from his chair and made his way between desks to Jay. "How are you? Good of you to come see us." He shook Jay's hand.

"It's nice to see you too."

"Rough time you've had of it, I hear."

Jay held up his splinted arm. "I'm only a little worse for wear."

"I'd say you got off pretty light, from the stories the younger Mr. Stanford has been relaying. Such a shame about his daughter and his fiancée."

"It is, but they're getting along well. They're looking forward to a visit from him."

"I'm sure. What can I do for you?"

Jay glanced around the room. "Can we speak somewhere a little more private?" There were too many eyes and ears for his liking.

"Of course. Mr. Braun is overseeing the gathering of relief supplies for both Chicago and Peshtigo, so his office is available."

"That's perfect." Jay followed Lawrence into the spacious room with large windows overlooking the Chicago River and Lake Michigan. From this vantage point, it was impossible to tell there had been any fire in the city at all. A turn of his head, however, revealed swathes of destruction where the fire had consumed much of what was in its path.

What had the people of the Midwest done to deserve this tragedy?

"Have a seat." Lawrence motioned to a leather chair on one side of the large walnut desk. He took the other one. "What can I do for you? I have been expecting you to come for a copy of the financial books."

"I did mail a letter requesting a copy of them, but it sounds like it never made it here."

"No, it didn't. What a fortunate thing that you put the monthly report into the mail just a few days before the fire. Without that, I don't know what we would have done."

"Of course. That's why we do it. That's also why we have multiple copies of the ledgers."

"If nothing else, the fire did teach us that. You have something on your mind other than that, though, don't you?"

Jay crossed and uncrossed his legs. He cleared his throat.

"Out with it, boy."

"There's no easy way to say it, so I guess I will have to spit out the words. Have you noticed any discrepancies with the records?"

Lawrence tapped a pen on the desk. "What do you mean?"

"Before the fire, I discovered money missing from the ledgers and numbers that didn't add up."

Lawrence leaned forward. "Do you mean that someone is skimming funds from the company?"

"That is precisely what I mean."

The older man slumped back in his chair. "Oh my. Do you have any idea who it might be?"

"I do, but at this point, I would rather not say. Not until I'm surer of my suspicions. For a while, I thought that perhaps I had made a mistake with the numbers."

"No, you didn't. You're too good with figures to make an error."

"No one is perfect, sir, but I did come into possession of information from an anonymous source that leads me to believe that someone else also found this discrepancy."

"How did you learn this?"

"Again, I would rather not say. I thought I would do a little investigating while I was here and see if anyone else noticed anything."

Lawrence shook his head. "It wasn't me, but I mostly review time sheets and take care of payroll. I'm not involved in the overall finances."

"I understand."

"It does concern me that there might well be someone stealing from the Stanfords. Mr. Stanford has been nothing but generous with us, and it's a shame to know someone is taking advantage of him."

Jay swallowed. "That it is."

"Let me collect what we have, and you can take a look at it, though I'm surprised that no one else has picked up on what you say is happening."

Jay nodded. There was a good reason for it. If anyone did figure out it was Hollis, they likely lived in fear of him discovering they knew. He wielded enough power to destroy them. Jay's arm was testament to that.

Lawrence returned several minutes later with a number of ledgers in his hands. "Here we are. I told the men working on these that you needed them to get things running in Peshtigo again. No one questioned that."

"Because it's true." Jay gave a wry half chuckle. He took the leather-bound books Lawrence handed to him and spent a good amount of time giving them a careful perusal, comparing numbers between the books. Everything was in order. He went to find Lawrence again. "How about the report I sent you from Peshtigo?"

"Ah, yes, I forgot that. Give me a few minutes, and I'll be back with it."

Jay took the time to go over the records once more. The ledgers appeared to be without fault. Not a decimal point out of place.

By the time he finished, Lawrence returned. "Accept my apologies for the amount of time it took for me to locate this. With everything that transpired both here and in Peshtigo, it got pushed to the side."

"No problem." Jay took the opened envelope, withdrew the paper, and compared his own figures with those recorded by the Chicago book-keepers. As expected, the numbers were the same. They weren't necessarily correct, but they were the same. "Thank you."

"Did you find what you were looking for?"

"Yes. Just what I expected. I would like to make a copy of my report, if I could, and I don't want to be in the way."

"You won't be in here."

"I do need to retrieve something from Mr. Hollis Stanford's office. His father said he would be working at the railyard today."

"Of course, though I would caution you to work in here. If he would catch you in his office, he would be none too pleased."

"I understand. It will only take me a few minutes."

"If you're sure, I'll leave you to it." Lawrence exited the room, and Jay made his way down the hall to Hollis' office.

This one was about the size of all the offices in Peshtigo combined. It boasted a spectacular view of the sparkling blue waters of Lake Michigan. Jay, however, did not take time to admire the scene out of the window. Lawrence was right. Any minute, Hollis could decide he was bored with the assignment his father gave him and come to his office, though it was far more likely that he would head to the nearest gambling hall.

Still, Jay had to make quick work of the task in front of him. With little trouble, he located more letters from creditors and Hollis' copy of the financial records. It was brazen of him to keep them here. But perhaps he believed—correctly so—that they were safer here, away from his father, the housekeeper, even the butler.

As suspected, the numbers Hollis kept didn't match with the official records Jay had. In fact, there was even more missing from the company than there had been a few weeks ago. Hollis hadn't been spending much time at the office at all. It also explained why he hadn't returned to Wisconsin where his favorite gambling lair had been destroyed.

A quick knock at the door sent Jay's heart racing in a matching tempo. Lawrence swung it open. "The younger Mr. Stanford just arrived. I have someone downstairs stalling him."

"Thank you."

If Hollis caught him in here, it might well mean an end to his life. He stashed the books away, hurried down the back staircase and out the rear door, all without encountering Hollis.

He blew out his breath, his heart hammering in his ears. The time had come for him to return north. Though he didn't have all he had come to the city to collect, at least the evidence of Hollis' embezzling existed. All he had to do was figure out a way to get his hands on it.

He had to calm down before he returned to the Stanfords to collect his belongings. Even if he could only get as far as Racine or Kenosha tonight, that would be good enough. Anywhere out of Chicago. If the incident before the fire taught him anything, it was that Hollis would stop at nothing to keep his secret from being exposed.

He strolled down the street, nonchalant on the outside, quite the opposite on the inside. Should he say something to Mr. Stanford? He deserved to know, didn't he, before Hollis brought him and the company to financial ruin?

And yet, it might kill the man. He was blind to the sins of his son. His only heir. Mr. Stanford had no one else to pass the company to without Hollis. Only Angelina, who was but a child.

He pulled himself from his musings to get his bearings and discovered himself in front of an art gallery in an area of the city untouched by the fire. Perhaps Mariah had visited this very one the last time she was in Chicago. Putting off having to decide what to do about Hollis, he entered the bright and airy shop where paintings filled the walls.

A tall man with a straight, regal bearing entered from a back room. "Good morning, sir. How may I help you?"

Jay gulped. "I came to see what you have on display."

The gallery owner eyed Jay up and down, no doubt assessing his ability—or lack thereof—to afford any of the pieces. "I see. Please, indulge yourself." The man stepped to a far corner but didn't take his eyes off Jay.

He perused the artwork displayed there. Still lifes. Portraits. Landscapes. Nothing caught his eye as much as Mariah's work did. There wasn't a single piece that was as vibrant as hers. As alive.

He stood with arms akimbo in front of one piece, not really seeing it but envisioning how Mariah would have painted it. When he left, she was so torn-up by the loss of her sight. The loss of her craft.

Could she paint from memory? From the images still locked in her brain? Asking a blind woman to paint might be crazy, but why not? True, he didn't understand much about art or about creating it, but if he could bring Mariah even a little joy again, it would be worth it. If all she could do was feel the brush in her hand, inhale the odor of the paint, relish the movement of the bristles across the canvas, it might be enough to cheer her.

He approached the gallery owner. "Excuse me, sir. Is there a place nearby where I might purchase some art supplies?"

The man stared down at Jay, never moving his head. "Do you think to paint something worthy of this gallery?"

What had brought on that line of questioning? Did Jay appear provincial? Was it the way he spoke or how he held himself? Or was the man one of the most condescending people Jay had ever encountered? He inhaled and exhaled and managed to keep his composure. "No, not at all. I'm asking because I know someone who is very talented."

The gallery owner gave Jay the directions, which he followed to the art supply store. The shopkeeper there was much more congenial and assisted Jay in procuring the right materials for Mariah. When all was said and done, he spent much more than he had intended, but to see the smile on Mariah's face would be well worth it.

At least, he hoped she would smile. Otherwise, he might be making one of the biggest mistakes of his life.

Chapter Twenty

MARINETTE, WISCONSIN
FRIDAY, OCTOBER 27, 1871

When I waked, I cried to dream again.

This quote from Shakespeare that Mariah had memorized when she was small was all too true for her now. The nights when she dreamed, oh how wonderful they were because then she could see again. See the faces of her family and those she loved so dearly. The towering green pines that had once surrounded the town. The brilliance of the blue sky and the shades of the yellow sun dancing on green leaves.

When she woke, though, it all disappeared, replaced by this awful, utter darkness.

It strangled her. Weighed her down. Down to the depths.

She was barely alive. Why had God even spared her?

Lydia knocked at the door. Each person had their own distinctive way of announcing their presence. A little trick Mariah had learned.

Lydia's skirts swished against the floor, her shoes giving a light tap. She brushed Mariah's cheek. "You have to live again. Sitting in a room in a rocking chair all the time for the rest of your days isn't the way to go about it. That's what Mama would say."

"But she isn't here to say it, is she?"

"I miss her too, Mariah, more than I can say. Her and Papa both. One thing I know, though, is that they would want us to carry on with the rest of our lives. What is helping me survive is staying busy. It passes the time and occupies my mind. You need to get up and try to do a little. You had been. What happened?"

"Can we talk about something else—anything else—other than my blindness and the deaths of our parents? Such conversation does nothing to cheer me up."

"What have you heard from Hollis?"

"That will do nothing to buoy my spirits either."

Lydia chuckled. "Then what will? You pick the topic."

"Tell me what it looks like outside the window. I've seen the view before, but I want to experience it now."

"Oh, I'm no good with colors or shapes like you are."

"You are good with words though. You wrote the most wonderful poems at school. Just tell me what you see."

"Okay. I'll try." Lydia moved away from Mariah, toward the window. "The trees are almost bare, so their bark stands out. Some are dark brown, like cocoa, others lighter, and the birches are white. Of course, the pines are there too, towering over everything. Mrs. Monroe's house across the street is as neat as ever, the clapboards painted pale pink, such a contrast to the end of fall.

"The street is quiet. Oh, no it's not. There goes Mrs. Harper, probably to the store like she does every Friday. Yes, she has her woven basket with her.

"Wait, someone else is coming. A man, by the looks of it, as I see no skirts. He's carrying something. Of course, it's Jay. He's back from Chicago already with his valise in his hand. He borrowed John's."

An undefinable twinge stirred in Mariah. She slid forward on the rocker. "Why is he back so soon? I hope all went well there for him. Perhaps he brings word of Hollis too. Angelina is anxious to hear from her father."

"And you are as well, I imagine?"

"Yes."

"That was an unenthusiastic response."

"Was it? I suppose it's because I don't know what is going on with him. He doesn't visit, hasn't written. We haven't even spoken about the wedding, which I presume is postponed at the very least. Perhaps he doesn't want a blind woman as his wife, but he hasn't voiced that to me one way or the other, which is most frustrating."

"I imagine it is. Well, I had better go downstairs and greet Jay. Are you going to come with me?"

"A very good try, Sister, but no."

"I have a feeling he would like to see you."

Mariah shrugged, and Lydia left the room without closing the door behind her.

Voices rose from downstairs, Angelina's the most pronounced, probably because it was the loudest. "Did you bring anything from Father?"

"He sends his love, which is the very best thing to send. Even better than a toy or a letter because you will always have his love with you." God bless Jay for trying.

And curse Hollis for not.

"Couldn't I have his love and a new doll?"

Laughter followed, then silence. They must have moved to the kitchen.

Yes, she would like to join them, but she was a burden, always needing help with one thing or another. Soon, maybe, but not today. She didn't have the energy to get up from the chair.

"Mariah?"

She startled and clutched her chest. "Jay, I didn't hear you come in."

"Your forehead was scrunched, so I imagine you must have been deep in thought."

"Yes, I suppose I was. How are things in Chicago?"

"Fine. I did manage a very brief glance at Hollis' ledgers there, and the numbers are off, just like they were here. And there are letters from creditors. Unfortunately, he returned to the office before I could decide what to do about everything. Also while I was there, he made it very clear that I am not welcome in his home."

"It really is his father's."

"True, very true."

"I heard a bit of your conversation with Angelina, and I guess that you brought nothing for me?"

"No. I'm so sorry. His aunt did mention the wedding at dinner the other night, so she is still planning on you joining the family after your period of mourning is completed."

"That decision needs to be between me and Hollis, which is difficult since he isn't answering any of the letters I dictate to Lydia. It is total silence on his end."

"Well, I didn't come empty-handed. I do have a gift for you."

Amazing how Hollis couldn't be bothered to drop her a line, but Jay thought about her enough to bring her a trinket. "You didn't have to do that."

"I know, but this will cheer you up. Maybe it will be good for you."

"What is it?"

"I'll hand it to you, and you can tell me. It's actually several small items and a couple of larger ones."

"Now I am intrigued." She again slid to the edge of the rocker's seat.

Jay dropped a few things in her lap. Some were light, a few others a little heavier. She picked one up, the metal of it cool underneath her touch. "Is this a tube of paint?"

"Pick up something else, and you'll know if you are right or wrong."

Her fingers skimmed against the items on her lap until she touched something soft. Bristles. A paintbrush. "You brought me painting supplies?"

"Everything you need to start again, including canvases."

"Painting supplies, Jay? Really?"

"Yes." Jay drew out the word.

"What were you thinking? Did you forget that I'm blind? That I can't see a thing? Not a single thing, Jay. Not the colors of the paint, not where I'm making my strokes, nothing."

"Use your instincts. You still have it inside you."

"Your skill lies in numbers and figures." Her voice rose in pitch. "You know nothing about art and nothing about being blind." Searing white heat rose in her chest. If the paint tubes wouldn't burst when they hit the wall, she would throw them.

"I only meant to help."

"Get out. Now. And leave me alone."

"But—"

She pointed in the door's direction. "Out."

He shuffled his feet as he left the room.

A moment later, Lydia's light footsteps announced her arrival. "What is going on? I heard shouting."

Mariah grabbed the paint tubes and brushes from her lap and held them up as evidence for her sister. "Jay brought me painting supplies. Can you believe it? He thinks I can paint. In fact, he went as far to even say that painting would be good for me."

"Oh, you poor dear." Lydia grabbed the items from Mariah's hand, a brush clattering to the floor. "I can't imagine what must have been going through his head, though I'm sure he means well. I'll just put the paints and brushes on top of the dresser, and the canvases on the floor beside it. Setting the table is one thing. Painting is another matter altogether."

"How could he be that insensitive? He has always been awkward, but not like this."

"I'm sorry he upset you so. Why don't I bring you a cup of tea to settle your nerves?"

"That would be lovely. Thank you for everything. For being understanding and compassionate."

"You know, Jay's heart was in the right place. He didn't mean to upset you."

"Don't go taking his side."

"There are no sides here." Lydia's voice took on a firmer tone. "Have some compassion on him too. He cares for you. A great deal. Something to think about. I'll be back with the tea soon."

Lydia was true to her word, and not too much later, Mariah held a warm, steaming cup, the scent of chamomile tickling her nose and tempting her to sip even though the tea would burn her tongue.

Had she been too harsh on Jay? He had never been cruel or insensitive before, not to anyone. Perhaps she shouldn't have gotten so angry with him. As Lydia had said, he was only trying to help.

Maybe that was what grated her nerves the most. Everyone thought they had the cure for her blindness, or at least the key for how she should deal with it, as it had been weeks now without improvement.

The floral aroma from the tea relaxed her, and she drank in the warmth of the light that flooded the room. As winter approached, the sun settled in the south. The room faced the right direction to capture it all.

She was down to the last dregs of the tea when Angelina burst into the room. "Mrs. Stuart is going to a church meeting, so she told me to come in here so we can play while she's gone. Isn't it going to be fun? I just can't decide what to do." It was the first time in a couple of weeks that she had wanted to spend time with Mariah.

She finished her tea and set the cup on the sturdy little table Lydia had situated beside the rocker. "That's a good question."

"If Father had sent me a doll, we could play with her, but now I don't have one."

"You know what? Lydia still has her doll from when she was a little girl. At least, I think she does. But where would it be? I haven't seen it since she got married and moved here."

"I could go look for it." Angelina's footsteps moved toward the door.

"No, honey, you can't do that."

"Why not?" Her voice held a hint of poutiness.

"Because it's impolite to search through people's belongings when you don't have their permission."

"But I want to play with a doll." She sniffled.

Mariah held her arms open. "Come here. I can tell you a story."

Angelina stomped her foot. "I don't want a story. I want a doll."

The girl was almost never this obstinate and disobedient. "Though I wish I could, I can't make a doll appear from thin air. These days, we all wish many things, but most of those aren't possible."

"Like how I wish my arms didn't have these burns? Or like you wish you could see?" Angelina sniffed again.

"Yes, like that. Those are the big wants we have, but there are little ones too, like wanting a doll to play with." Though it would be nothing for Hollis to send one to his daughter, a simple gesture that would have brightened her days.

Angelina touched Mariah's arm. "I'm sorry."

Mariah squeezed the little girl's shoulder. "I forgive you. It's difficult to be patient and to do without what we wish we could have. In time, life will go back to normal." At least for Angelina it would. "Right now, we have to make do."

Angelina moved away from her. "What's this? They look like paints. And there are brushes."

"Those came from Mr. Franklin. He brought them."

"Since I don't have a doll, may we paint together? Please?"

"I don't know."

"I asked politely."

"You did." But the thought of putting brush to canvas sent a chill all the way to Mariah's fingertips.

"Then can we?"

Only a few weeks ago, Mariah would have given in to her request without any thought. But now? Well, everything had changed. "Don't you remember that I can't see?"

"But I can. Maybe we can paint together. I can tell you where to put the brush, and you make the picture."

Mariah's heart fluttered, stopped for a split second, and fluttered again. She drew in a deep breath. "I don't know. I don't think I can."

Chapter Twenty-One

Jay settled behind his desk in the borrowed office, the whirring of the mill's saws a constant din in the background, which did nothing for the terrific headache building behind both eyes. No matter what, he couldn't do anything right. He had purchased the painting supplies for Mariah out of nothing but good intentions, never thinking she might not want to paint again.

Or might be too frightened to try.

The loss of her eyesight had to be terrifying. To him it was unimaginable. The darkness must be overwhelming, especially to a visual person like her. Almost everything she did required her sight.

What a fool he had been. What a complete and utter fool. An ant possessed more common sense than he did. What was it about him that had him blundering his way through life?

The one good thing from his trip to Chicago was that he had retrieved the ledgers. Not Hollis' ledgers, the ones that kept track of his spending, but the ones Jay and the bookkeeper in Chicago had. Now he could get to work and take his mind off the devastating fire, at least for a little while.

Which was something Mariah and Angelina couldn't do.

He had also failed to bring back the proof that Hollis was embezzling. It was there. He had seen it with his own eyes. If only the person who sent Mariah the original note would contact her again.

Then again, he might not even be alive. He could have been a victim of the fire. The informant's identity might forever remain a mystery.

He forced himself to concentrate on his work and managed to get a bit done when a knock came on his door. Shawn peeked in. "Ah, ever the faithful, hardworking employee."

"Someone has to be."

Shawn chuckled. "I don't know if you heard the news, but the Stanfords' train has arrived, and the goods are being off-loaded into the wagons now. By the time we make it to Peshtigo, they should be there for us to help."

"How did you hear so fast?"

"A rider came. Mr. Stanford wants us to be there to lend a hand and represent the railroad."

Jay sighed, set down his pen, and wiped ink from his fingers. "I'm surprised he didn't come himself."

"Me too, but I guess he's pretty busy."

"I can vouch for that." Jay rose from behind his desk. "Let's get over there then."

The livery had no more horses available, so Shawn and Jay had to make the seven-mile trek by foot. At least the heat had passed long ago and now a chilly November wind blew.

They had gone a fair piece when Shawn turned to him. "You're very quiet."

"I have a great deal on my mind."

"These days, we all do. Does it have to do with what we discussed before? Did you discover additional information in Chicago?"

"Yes and no. It's a frustrating search. Between that and Miss Randolph, my mind is well occupied."

"Miss Randolph. Hmm." Shawn scratched his head.

"Oh, no need to play it like that."

"Fine. What is going on with the beguiling Miss Randolph?"

"I have been a fool yet again."

"Now what?"

"I brought a souvenir home for her."

"And what is so wrong with that?"

"I brought her paints, brushes, and canvases."

Shawn scurried in front of Jay and came to a halt. "You did what?"

"I know, I know." Jay waved his hands.

"That is the craziest thing I have ever heard. What were you thinking?"

"She has been so sad since the fire. She lost her mother and father, her sight, and her home. Everything that mattered to her. All I wanted was to cheer her up."

"In case you haven't heard, Miss Randolph is blind. Unless her condition has changed."

"It hasn't, and the doctors can give no definitive prognosis. I thought maybe this would help her resume her painting. If there is a way for a blind woman to do it, Mariah is the one to figure it out."

"I believe I may need to have you committed to an insane asylum."

"That might be for the best." At least there, he wouldn't hurt anyone with his bumbling actions.

"I was only joking. She has to know that even though it might not have been the most sensible, thoughtful gift, it came from your heart. You meant well."

"My good intentions can do nothing to mitigate her misery."

"Next time you think to bring her a gift, consult me first."

That brought a wry smile to Jay's lips. "The last I knew, you were also single, so I don't believe your skills with the fairer sex are so superior to mine."

The teasing grin slipped from Shawn's face, and he fell in step with Jay again.

"What's wrong? Please don't tell me that I've once more said the wrong thing."

Shawn shook his head. "You had no way of knowing, but I had my eye on Miss Adelaide McClean. Now..."

"Oh, I'm so sorry. You never said anything. Even after the fire, you never let on that you were interested in her."

"There isn't a person who once lived in Peshtigo who wasn't touched by the fire. No one who didn't lose someone."

"That's the truth."

The rest of the walk passed in silence until they came to the burned-out village. From the huddled tents rose the wails of infants. Children raced each other around the makeshift dwellings, some of them without coats, a few with rags wrapped around their feet.

Hatless men shuffled as they meandered up and down the tent village, their eyes as empty as their pockets.

No sooner had Jay and Shawn come upon the scene than the jangling of harnesses met them, and the wagons rolled into town.

What a commotion that caused. The men, previously aimless, now hurried in the direction of the supplies. The children stopped their play, and the women ducked out of the tents, their eyes squinting against the fall sunshine.

As if they were a school of fish swimming in unison, they collectively made their way toward the wagons.

Shawn and Jay hurried ahead of the group and turned to face them. Shawn took over as spokesman, which was just as well with Jay. "Excuse me. On behalf of Stanford Rail Industries comes this trainload of goods and supplies for you. Let's handle this in an orderly fashion. Mr. Franklin will help you queue up and make sure everything is distributed equitably."

"Get down from there." Hollis emerged from behind one of the wagons. "You are not to speak on behalf of my father, myself, or our company. You are a hireling."

Not much flustered Shawn. "Welcome, Mr. Stanford. It's good to have you with us. Please, direct the distribution of this generous gift from the railroad."

Hollis stepped closer to Shawn but spoke loudly enough for Jay to overhear. "Sarcasm does not become you. Put your muscles, if you have any, to work and start unloading these wagons."

Shawn and Jay went to the closest one and hauled off sacks of flour and barrels of clothes and shoes. The people crowded around them, pressing in, grabbing whatever they could reach.

Hollis did nothing but stand with his arms crossed and survey the scene.

For hours, Jay and Shawn worked with the other men to unload and distribute supplies. Shawn didn't make another public announcement, but he and Jay quietly organized lines and made sure no one got too much or too little.

It would be enough for a few weeks, but any time now, the snow would fall. Before long, the rags around people's feet wouldn't be able to keep out the biting cold. And there would be no food available to them until crops could be planted and harvested.

Who knew how well they would grow in the ashy soil?

Jay's muscles ached, every single one of them, and he was bone weary by the time the last wagon turned around and headed to the end of the tracks to await more provisions. Now he and Shawn faced the daunting trek all the way back to Marinette.

They hadn't gone far before Hollis passed them, working his sleek white steed hard. Too hard, though Jay would never dare to say so unless the animal was in mortal danger.

Night had fallen early as it did in late fall, and darkness covered the land by the time they entered Marinette proper. Shawn broke off to go to his accommodations, and Jay continued toward the Stuart residence.

What a day it had turned out to be. Just the idea of Hollis being in the same town as him quickened his step. He turned down the street where the Stuarts lived and had their simple clapboard home in sight. How wonderful it would be to lie down in bed, pull the covers over himself, and sleep.

Behind him, a crunch sounded. He whirled around. "Who's there?"

Only the barking of a dog in the distance answered him.

Now he was losing his mind. He took a few more steps, and the noise came again—in perfect pace with his steps. His heart rate kicked up. "Who's there?" he called again.

All was still and silent. Jay held his breath until he almost blacked out. As soon as he continued on his way, the same thing happened.

This time he stopped, every nerve poised and ready for whatever might be coming.

But nothing could have prepared him for the blow to the side of his head. The world around him whirled, and he staggered backward. His knees buckled, and he fell to the ground.

"You mind your own business. Do you understand me?"

If Jay opened his mouth, he would vomit.

"I asked if you understand? Or are you too stupid?"

"You are. . ." Jay struggled for breath.

"What? What am I? Whatever it is, it's a sight better than what you are."

"Took money."

Hollis' boot connected with the side of Jay's head.

The world went black.

Chapter Twenty-Two

Voices came from below the window where Mariah was laying out her nightgown on the bed, preparing to retire for the night. There was shouting and a commotion. She moved to the window behind her.

As she reached it, a *thump* came.

She flung open the sash. "Who is there? What's going on?"

The bedsheets rustled. "Miss Mariah?" Angelina's voice was thick with grogginess.

"Go back to sleep, sweetheart. I heard a noise, likely a cat searching for a midnight snack."

"Okay." The sheets moved again.

Mariah felt her way along the bureau and straight ahead to the door. She had memorized this section of the room and no longer stubbed her toe on the bed, always a blessing.

Once she entered the hall, she stood for a moment. Silence. Lydia and John must still be downstairs. She shuffled along until she came to the staircase and made her way to the first floor. The hum of quiet voices greeted her.

"It's so sad. I wish we could do something to help cheer her up." Lydia. Was she discussing Mariah?

"She'll come around in time. Just be patient with her. This can't be easy," John answered his wife.

Mariah clomped a little harder than was ladylike to announce her presence. "Lydia? John? Did you hear that noise outside?"

"Noise? No. We were talking."

"There was a commotion, then a thump."

"Oh, dear. John, would you investigate, please?"

"Already on my way out the door."

"Are you sure about what you heard?" Lydia's voice came closer as she spoke.

"I'm blind, not deaf."

"My apologies. I don't want to upset you."

Mariah squeezed her eyes shut to keep her tears from falling.

"Lydia, come quickly." John was breathless. "It's Jay."

Mariah gasped. "No. What happened?"

"I'm not sure, but he's on the ground and not responding. Lydia, I need your help to get him in the house. He's right outside the door."

"Of course."

For a few moments, only the ticking of the wall clock kept Mariah company. That and the pounding of her heart against her ribs.

"Bring him to the davenport." John's voice was strained. "Mariah, he's bleeding pretty badly. Get a washcloth from the basin in the kitchen. And some towels too."

She fumbled her way along, running into the dining table before locating the washcloth and the towels, then reversing course, making her way to the couch.

Lydia took the washcloth from her. "I want to clean away some of this blood to find what injuries he has sustained."

Unable to see, Mariah couldn't even help her sister care for Jay. She balled her hands and blew out a breath.

"From the looks of it, someone punched him. Maybe even kicked him." The tightness of John's words gave away his anger.

"The thump I heard must have been from when he hit the ground. Did you see anyone out there?"

"No. It was too dark, and by the time you came down and informed us, whoever it was had disappeared."

Mariah knelt beside the couch and touched Jay's head, careful not to bump him and cause him any discomfort.

He moaned. Mariah blew out a breath. He was alive, so that was a positive.

"Jay?" She leaned in. "Jay, you're safe now. I'm here and so are Lydia and John."

He groaned. "It hurts."

"Where?" If only she could see his injuries.

"Everywhere."

"What happened?" Mariah brushed his hair from his forehead.

"Don't know. Coming home."

"Yes. John found you right outside the door."

"Helped in Peshtigo. Supplies."

Mariah nodded. "We heard about that."

"Late. Dark."

"Yes. We were all just about to go to bed."

"I have some soup on the stove I can heat up." God bless Lydia. "It might warm you through."

"No. Ow. I shouldn't have tried to shake my head."

"Just stay still and allow Lydia to take care of you." Mariah directed her attention toward where John had been standing and hopefully still was. "Does anything appear broken?"

"I'm not a doctor, but there is nothing visible."

"Perhaps we should call for one."

"That's a good idea. Lydia, why don't you get Jay some soup while I go for the doctor."

Within moments, John had left, and the kitchen door squeaked behind Lydia, leaving Jay and Mariah alone.

"Are you sure you don't remember who did this to you?"

Jay sucked in a breath. "I didn't at first, but it's coming back."

She licked her lips. "Who?" She prayed he wouldn't say what she believed he would.

"Pretty sure it was Hollis."

She shook her head, just a small back and forth motion. "So he's in town."

"Yes. I remember him giving orders in Peshtigo."

"That sounds like him."

"He threatened me in Chicago. Made good on it tonight. Not all the way, but he tried."

"Threatened you how?" Mariah could barely breathe.

"My life. Said he was going to kill me."

Mariah rocked back on her heels. All her dreams of a life with Hollis crashed around her in that moment. How could she ever marry anyone like him? He was a monster. Evil.

What he could have given her—a life of leisure, an art show, a daughter—no longer mattered, not only because she had lost her sight and her work but because of who he'd shown himself to be. All along, she had closed her mind and turned her back on the evidence pointing to the kind of man she was about to marry.

Of course, ending her betrothal would break Angelina's heart. How could she do that to the child who was already struggling with her father's absence and her injuries? Would it be right for Mariah to walk away and leave Angelina with no one who truly, fully loved her, other than her grandfather?

"I don't know what to do. Perhaps I should break my engagement to him. I could never wed a man who would do such a thing. How he has treated his injured daughter is also not right. In fact, I don't know what attracted me to him in the first place."

That wasn't the complete truth. The attention from a wealthy, handsome man who promised her the world. That was what had drawn her to him. "What a fool I've been."

"Don't."

"But I have been selfish, ready to do anything to get what I wanted, what I thought I deserved. Only the hurt Angelina would suffer if I left is holding me back."

"Good, because I meant don't break off your engagement."

"That blow to the head has affected you. Why would you want me to marry him?"

"I can't prove it."

"His skimming?"

"Yes."

As soon as the full impact of what he was asking of her hit her, she stood. "You want me to stay betrothed to him so that I can snoop around and discover if he's taking money from the railroad?"

"Yes."

"I'm not sure I want to. That I can. He will likely come to see me, or at least his daughter, while he is here. With my blindness, he may want nothing to do with me. I'm not an asset to him. How can I host lavish parties and balls and everything that goes with being a part of society when I can't see?"

"Convince him."

She laughed. "You make it sound so easy."

"You can do it."

Angelina. She had to think of her and the impact of this on her fragile spirit. Perhaps marrying Hollis would be the least selfish choice she could make.

"Miss Mariah?" Angelina's little voice came from the top of the stairs.

"What is it, sweetheart?"

"I had a bad dream. I'm scared." She broke down into heart-wrenching sobs.

Mariah maneuvered her way around the couch and up the stairs to the crying child. Once she was at the top, she picked her up. "Shh, shh, don't worry. I'm here, and I'm not going to let anything happen to you."

"When I woke up, you weren't in bed with me."

"I came downstairs to talk to the grown-ups, but I was in the house the whole time. I didn't leave."

She clung to Mariah's neck. "I dream about the fire every night." A sob cut off her words. "That it's coming for me, and I can't run away."

"You're safe now. I understand about your nightmares, but you're safe. Nothing is going to hurt you."

"Don't leave me."

Those three simple words almost broke Mariah. If she called off her engagement to Hollis, she would leave Angelina without a mother. She would only have a series of nannies, women who may or may not care much for a precocious child.

What could Mariah do? What *should* she do?

◆◆◆

The pounding in Jay's head matched the pounding in his heart. The blow to his head must have made him insane, telling the woman he had loved since he first met her not to break her engagement to a despicable man.

Wasn't that a dream come true for him?

Yes, it was. But Hollis had to be stopped. No longer was he simply taking money that didn't belong to him—though Mr. Stanford would have given him whatever he wanted—but now he was violent and would do anything, including murder, to keep his deeds from being brought into the light of day.

And Jay had asked her to stay with a man she didn't love.

She didn't love him, did she?

What a muddled mess he was making of everything. Not unusual in and of itself, but why did he have to bumble so much when it came to Mariah?

He must have drifted to sleep, because a light touch on his shoulder startled him and sent his head to pounding again.

"Oh, I'm sorry. I didn't mean to frighten you." Lydia stood over him. "Dr. Henderson is here. Where did Mariah go?"

"Angelina had a bad dream, so I think she's with her."

"I'll check to see if she needs anything."

Dr. Henderson evaluated Jay, poking and prodding every inch of him, only increasing his headache. At last he stood back. "You're lucky to be alive. A blow to the head like that can be fatal. Take it easy and rest for the next few days, at least until that pain in your noggin subsides. Do you know who did this to you?"

"It's something I'd prefer to handle with the authorities." The doctor didn't need to know. No one other than Mariah did.

At this point, it was his word against Hollis', and no one was going to believe him over the most powerful and influential man in that part of the state. Then when—if—Jay was able to show that Hollis had been embezzling, Hollis would cry foul and accuse Jay of jealous intentions to bring him down.

"All right, then, but whoever beat you like this deserves to pay for his crime."

"I agree." And Lord willing, at some point, he would.

"Take care. John, send for me again if anything at all changes with Jay's condition."

"Thank you, Dr. Henderson. You've been very kind." John stood behind Jay, just out of his line of vision.

"Feel better. I'll see myself out."

"Oh, I missed the doctor." Mariah appeared at the edge of his line of sight as John exited the room.

"You did, but he said I'm fine. How is Angelina?"

"Sleeping. I didn't tell her Hollis is in town, in case he doesn't. . ."

He reached for her and touched the top of her hand, just a whisper against her skin. "Are you afraid that he will or that he won't?"

"For her sake, because he is the only parent she has, I hope he does. Only for her sake. She's so young, and he is her father. No matter what kind of person he is, every little girl deserves affection from the first man in her life."

"You're right, and I've been thinking."

"I'll do it. Or won't do it, as the case may be. I won't break my engagement."

"That's what I've been thinking about." He turned to his side just a little to raise himself on his elbows so he could see her. "I asked too much of you. You don't need to do this for me. Not because of some missing funds."

"You're right. It's not about the money. It's not about me or him. Keeping my commitment to him is about Angelina. Right now, she needs someone in her life who is going to be there, who will love her and take care of her. I don't know if I'm the right person for the job, but at this moment, I'm the only one who can do this."

"Are you sure?" This time, he touched her hand for longer, lingering.

"Someone has to be there to comfort her when she has nightmares."

"And who will comfort you?"

The question hung in the air.

Chapter Twenty-Three

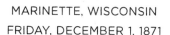

MARINETTE, WISCONSIN
FRIDAY, DECEMBER 1, 1871

Why, when Mariah had been expecting the knock at the door, did it startle her so when it came? "I'll answer it."

Lydia was in the kitchen with Angelina, the two of them giggling as they baked up a venison stew that sent Mariah's stomach to rumbling. "Thank you."

She turned the knob. "Hello, Hollis."

"How did you—?"

"You have a distinctive knock." She held back the part about it being decisive to the point of demanding.

"Oh." He dropped a kiss on her cheek, his lips rough against her skin.

No shiver of pleasure ran through her, not like the night when Jay was injured and had touched her hand. Light and brief, but enough to make her heart dance. Praise the Lord that he suffered no permanent damage and was back at work.

No one had seen Hollis the rest of November. He hadn't stopped by to visit either her or Angelina. It was as if he had fallen off the face of the earth. Now he was back. "Jay told me you were in town. I'm surprised you didn't stop by sooner."

He brushed past her before she even had a chance to invite him in. Had her mind been blind before her eyes went dim so that she didn't see—or want to see—the caliber of man Hollis was? He dangled fame and fortune in front of her, and she bit from that carrot.

"I have been busy with railroad matters. The fires in both Peshtigo and Chicago have consumed much of my time."

"We could have accommodated you here. Lydia would have loved to have you."

"I didn't want to be an inconvenience."

They moved to the parlor. "Please, have a seat. I'll let Lydia know we would like some tea. Angelina is in the kitchen with her." She moved past the couch, and he caught her by the wrist.

"Wait. Sit." Two commands.

Commands which she obeyed while he pulled her right beside him. She fought the urge to lean away. "What is it, darling?"

"I've come for a few reasons. First of all, I want to discuss our upcoming marriage."

She allowed her shoulders to relax. "What a relief that is."

Muffled voices and the occasional childish laugh came from the kitchen. "I'm not breaking our engagement, but it would be best, I believe, to postpone it. At least until you are stronger and your eyesight has returned, not to mention that you are in mourning. With the chaos surrounding the fires, this is no time to be holding a society event."

"I do believe that to be best. There hasn't been a moment to do any planning, and up to this point, I haven't been strong enough to travel to have my gown fitted."

"Of course. Once you are better, we can discuss setting a new date."

"Thank you. Though I'm eagerly anticipating becoming your wife, your reasoning makes sense. It's the best course of action at this point."

"Good. I'm glad you're agreeable. I was afraid of a storm of tears."

"Don't you know me better, Hollis? I'm not one easily given to such displays of emotion." No, instead she bottled up every tear, every scream, every wail, and held it in. That was how she had been from childhood, or so Mama had said.

"Then there is the matter of Angelina."

"Yes. Let me get her. You must be anxious to see her. Her arms, while they will always be scarred, have healed nicely. With long sleeves, no one will know the difference. Her nightmares, though, are another matter altogether."

"Nanny has left the position."

"What? Why?"

"Like all the survivors, she was traumatized by the fire and has gone to her sister in New York, believing the brisk salt air from the ocean will help."

"Of course. I can't blame her." And Mariah couldn't. Then again, the memories were forever etched into her brain, and they would remain with her until her dying day. Wherever she went in the world—whether to Peshtigo, New York, or China—they would travel with her.

"That leaves me with something of a dilemma. I have no one to care for Angelina. Father is keeping me on my toes with work, and even if that weren't the case, she needs a woman's touch."

Mariah ran her hand back and forth on the soft velvet of the settee. "You would like her to remain here?"

"For the time being. She could spend a happy holiday season with you, and perhaps after the New Year I will have secured a new nanny and she will be able to return home."

"Are you remaining here for Christmas?"

"I'm afraid not. As I said, Father is working me hard, and I'm needed in the city at the main offices."

"Oh." How could he not long to spend the happiest day of the year with his little girl? Was he truly not bothered by missing out on her opening gifts and exclaiming over the candles on the tree and the goose on the table?

"Is that too much for you? Without your vision, it will be a difficult task. With Mrs. Stuart's assistance, though, I feel you are quite capable."

She fiddled with a ribbon from her gown. Had he meant those last words as a solace or an insult? "I had thought we might spend the holidays together. I would very much like that."

"Unfortunately, darling, that is not meant to be. The fire has disrupted our lives and our plans. By next year, things should return to normal, but until then, we must learn to deal with our disappointments."

Oh, it wasn't that she was disappointed. How would she be able to get proof of his crimes when he wasn't even in town? How would she get him to slip up and tell her about his gambling debts when they wouldn't be together to converse? Still, she had to maintain the charade. "Of course. How selfish of me. We have a roof over our heads and clothes on our backs. That is much more than many do. We must all make sacrifices."

"Thank you." He placed another brief and very chaste kiss on her cheek, then the shifting of weight from the couch told her that he stood.

She also came to her feet. "Let me get Angelina to say hello to you. She's going to be so excited. Of course, you must stay to dinner."

"I'm afraid that I must be going. Please, leave Angelina be. It sounds like she is having fun, and I don't wish to disrupt that. Since I have a train to catch, I don't have much time, and it will only end with her in tears."

Mariah couldn't deny the swelling in her throat either. Not because Hollis was leaving her but because he was leaving his little girl without so much as giving her a hug. What kind of father was he? While it was true that the upper classes often left the raising of their children to nannies, did that mean they didn't love them?

"I did bring each of you a gift." He handed Mariah a velvet box. "Open it."

She swallowed hard to rid herself of the lump and did as he asked. She fingered a chain with what had to be a gemstone by the feel of it.

"It's an emerald. I love the way they bring out the color of your eyes. Do you wish me to put it on you?"

She shook her head. "Not right now. Thank you. I'm going to save it for special occasions."

"The other box is a locket for Angelina with my picture in it."

"She'll be so pleased to have a photograph of you to carry with her. That was very thoughtful." Mariah almost choked on her words. Angelina would have rather had her doll from home. Better yet, she would have loved to have her father spend time with her. "I will give her your love."

"Please, do that. And don't trouble yourself. I'll see myself to the door. Merry Christmas, Mariah. Thank you for caring for my daughter." A cold gust of wind blew through the parlor, and he was gone.

Less than a minute later, Angelina danced into the room, her shoes swishing on the floor as she skipped. "Miss Mariah, we made cookies for dessert. Miss Lydia says they're a special treat. I can't wait to have one."

Mariah stashed both jewelry boxes into the pockets in her skirt. "You will save me one, won't you?"

"Maybe." Angelina drew out the word then giggled. "Could I save one for Father too?"

"Why would you say that?"

"Because it's almost Christmas. He has to come for Christmas, doesn't he?"

Mariah sat on the sofa and held her hands out for Angelina, who came to her. "You know the fires here and in Chicago have made life hard for everyone. Your father is very busy with the railroad. There is more work than ever for him. I'm not sure if he will be here."

Angelina puffed out a breath. "But I want him to come. I miss him."

"I know you do." Mariah hugged her. "I'm sure he'll send some wonderful gifts for you."

"That's not the same."

"I understand. Do you remember what I said Christmas is all about?"

"About Jesus in the manger?"

"Yes. Remember that. There are many children in Peshtigo and Chicago who don't have fathers anymore. They will never see their papas again."

"Like you?"

Mariah swallowed away the threatening tears and nodded. "Yes, like me."

"I still want him to come."

"Maybe he will, sweetheart. Maybe he will."

<hr />

After Mariah broke the news to Angelina about Hollis not spending Christmas with her, the child was out of sorts for the rest of the day. She turned down the cookie Lydia offered her after dinner, and soon afterward, asked to go to bed.

What six-year-old wanted to go to sleep early?

One with a broken heart.

Lydia and John sat with Mariah and Jay in the parlor. Lydia embroidered while Mariah tried her hand at crocheting, a hobby she had enjoyed when she had her sight. She practiced the chain stitch until she had a long snake of yarn. What was it useful for? She ripped out the stitches and dropped the hook in her lap. "Hollis was here today."

"He what?" Lydia's voice rose. "When was this? I was home all day and didn't see him."

"When you and Angelina were making cookies."

"You should have invited him for dinner."

"I did. He said he had a train to catch and that he didn't want to see Angelina because she would end up crying when he had to leave in a few minutes."

"That's dastardly of him." Jay's words were tight, as if he spoke them through clenched teeth. He likely did.

"He's not coming back for Christmas. He asked me, with Lydia's help, to look after Angelina for the time being. Nanny quit." Mariah clutched the arms of the chair where she sat.

"If I could get my hands on him, I would—" God bless her brother-in-law.

"We have postponed the wedding until after I regain my sight." Hurt as she was about his attitude toward Angelina, she hadn't had time to examine that aspect of his visit.

Was he ashamed of her? Did he believe she couldn't be a good society wife if she couldn't see? Honestly, it would be difficult without her sight for her to arrange teas and balls and do everything expected as the wife of one of the wealthiest men in the Midwest.

Not to mention that she was in mourning, and in society, one didn't marry for a period of time after a loved one's death. Nothing like in a small lumber town where, often out of necessity, that wasn't the convention.

"Are you still considering marrying him?" Lydia's question cut Mariah to the heart.

She had to answer her sister with a modicum of honesty without giving the real reason for maintaining the relationship. "I don't know. This must all be because he is overwhelmed with the work he has to do following the fires. You can imagine the immense financial toll this has taken on his family as well. And we are in mourning, so it wouldn't be appropriate. All things considered, postponement was our only option. Once life settles down again, I will reevaluate."

"I hope you make a wise decision." Lydia was every bit the older sister with that statement. "John, Mariah, are you coming up? I'm afraid I'm rather exhausted after a long day in the kitchen."

"I believe I will turn in." Mariah set her yarn and hook in the basket at her feet.

As she made her way to the stairs, Jay tugged on her elbow. "You do know that Hollis isn't too busy with work to come for the holiday, don't you? I heard that he is planning a spectacular New Year's ball."

"A ball? Without me? While I'm in mourning?" What was Hollis up to?

Chapter Twenty-Four

MARINETTE, WISCONSIN
FRIDAY, DECEMBER 15, 1871

Lydia had taken Angelina to the store and perhaps—just perhaps—to play in the snow with some of the local children. The men were at work, leaving only Mariah at home. With a bit of a cold coming on, it was best she stay inside.

She sat in her rocking chair beside the window. In her mind's eye, the snow fell like feathers, drifting toward the ground, covering roads and gardens and houses alike. If she could see, she would have her paints out and would be commemorating this snowfall by impressing it on the canvas.

It was so clear in her mind's eye. Every detail was there in full color. Her fingers knew just how she would paint it.

Her fingers knew.

Though she couldn't see the paints and other supplies Jay had brought, she turned toward where Lydia had left them on the dresser. The last she had checked, they were still there.

When she got up and felt around this time, they hadn't been moved.

Her heart pounded against her chest, the sound echoing in her ears. Could she do it? Did she dare try? She touched a canvas, her fingertips registering the little bumps all over it. Between it and the next one, there was a small palette. She picked up a brush, its bristles soft, the wood handle smooth.

How would she get the colors correct though? No one was home to help her, and she wasn't going to tell anyone about this painting trial until after she made a go of it.

If she did.

She returned to her rocker and worked to put together a plan. If she started in the middle of the canvas and worked in quadrants, she wouldn't lose her place as easily.

She tapped the end of a paintbrush against her chin. One of Angelina's first attempts at painting, she had dabbed the paint with a heavy hand, leaving behind thick globs.

What if Mariah did the same? The globs could be snowdrifts and would further help guide her. She could feel them. Her fingers might get very messy, but she could always wash off the paint.

Yes, it was unconventional at best, but did she dare try? If she only showed the painting to Lydia to get her honest impression, then no one else need ever know. She could dispose of the disaster and be certain that she was done painting forever.

Which would break her heart as much as Angelina's broke when she learned Hollis wouldn't be spending Christmas with them.

But if it worked. . .

In all likelihood, it was a losing proposition. But how would she know if she didn't take a chance?

If she had been too afraid to pick up a brush the first time, when she was just a child, she would have never created all the works she had. This was no different.

She repeated this to herself as she set up the canvas and the brushes. Though she couldn't see out the window, that was where she, out of habit, placed her supplies. If the sun were out today, it would warm her face and hands.

The first problem arose. She had no easel. The windowsill might work. Then there was the ill-fitting petticoat she had gotten from the charity supplies soon after her release from the hospital. Ripped up, it could serve as a drop cloth and a towel.

Once she had that set up to her liking, she turned her attention to the next, even bigger obstacle. What colors were the paints?

She picked up a tube, a newer invention but one that made painting so much easier. She didn't have to mix pigment with oil to create the color. The problem was that each tube felt the same, the smooth metal of it cool. How could she tell which was which?

Then she ran across a metal tab at the bottom of one tube, and she traced the raised portions of it. She crinkled her forehead and concentrated. Was that an R? R-E-D. Red. Had someone put this on there just for her? She had never seen anything like it before on any of the tubes she had owned.

Jay. It had to be him. There was no other answer. She had gotten angry at him and told him to leave without giving him an opportunity to explain what he had done. He had been so thoughtful of her, and she had treated him terribly for it. When she saw him next, she owed him an apology. A huge one. If, that was, this painting turned out and she told anyone of its existence.

She pressed her hand to her stomach to still the fluttering there, took a deep breath, then squeezed out some of what she believed to be white paint onto the palette. She went by memory to figure how much she needed.

Once she had her colors lined up on the palette, memorizing where she placed each one, she dipped her brush into the white and dabbed a generous amount onto the canvas using the fingers of her left hand as a guide. Even though it wasn't necessary, she closed her eyes and painted a picture in her mind at the same time she painted it on the canvas.

She worked and worked, engrossed in the task in front of her, praying the scene she was creating matched the one in her brain.

"Mariah?" Lydia's soft voice in her ear startled her out of her picture world. "You're painting."

Mariah turned toward her sister. "I had this picture in my mind of the snow outside the window, and I had to put it on canvas. Is the door closed?"

"Yes. You didn't hear me knock, but I peeked in anyway, thinking you might be napping."

Mariah straightened her spine, ready to receive the blow. "Be honest with me in the way that only sisters can be honest with each other. What does it look like? Is it any good, any at all?"

"How did you do it?" Lydia was breathless.

"Will you answer my question first?"

"Oh, yes. I'm sorry. It's unbelievable."

Mariah sighed. "That isn't really an answer." Maybe she had to be more specific. "Can you tell what it is?"

"It's a beautiful snowscape. The tree branches are covered, some of them bending under the weight of the snow. Small white hills rise in the distance."

Mariah bit the inside of her cheek. "That's what I painted. But does it look like a two-year-old did it?"

"Not at all. It's not perfect. There are areas where some things are out of place. The proportions on the tree are pretty much what they should be, and this is good work. Not to mention that the thick paint is unique. I want to reach out and touch it."

Mariah could only manage to speak in a whisper. "It's not bad then?"

"It's better than not bad. It's amazing, especially since this is your first one after the fire. It is the first, isn't it?"

"Yes. I know I'll need practice, but I had to find out if it was good enough for me to take a try at it."

Lydia hugged Mariah's shoulders. "It is." She sniffled. Lydia always did cry at the drop of a hat. "I'm so proud of you. It must have been hard for you to pick up that brush and start, but you did it. You are the most amazing person I know. You have to show Jay."

"No." The word left Mariah's lips without thought. "I don't want him to see it yet, though I do owe him an apology." She explained how he put the tags on the paint tubes so she would know the colors. "Then I lined them up on my palette and started painting."

"Why wouldn't you want him to see it? He was right all along. You can create art, even without your sight. He knows your talent and believed in you when you didn't believe in yourself. Don't you think he deserves to be rewarded for his optimism?"

Lydia had a point. If not for Jay, she would be sitting in the rocking chair, crocheting one long chain of yarn and feeling sorry for herself. This had given her purpose again.

She was so light, she might float into the sky like a hot air balloon.

"Miss Mariah, you'll never guess what we did." Angelina burst into the room. "Oh, you made a painting of snow. It looks just like it does outside. Miss Lydia took me to the schoolyard to play with the other children, and we built a snowman. I like your picture, but it needs a snowman."

All the pent-up grief, anger, and loss evaporated, forgotten for a moment, and laughter exploded from Mariah's lips. Lydia joined in, and then Angelina. Oh, what a blessing laughter was. Far too much time had passed since her last good giggling fit.

"What's going on?" Jay's question brought their laughter to an end.

"No. I didn't want you to see it yet." Angelina must not have closed the door behind her.

"Is that. . . ? Did you. . . ? You did. It's incredible. Different from anything I've ever seen. We both know I'm not an art critic, but I love it. This is so very good."

"Angelina, let's see if I have that Christmas bow for your hair that I was talking about earlier. We'll be right down the hall." Discreet but proper. That was Lydia at all times.

Mariah stood, bumping against the chair, which Jay scraped back. "I'm sorry I got so cross with you the day you brought the supplies. It was a kind gesture on your part, and I didn't appreciate it the way I should have. When I decided to try to paint, I didn't know how I would figure out the colors. But it was you who made those tabs, wasn't it?"

"I thought they would help. I didn't know another way for you to distinguish them even though I smelled each color. For the record, orange doesn't smell like an orange."

"No, it doesn't." She couldn't stop the smile from breaking out on her face. "Thank you, my friend. This means the world. You have given my purpose back to me, and that is a gift beyond measure."

"You could also become a writer, you have such a way with words. All I wanted to do was to bring you a gift that would return the light to your eyes. I hated that you were so sad."

"It's difficult not to despair in times such as these."

"Yes, it is."

"I miss Mama, Papa, and Lucy more than I can put into words. And learning to navigate this dark world has been terrifying. Why would God allow such misery to befall us all? Where was He on that terrible night? What did we do to deserve His judgment?"

Jay clicked his tongue. "All of us are left with the same questions, ones for which I don't have the answers."

"I wish I knew. I wish I could talk to God and ask Him. You're right, I've been giving in to despair over the entire situation. When I picked up my paintbrush, though, and touched those bristles to the canvas, for a moment, I was caught up in a snow scene. I saw it in front of me, as if I was looking out the window. Goodness, I even shivered from the cold as I worked."

"That might be because you are next to the window and darkness is coming."

"Has the snow stopped?"

"Almost. I can't tell which is more beautiful—God's creation or yours."

"His is always infinitely better than mine, than any artist's. We only form dim representations of His perfect work."

"I see what you're saying, but He has also given you a great talent."

"Thank you again. I can't say it enough."

"While you were busy here, I was at work, having a difficult time concentrating on the job in front of me. You're upset that Hollis isn't coming for Christmas and that he didn't invite you to the ball."

"Yes. He hurt both me and his daughter."

"As I tried to make sense of the numbers on the page today—"

"A creative talent in its own right."

"—I came up with a plan, a way to force Hollis' hand. Are you interested?"

She wiped a brush with the old petticoat. "Yes. Yes, I am."

Chapter Twenty-Five

My friend. That was how Mariah had referred to Jay. After all this time, after all they had survived together, he was nothing more than her friend. And it may never change.

She had said she was keeping her betrothal to Hollis because of Angelina, because she didn't want the little girl to be without a mother. How wonderful of her to be so generous and gracious to a child who, in the eyes of the world, had so much but, in reality, possessed so little.

The longer she remained a part of Angelina's life, though, the harder it would be for her to walk out of it. Every scenario he played in his head ended up with Mariah marrying Hollis for Angelina's sake.

She was the type of person who would sacrifice her own happiness for the happiness of others. Even for him, after he asked her not to break her engagement.

At least he had been able to bring a bit of joy to her life. His fumbling attempts at a gift had turned out to be good after all. She had talent. Quite a bit of it.

If only she didn't need Hollis to secure an exhibition in a Chicago gallery. What a sensation she would be when the world discovered that the paintings were created by a blind artist. A female one at that.

Word about her would spread to New York and then to London and Paris. He would be nothing but a distant memory, slaving over ledgers in a burned-out town no one cared about.

Oh, if his mother were here and could read his thoughts, she would scold him for such melancholy. She would sit him down at the tiny kitchen table with the uneven legs and make him count his blessings.

It was the only way they had survived the crushing poverty that plagued them from his birth until Mr. Stanford recognized his gift with numbers. That was how both he and Ma referred to it.

It hadn't prevented her premature death, though, from consumption. No amount of money could overcome the poor living conditions she had endured for more than thirty years.

So he drew a sheet of paper from his desk drawer and dipped his pen into the inkwell then listed all the blessings he could. Food, clothing, shelter, friendship, employment, salvation. Many more.

"Are you busy, Jay?" Shawn stood in the doorway, hands tucked in his pants pockets.

"Is it lunchtime already?"

"It is. You've been rather engrossed in your work."

Jay raised and lowered his eyebrows. "Not work, necessarily. Just picking myself up out of the doldrums." He set the paper to the side and stood. "I'm ready to go."

"Remind me why you want me to accompany you to the tailor?"

"Because I have to reach into my small amount of savings and purchase myself some evening clothes. Well, first I have to see if I can afford them. Otherwise, I may need to beg some from Mr. Stanford, though he is more rotund than I am."

"And this is because you're going to attend a ball you haven't been invited to?"

"Yes, that's correct." He and Mariah would be attending. She would be the beautiful distraction that would allow him to slip away and see if he could finally discover the evidence he needed to tie Hollis to the missing money.

"I thought we were beyond feeling the fire's effects, but perhaps I was wrong. The smoke and flames have addled your brain."

"No, my brain was already like that."

Shawn slapped him on the back as they left the office. "You can be funny if you have a mind to."

He was serious, but he let the comment go. "Mr. Stanford the younger has been avoiding both his daughter and his fiancée."

"And you aim to correct that."

"Yes. I feel that he is doing so because of Miss Randolph's blindness and because of his daughter's scarring. He needs to see that he's a very blessed man and that they need him."

"What about your attraction to Miss Randolph?"

"It's of no consequence. I'm her friend and nothing more." There was no need for him to sink to the depths of despair once again. "Now, I need your assistance with this. I have no idea what I'm doing."

"You picked the wrong person to bring with you. You should have selected Miss Randolph. She would have been able to advise you better."

"If I can't afford what I fear this is going to cost, I don't want her to know, and I certainly don't want her to feel sorry for me and offer to pay for my clothes."

"She has that much money?"

"I don't know. Her father must have left her some kind of living, and I believe her brother-in-law has a secure income."

"Once she marries Mr. Stanford, she will have plenty of cash."

Perhaps bringing Shawn on this errand had been a mistake, but one too late to correct now as they arrived at the shop. The window offered a view of the tailor pinning a man's pants. Shawn led the way inside, where a jingling bell announced their arrival.

The tailor nodded at them and spoke around the pins in his mouth. "Good afternoon, gentlemen. Please, make yourselves comfortable. I will be with you as soon as I finish with Mr. Rhodes."

The young, wiry man went about his business, and Shawn and Jay settled into the two chairs in the far corner. In no time, the pants were pinned, and Mr. Rhodes left to change into his everyday clothes. The tailor smoothed his mustache and smiled at Shawn and Jay. "How may I help you?"

Jay dipped his head. "I have an event on New Year's Eve that I require a set of evening clothes for. Something befitting Chicago society. I was wondering how much the cost would be."

The tailor sized up Jay then clucked his tongue before quoting him a price.

Jay's mouth fell open, and he stammered more than usual until he managed to form the words. "That much? Why, that's a week's salary for me. I'm sorry to have wasted your time."

Face burning, Jay hurried out of the establishment, ready to rip the bell from the door on his way out.

"Wait for me." Shawn slid on the ice as he hurried to catch Jay.

"My apologies. I have never been so embarrassed in my life. I had no idea clothing could require such a hefty sum."

"That was more than I was expecting too. Guess we'll never be society gentlemen, will we? That amount could feed my family for several days."

"Ma and I could have eaten well for a month on that. And to think that Mr. Stanford bought me some when he was training me."

Shawn halted. "What do you mean? This isn't going to be your first ball?"

"My second. The first one I spent standing against the wall at the edge of the action vowing I would never attend one again. Not that I thought I ever would have the chance."

"Look at you now though. The chance has presented itself. Wire him and ask if you can borrow his evening clothes. Let him know your plans."

"The trouble with that is I don't want Hollis to find out we're coming. He would do everything in his power to discourage Mariah from attending." Without Mariah, his plan wouldn't work. Or wouldn't work as smoothly. No, he needed her to be there, the stunning diversion, so that he could expose Hollis once and for all.

"Tell him that too. Let him know that Miss Randolph wants to surprise his son."

"Some surprise it's going to be."

Marinette, Wisconsin
Saturday, December 30, 1871

Mariah stood in front of Lydia and allowed her to adjust the hat on her head, part of her maroon traveling ensemble. Thankfully Hollis had left a stipend as a Christmas gift for her to purchase anything either she or

Angelina required, so they had all the clothing they needed and then some. The pale blue evening gown, ordered at the last minute, was packed in the trunk that Jay would soon load onto the sled he hired from the livery.

Lydia stopped fiddling. "Perfect. You are beautiful."

"I won't look like this when I step off the train in Chicago."

"No matter. You'll start off smart at least. And how kind of Mr. Stanford to send his private railcar here for you. I can't believe they managed to fix the part of the line that had burned and bring it here in such a short amount of time."

"It does make the prospect of traveling a little less daunting, that is for sure."

Lydia took her by the hands. "Your palms are sweating."

"I'm frightened. What if Jay and I get separated? What happens if I lose Angelina in the crowd? How will I ever manage this?"

"You painted a beautiful picture from your memory. You were resourceful and got it done. I have no doubt that you will be the toast of Chicago and the talk of the town by the time this old year ends."

"I do hope you're right."

"I'll be praying for you, my dear sister. Mama would have been proud of you." Lydia kissed her cheek.

Mariah's throat burned, but the jangling of harnesses announced John's arrival with the wagon. In a short time he had loaded her trunk, which also contained some of Angelina's belongings, while Jay helped Mariah and Angelina into the wagon and covered them with thick furs. Thank goodness they didn't have far to travel. They were headed out on the first train to leave Marinette.

The girl bounced on the seat. "We're going to Chicago to surprise Father. I can't wait."

She jostled so much, Mariah clung to her arm to keep her from falling out of the wagon. "Be careful. We can't lose you. When we get to the train, be sure to stay right with me and Mr. Franklin. You need to get safely to your house, otherwise you won't see your father."

Angelina calmed, though not completely. As they wound their way through town, she squirmed beside Mariah.

It wasn't long before John pulled the team to a halt, and he retrieved their trunk while Jay assisted Mariah and Angelina down and led them to the station. "Wait here with Miss Mariah while I see to boarding the train, and I'll be back soon," he said to the excited little girl.

Angelina clung to Mariah's hand as they stood in the midst of the crowd. Or as much of a crowd as there would be at a small town at the end of the line. Then she tugged on Mariah's arm. "Look. It's Johnson." She raised her voice. "Johnson! Johnson!"

"Ah, Miss Stanford, Miss Randolph, how good to see you." Al Johnson was the man who saw to the Stanfords' needs in their private cars. "Shall I escort you on board?"

"We have to wait for Mr. Franklin." Angelina used her best grown-up voice, and Mariah had to stifle a laugh behind her gloved hand.

"Then I will wait with you and make sure you all get to the car together. How excited you must be to see your father."

Angelina and Johnson chatted away while Mariah's shoes pinched her feet. This was, by far, the longest she had been away from a familiar location since her release from the hospital, and fatigue pulled at her shoulders. Finally, Jay arrived, and Johnson led them to the train.

She sank into the plush seat, the red of it seared into her memory. The journey hadn't even started, and she was ready for it to be over.

Johnson cleared his throat. "Excuse me, miss. Would you care for a cup of tea?"

"Thank you. A cup of tea would be wonderful."

By the time she and Jay returned to Marinette, Hollis' deeds would have been exposed. No matter what it took.

Chapter Twenty-Six

CHICAGO, ILLINOIS

By the time Mariah, Angelina, and Jay arrived at the Stanford home, it was late. Jay carried Angelina from the waiting carriage to the house. Despite her excitement earlier in the day, she had fallen asleep somewhere between Racine and Kenosha and didn't even stir when they arrived in Chicago.

Hollis was out for the evening, the driver had informed them, which was just as well with Jay. It would be enough when they saw him tomorrow. Strange how he was safer in the Stanford home, right under Hollis' nose, than he was on the streets of Marinette.

Mariah and Angelina went straight upstairs and to bed, but Mr. Stanford invited Jay to join him in his office, which he did. Mr. Stanford poured himself a glass of whiskey. "You still don't drink?"

"No, sir, I don't." It was the drink that had ripped his family apart and killed his father. Even though he was a small child when Pa died, he vowed he would never touch the stuff.

"How about a cigar?"

"I will smoke one."

"Very good. These are the best. From Havana." Mr. Stanford

prepared the cigar and handed it to Jay, who lit it and sat back in his leather armchair.

He took several puffs. "Thank you for sending your car to bring us here. Miss Randolph was much more comfortable than she would have been in the coach. The trip was frightening enough for her."

"I'm sure it was, so it's a good thing she knows her way around this house. The most important rooms anyway. How is she doing?"

"She has her good days and bad days, like all we survivors do. Life is scary for her in general, but she has started painting again. You should see the snowscape she created the other day. Not perfect, but far better than most artists I've seen. Beautiful and very different."

"That's good to hear. It's so kind of her to keep Angelina, though I would prefer my grandchild to be here with her father and me. I suppose it's best that she have a female influence in her life."

"Mariah has enjoyed having her. She's a light and keeps everyone smiling. The fire affected her too, as you can imagine. Many nights, she has terrible dreams. Traveling near Peshtigo on the train was hard for her."

"I'm sure." Mr. Stanford nodded, musing. "I'm sure. What I saw here in Chicago was enough for me. I can't imagine how much more terrifying it must have been in Peshtigo for a six-year-old. How about you?"

"Nothing in the past three months has been easy, but we have it so much better than most people. Many are still in tents, cooking what little food they have over open fires. They're cold and hungry."

"Such a shame. Between this trip and the last, you saw some of the devastation here, didn't you?"

"As I said the first time I came after the fire, it doesn't compare to Peshtigo. Not to minimize what Chicago has suffered, but everything in Peshtigo is gone. Everything. As far as you can see, there is nothing. The river is the only landmark remaining."

"Heartbreaking." Mr. Stanford took a gulp of whiskey. "Now tell me why you came with Miss Randolph and Angelina."

"With Miss Randolph's lack of vision, it would have been impossible for her to travel alone. Not to mention the impropriety of it all. They needed an escort."

"And you were happy to oblige."

Did he think Jay was interested in Mariah? Was he that transparent?

"There are business matters I need to see to while I'm here, so it worked out that I was able to accompany them."

"Is that the full truth?"

No, but Jay wasn't ready to divulge the information he had on Hollis. Not yet. The timing had to be perfect. And the business he was seeing to did involve Hollis.

"My son told me he didn't invite Miss Randolph to the ball tomorrow night because he was afraid the travel would be too much for her, and he mentioned that he wasn't ready for Angelina to be home as he hasn't yet secured a nanny."

"The girl misses her father, as you can imagine." Jay uncrossed his legs and leaned forward. "All she wanted for Christmas was to see him. The necklace he gave her was far less valuable than a visit. In addition, he has hardly seen Miss Randolph since the fire, and they were to be married soon. Is he ashamed of them?"

Mr. Stanford set his glass on the mahogany desk, the cigar glowing in his other hand. A curl of smoke rose to the high ceiling. He inhaled. "I can't explain my son's behavior, nor can I condone it.

"When he said Miss Randolph wasn't invited to the ball, I was astounded." He fiddled with a pen, turning it round and round. "Your question is good. One I have wrestled with these past months. I love my son, but I question some of his actions. Many of them. He isn't too busy with work to go out most evenings."

Jay nodded. "Miss Randolph was heartbroken when I told her of the festivities, so yes, I suggested that we travel here."

"You're forcing Hollis' hand."

Jay laid his cigar on the edge of the glass ashtray. "I question his love for Mariah and his desire to marry her. As for Angelina, I suppose I am forcing his hand and testing his dedication to the daughter he claims to be devoted to. If that were the case, then where was he when she was in the hospital? She needs him. Not a new nanny, but him."

"I agree with you, but to confront him with his fiancée and his daughter? I can't guarantee what his reaction will be."

"That is why I question his love for them. If it was genuine, then we would both be certain that it would be enthusiastic. Instead, we are left to wonder what is to come."

Lines formed in Mr. Stanford's brow. "I fear I've spoiled him far too much and was too lenient with him when his mother died. Who knows what kind of trouble he gets into when he goes out each evening. I'm worried."

Jay had no words of comfort. Mr. Stanford should be worried about his son because he was in far worse trouble than he realized.

◆ ● ●

Chicago, Illinois
Sunday, December 31, 1871

Beside Mariah in the big bed, Angelina stirred. Mariah tucked the covers under the girl's chin, and she settled down. The fires hadn't yet been lit, so it was too early to rise.

Now that she was here, in this big house with rooms that echoed, her stomach flip-flopped. Even Angelina wasn't at ease, not wanting to sleep in her own bedroom last night.

What would Hollis' reaction be when he discovered they had come? Since he had been out last night, he likely would be sleeping late and wouldn't be at breakfast, and with such a big house, he may not see her until the evening.

Had it been a good idea to come? Mr. Stanford must have thought so, because he sent his private railcar for them. He welcomed them with open arms and hugged his granddaughter when they walked through the door.

She turned over on the soft mattress, searching for a comfortable position. For all she knew, it could be the middle of the night. Going back to sleep was a struggle she soon abandoned.

A soft knock at the door was followed by quiet footsteps across the room and rummaging near the fireplace. The maid had come to start the fire to warm the room, so it was morning. Early morning, but morning at least.

Once the maid had finished her duties and left, Mariah slipped from the bed to await another maid to help her dress. While she sat in the armchair beside the crackling fire, she turned her doubts over and over in her mind.

The only conclusion she reached was that they were here now, so there was no turning back. She had to see her plan through. Her part was easy. It was Jay who could be caught, and then. . . Hollis might be furious with her, but if she could put off seeing him until they met in a ballroom filled with people, he would have to hold in his anger and act in a civil manner toward her.

She prayed he wouldn't reject Angelina when he saw her. She would keep the girl in the nursery today and wait to tell him of her arrival until the ball. Again, having an audience when she divulged the news would be best.

Just the idea of him close to her sent chills up and down her arms, her hair prickling. This was for Jay. It was also for Angelina, though if Jay managed to find what he was searching for, if he got the proof he needed, then the child would lose her father in addition to her mother.

After both she and Angelina were dressed, they made their way to the dining room, Angelina taking Mariah by the hand. The aroma of bitter coffee mellowed with cream woke her senses, and that, combined with the fragrance of bacon, stirred her hunger.

"Ah, good morning." Mr. Stanford came and greeted Mariah with a kiss on both cheeks.

"Grandfather, how about me?"

"Yes." He must have lifted his growing granddaughter in his arms. "It is always good to see you, pumpkin." He gave her a loud kiss and then her shoes hit the floor again. "What will it be for breakfast for two of the loveliest ladies I know?"

They put in their orders, and the maid served them. After Mariah said a silent grace over the food and before she took her first bite of eggs, Mr. Stanford dove in with the questions. "So, you are here to surprise my son?"

"Yes. I've been told you knew I wasn't invited?"

"I urged him to include you, but he doesn't listen to me. He hasn't for years. Only when I threaten to cut him out of the inheritance."

Interesting. Even Hollis' father acknowledged his son's greed and lack of ambition, but he did nothing about it. Mr. Stanford was a good man but had a blind spot when it came to Hollis. "I hope that my coming will be a good surprise for him. If nothing else, I'm sure he will be happy to see Angelina."

"When can I see Father?" Angelina spoke around the biscuit in her mouth.

Mr. Stanford's cup clinked against the saucer. "Children are to be seen and not heard."

"Sorry," Angelina mumbled.

Mariah wiped her hands on the linen napkin in her lap. "I think it would be so much fun to surprise him at the ball. You may come as my guest, Angelina, at least for a few moments. Then it's off to bed with you. Perhaps Gloria will help us pick out a suitable frock."

"You may speak." Mr. Stanford chuckled.

"I can go to the ball? Really? And surprise Father? This is going to be the best day ever. I mean ever and ever, since I've been alive."

"Then we have much to do today. Perhaps we should follow your grandfather's rules and finish our breakfasts. I daresay it will take us all day to prepare everything and finish our toilettes."

Angelina's fork scraped against her plate in a rapid rhythm.

"Don't forget to chew." Mariah sipped her coffee, her stomach one big knot that refused to allow her to eat, no matter how tempting the aromas.

After another cup of coffee and a few sips of fresh orange juice, Mariah took Angelina and returned to their rooms. The rest of the day passed in a blur as Angelina tried on dress after dress. Mariah was able to attest to the fit of each one but had no way of knowing if the colors suited Angelina or not.

Once they decided on an ensemble, Gloria got busy helping Mariah into her gown and worked on braiding, curling, and doing up her hair. She topped off everything with sapphire jewelry Mr. Stanford loaned her that Gloria proclaimed brought out the blue in the gown.

Part of her was uncomfortable being out in society during her official period of mourning. At home, she hadn't worn black except for church services. She did keep her colors subdued, but imagining the light color of this gown set her to squirming, even though part of the plan was for her to make a grand entrance and draw everyone's attention so that Jay had time to search for what he needed.

Angelina came to her and grabbed her by the hand. "Aren't you ready to go yet? It takes grown-up ladies a long time to get ready for a ball."

"Everything good is worth waiting for." Mariah smiled even though Gloria tugged on her hair. A few minutes later, the maid declared she was finished.

"You look beautiful, Miss Mariah. Can we go now?"

"Yes, we can." She took Angelina by the hand and allowed her to lead the way to the ballroom.

Once they arrived, the footman at the door announced them by name, and the room fell silent.

Chapter Twenty-Seven

Jay stood in the far corner of the ballroom, half hiding behind a potted palm, a cut-crystal glass of sweet ruby-red punch in his hand. When the footman announced the arrival of Miss Mariah Randolph and her companion, Miss Angelina Stanford, he covered his mouth to stifle the chuckle.

Leave it to Angelina to talk her way into being allowed to come to the ball. Perhaps her presence made the entrance easier for Mariah.

When his sight snagged on Mariah, however, his breath caught in his throat. The pale blue gown, the color of the sky on a perfect winter's day, hugged her curves before it flared into a full skirt. Diamonds and sapphires twinkled in the jewelry around her neck. Though she couldn't see the guests milling in the room or the couples dancing across the parquet floor, her presence commanded attention.

Attention from one man in particular. As Hollis stepped toward Mariah, the music halted and the crowd parted.

Jay held his breath.

"Father, Father." Angelina broke from Mariah's grasp and rushed toward Hollis.

He watched her come, his mouth open in a wide *O*. She hugged his leg, and he patted her head. Not quite the reaction of a father who had been parted from his injured daughter for far too long.

Mariah was left standing at the top of the wide marble steps that led into the ballroom, but before Jay could make his way to her, the elder Mr. Stanford came to her rescue and offered his arm. She smiled at him and allowed him to lead her into the festivities.

The music resumed, and the couples returned to their refined waltzes and quiet conversations.

"She made quite the entrance, didn't she?" an older woman, feathers standing up straight in her hair said to another matron beside her as they moved in front of Jay.

"Rather. Such a shame about what happened to her. Lost everything, poor soul, including her sight."

"Truly? I hadn't heard that." The other woman, who clutched a glass of bubbling champagne in her gloved hand, shook her head. "That is a shame. All in all, though, she is beautiful and rather elegant. I couldn't believe it when I heard the announcement of Mr. Stanford's engagement to a provincial woman from Wisconsin, of all places, but now I understand."

"Amazing, isn't it, how the backwoods could produce such a refined beauty."

They moved away, and the dance ended, the couples clapping before the orchestra struck up another tune. Mr. Stanford left Mariah in the company of a group of other young women and headed toward the refreshment table. Jay took the opportunity to thread his way through the crowd toward her.

Hollis, however, beat him there. He offered Mariah his arm, and he led her toward the doors leading to the balcony.

Jay followed. He was not about to allow Mariah to be alone with Hollis for one moment. Not a single one. Not after what Hollis had done to him.

He trailed them through the door left slightly ajar to bring fresh air into the room full of dancers, but he remained hidden in the shadows. They proceeded toward the railing.

Hollis spun to face Mariah. "What on earth are you doing here?"

"Imagine my surprise when I learned that you were holding a ball and I wasn't on the guest list. I am to be your wife, and it's only right I should attend as the hostess."

"We aren't married yet, and you are in mourning. What a scandal you are sure to cause when word gets around."

"Still, we don't want tongues to be wagging all over the city by my conspicuous absence either, do we?" She tipped her head and stared at Hollis.

Even under her unseeing gaze, he squirmed. Ah, she may not perceive him with her eyes, but she certainly did with her soul. "You brought Angelina with you?"

"I couldn't very well come without her, could I? She would have been heartbroken if I had left her in Marinette with my sister, a virtual stranger to her."

"They were getting on well enough when I visited."

"Yes, when you stopped by without so much as saying hello to her. She misses you, Hollis. When will you realize how she longs for a close relationship with you?"

"You don't understand. It is not the way of upper-class fathers to play with their children. That is the job of nannies. I have indulged her more than I should have as it is."

"My father and I shared so many thoughts. I learned a great deal from him." Her voice caught on the last word, and it was all Jay could do to stop himself from rushing forward to offer her a handkerchief.

Hollis did no such thing. Instead, he scoffed. "You don't understand, but you will come to learn in time. Let's go. It's cold out here, and I would rather be inside. I'll leave you with the matrons, and you can depart on tomorrow's train."

"With you leading, I'm more than capable of dancing."

"Don't be ridiculous." Hollis gave her a rather rough tug and pulled her inside then hustled her to the nearest chair before rushing out of the ballroom.

Mariah sat there, her back as straight as Queen Victoria's, her hands clasped in her lap. How her heart must be breaking at Hollis' treatment. Jay went to her and tapped her on the shoulder. "Mariah?"

She clutched the strand of diamonds and sapphires at her throat. "Oh, Jay, you gave me quite a fright."

"I'm sorry. I wasn't trying to sneak up on you." He did that all too often. "I was on the balcony and heard what Hollis said."

"I shouldn't allow it to bother me as much as it does, but it hurts, and I can't help it." Even throughout her speech, she kept a smile on her face.

The orchestra played a new tune. "Would you care to dance? Let's show Hollis that you deserve to be here and deserve to be treated with honor and respect."

She blinked a few times then nodded. "Yes. That would be lovely."

He helped her to her feet and led her to the center of the ballroom. Though Mr. Stanford had included dancing as part of Jay's education, it had been many years since he had waltzed with a young lady. He held her by the waist, and they moved together to the rhythm of the music. At first, he counted the timing and watched each step, but Mariah was an accomplished dancer, and he relaxed, only stepping on her toes a handful of times.

He squeezed her hand. "I don't want to make you self-conscious, but everyone is staring at you." It was true. He caught many not-so-subtle glances in their direction from other young people as well as the older men and women.

"Oh. I didn't mean to put you in the spotlight."

"For once I don't mind, because they aren't paying a bit of attention to me. All eyes are on the beautiful woman who has allowed me to have this dance."

"Excuse me."

Hollis. The one and only person who could ruin the moment just did so. "I would like the pleasure of dancing with my fiancée."

Jay released her and stepped away. What else could he do? He wasn't about to make a scene in the middle of the ball.

Hollis' timing was suspect though. A few minutes earlier, he was angry with Mariah for showing up and left her on a chair without a partner. The moment the ballroom fixed its attention on her, he came to claim the dance.

Curious.

Very curious.

Jay kept an eye on the couple as Hollis partnered the next three dances with Mariah. Angelina must have been whisked off to bed as soon as possible, because she was nowhere in sight, so Jay sipped his punch as Mariah chatted and laughed with Hollis.

Had she fallen for his charms again? Forgotten about the kind of man he was?

No. He shook his head as if that would banish such thoughts. She had a good, forgiving heart, but she wouldn't forget what Hollis had done. Was doing. Instead, she was playing her part in their scheme to perfection.

When the next song began, Mariah waved Hollis off, and he brought her to a seat, this time in the midst of the young ladies. Jay inched closer to where they were gathered.

Before long, Mariah had a glass of punch and a plate of tiny sandwiches without crusts and miniature cakes in her hands. The women her age surrounded her, inquiring about the fire and her eyesight and her painting. She answered each question with grace and a smile.

"Aren't you the dashing young man who first danced with Miss Randolph?"

He turned to find a dark-haired, fair-skinned young woman batting her eyelashes at him. "I am."

"I couldn't help but notice. You are a very good dancer."

"Thank you." Was she fishing for a dance? He would never get the words past his lips without making a mess of it. Besides, he was here to keep an eye on Mariah.

"Any young lady would be flattered to have a dance with you."

Ah, so she was hinting at what he had suspected. He glanced at Mariah, still surrounded by young ladies, and now with a line of men likely waiting to partner with her, so he returned his attention to the woman beside him. "Would you care to dance?"

"Thank you. That would be wonderful."

Miss Waldon, as Jay soon discovered was the young lady's name, kept up the conversation, though he didn't relax with her the way he had with Mariah. The orchestra must have played the longest waltz in the history of waltzes, but it came to an end at last.

They clapped with the rest of the crowd, then Miss Waldon turned to him. "It is warm in here, and I am so very thirsty."

"Would you care for some punch?"

"Oh, how thoughtful of you. I will meet you over there." She nodded in Mariah's direction.

"Very well." He left her and, after a short wait, secured two glasses of punch. Before he made it back to the ladies, however, Hollis stepped in front of him and stopped his progress.

"Well, well. If it isn't Mr. Bookkeeper," Hollis sneered. "I don't recall you being on the guest list."

"I'm here at the invitation of your father."

"Strange, since this party was to be for me. I have half a mind to have one of the footmen escort you from the premises."

"Is there a reason you initially avoided both Miss Randolph and your daughter?"

"Awfully bold of you to ask such a question. I should have kicked you twice."

"You have yet to answer my question. Are you ashamed of them?"

"Ha." There was no mirth behind Hollis' single-syllable laugh. "If you haven't noticed, my fiancée is the talk of this evening's festivities. I've danced with her, and we've had a pleasant chat."

"Yet you didn't invite her to attend this evening's festivities. Again, I have to wonder why."

"That, Mr. Ink-Stained Hands, is none of your business."

Jay tamped down any offense over Hollis' name calling. If Hollis got under his skin, he would win this little game. Jay was not about to allow that to happen. "I'm the one who answers Angelina when she asks me every day when you're coming for her. Miss Randolph is the one who comforts her when she has a nightmare."

"I'm a busy man with many important matters to tend to."

"Is that so?"

"You would dare question me? Without my father's generosity, you would be living in Chicago's gutters. If you had managed to survive the fire, that is."

"I did survive Peshtigo's, no thanks to you."

"If I were you, I would watch my step. Accidents have this funny way of happening when you least expect them."

"You don't deserve a wonderful woman like Mariah." The stares of several people bored into Jay's back.

"Lower your voice, man."

He did but only because he wasn't ready to play his hand yet. "You have been blessed to have a beautiful woman in your life and a bright little girl. My advice would be to treat them right."

Hollis leaned in and whispered in Jay's ear. "My advice to you would be to stay away from both Miss Randolph and my daughter. You are acquainted with what the consequences will be if you don't."

Chapter Twenty-Eight

"It is awfully brave of you to travel all this way to be here tonight. I'm sure Mr. Stanford is pleased to have you by his side." The woman with a high-pitched voice wore far too much floral perfume. It was enough to make Mariah's eyes water.

"I brought Angelina to visit her father."

"Oh, yes. I heard the poor tyke survived that awful fire." The woman must have stepped closer, because the scent of the perfume wafted ever stronger. "Of course, we had such a terrible time of it here too. Father and I watched it from an upstairs window. The flames shot into the air. We were afraid we might have to leave the house."

Mariah wouldn't turn this into a competition about who had it worse that horrific night. "That must have been so frightening."

"Oh, it was. I didn't know if I would live or die. It is such a shame about those who perished. Mother and I went through all our old gowns and donated several of them to the relief effort. It was the least we could do."

The other women murmured in ascent.

"What is it like to be blind?" The woman punctuated her words with a giggle, as if all the world was a joke.

"I am slowly getting used to it, though I pray I will be able to see again one day."

"I can't imagine." More giggling. "Life must be awfully dull for you if you can't see. Then again, what is there to do in such a backwater town?"

"I have been caring for Angelina."

"Oh." The giggler didn't laugh at this. "I had the impression you were betrothed to Mr. Stanford."

"I am. While he has been busy here, Angelina has been staying with me at my sister's residence, healing from her own injuries."

"Oh, what a kind soul you are." A rustle of the woman's skirts brought another waft of perfume. It was enough to churn Mariah's stomach.

"Angelina is sweet, and it is my pleasure."

"You will hire a nanny once you and Mr. Stanford marry, won't you?"

"I suppose we will have need of one for when we are otherwise engaged, but I don't see a great need to hire someone to care for her. I enjoy spending time in her company."

"Who is that Hollis is speaking with? I don't remember seeing him before." Several giggles followed this question.

"Does he have curly, sand-colored hair?"

"He does, and he is quite a bit taller than Mr. Stanford. He is rather handsome."

There was no doubt they had spotted Jay. And yes, he was handsome. How wonderful it would be to see his face again. Perhaps the Lord would grant her request and restore her eyesight. "That must be Mr. Jay Franklin. He is employed by the railroad and is a good friend of my family. He accompanied us here from Peshtigo."

"Goodness." The perfume wafted ever stronger as the woman fanned herself. "Do leave a few of the men for us."

Mariah waved her hand, more in an effort to dissipate the scent than to dismiss the woman's comment. "Keep in mind that I'm engaged to Mr. Stanford." A pain stabbed her heart at the thought of anyone else claiming Jay's affections, because in truth, she was beginning to think of him as more than a friend.

But did he see it that way?

She held back a sigh.

A peal of laughter rang out. "Oh, Mr. Stanford is headed this way. I do believe he is going to ask you to dance."

"I certainly hope he will. I have sat out too many numbers already." Other than the three dances they shared and the rather pointed conversation, short as it was, he hadn't paid her one bit of attention all evening, which was fine by her but sure to send many tongues to wagging. And she needed to keep the attention on the two of them. Apparently, Jay hadn't left the ballroom yet.

"Miss Randolph." Hollis picked up her hand and kissed it. "May I have the pleasure of this dance?"

"Of course. Thank you for asking." She rose and allowed him to lead her to the ballroom floor.

They moved together in harmony, but he didn't speak to her. After a few minutes, she dared to break the silence. "Is something troubling you?"

"No. Why would you ask?"

"You are distant, and we have only shared a few dances all evening."

"You were more than happy to pair with Mr. Franklin."

"Who else was to partner me?"

"Let's not ruin this evening by talking."

"Don't you want me here?"

They made several turns, just the right amount of distance between them. "You surprised me, nothing more. I didn't know how you would be received by society, and so I meant to spare you any unkindness by others."

"What unkindness? They have been very solicitous of me and have treated me well."

"Yes, I see that."

"What did you have to say to Mr. Franklin?"

"Nothing. I'm surprised you came from Peshtigo with him with no other chaperone. Some may view that as very inappropriate."

"We had Johnson taking care of us the entire way, and Angelina was along as well."

"She is nothing more than a child and doesn't understand enough to be considered a chaperone."

"Get to know your daughter, Hollis. She is a bright and lively girl who loves you deeply. When you deny her your attention, you are missing out on the greatest blessing in your life."

"I would thank you to not lecture me on how to raise my child. I'm quite capable on my own."

"As you wish."

The dance concluded, and Hollis led her back to the spot where he had found her. Always the gentleman, he kissed her hand before he walked away.

"Oh, what I wouldn't give for Mr. Stanford to dance with me. He is divine, and you are one very fortunate woman. Many hearts in Chicago broke when he announced his engagement to you."

The gale of giggles scraped on Mariah's nerves. She clasped her hands in her lap and nodded. "I am indeed blessed."

"Isn't the wedding to be soon?" The young woman who spoke this time had a sweet, timid voice.

"It was, but we have postponed it. My health hasn't allowed me to do much planning, and Mr. Stanford has been occupied with railroad business." She left out any mention of her being in mourning. That news would cause a scandal because she was wearing light blue and dancing after less than three months. "As soon as life returns to normal, we will choose another date."

She spoke the words, though she had no intention of ever marrying Mr. Hollis Stanford.

———— • • ————

Jay strolled the perimeter of the room, the cups of punch still in his hands. The woman he had gotten the drink for was now dancing with another man. When a waiter passed him, he placed both glasses on the silver tray.

He wiped his sweaty palms on the pants Mr. Stanford had been kind enough to lend him. He had bluffed his way through the discussion with Hollis, but it left his stomach bouncing around in his midsection.

Hollis was capable of doing away with him, given the opportunity. He had proven that once already. There was nothing stopping him from finishing the deed himself or hiring someone so he could keep his hands clean.

What they needed was for Hollis to dance several sets with Mariah, but other than when he had cut in on Jay, and one other brief dance, he hadn't done so to this point. He headed in her direction to urge her to keep Hollis occupied for a lengthy amount of time. Jay would need at least thirty minutes.

Before he reached Mariah, another man, a thin fellow who towered over even Jay—not an easy feat to accomplish—led Mariah to the dance floor.

Jay's chest burned. Though it wasn't right for him to be jealous, he was. He had no claim on Mariah, but it tore him up to stand along the side while she danced with another man, held in his arms. It was one thing when it was Hollis. She had told Jay she didn't love the man and didn't want to marry him.

Could she ever care for such a bumbling fool as he?

He could attempt to pull himself from the doldrums by asking another young lady to dance, but he had no heart for it. It was Mariah who had fit in his arms like a hand in a glove. Almost as if they were made for each other.

That line of thinking wasn't helping. Though he wasn't hungry, sampling one of the cakes on the dessert table would give him something to do while biding his time.

The dance ended, and another partner claimed a dance from her. And then another and another.

The woman in the pink dress sashayed past him, and he stopped her. "Miss Waldon?"

She stopped in front of him and flashed him a dimpled smile. "Yes?"

"Would you care to dance?"

"It would be my pleasure, Mr. Franklin." Soon they were gliding across the floor, and he guided them in Mariah's direction. Of course she couldn't see him, but he was near her nonetheless.

"Have you lived in Peshtigo all your life?"

"No. I'm originally from Chicago." He kept his eye on Mariah.

"Truly? How wonderful." She launched into a monologue extolling each of the city's virtues, once again monopolizing the conversation. All the better for him. Here he was, a grown man, jealous as a schoolboy with his first crush. When the music ended, he released his partner and returned to his haunt along the room's perimeter.

This time, he made it to the refreshment table where all manner of little cakes and cookies, all even in size and shape and highly decorated, awaited him. If Ma could see this. Each year on his birthday, she had scrimped and saved to have enough sugar to make a small creation for him.

In some ways, those little cakes, made out of a heart full of love, were much more special than these fancy ones. He picked up one decorated with pink frosting and a chocolate drizzle and bit into it.

Nothing like Ma's. Hers were better.

By this time, Mariah had returned to her seat, once again holding court. He headed toward her, and out of the corner of his eye, he caught sight of Hollis making his way in the same direction. Good. He slowed his pace.

Before he reached the edge of the room once more, someone tugged on his arm. Hard enough to pull him to a sudden stop and spin him around. He worked to wrest himself from the man's grip to no avail.

"Don't fight me."

Jay caught sight of the man holding him. His hair and beard were dark and unkempt, as were his clothes. He stood in contrast to the guests, each dressed in their finest, not a hair out of place. "Who are you?"

"I know what you want."

"I don't know what you mean." Could he be speaking about Mariah? Or the proof of Hollis' dirty deeds?

"You do. You lost something valuable in that fire, didn't you?"

"Everything." Jay scrunched his eyebrows.

"I don't have time for you to play coy. You were searching for proof. Had found some of what you needed. Had it in your possession. But you don't now."

"How do you know?" Goose bumps broke out on Jay's arms, and his heart pounded in his ears, drowning out the music of the string quartet.

"I have my ways. And I have what you need, what will get you everything you ever wanted."

"I—"

"Do you want what I have?"

"Yes." Jay didn't have to think about it.

"It will cost you."

"How much?"

"Not in dollars."

"Then what?" Jay spoke around the swelling in this throat that threatened to cut off his breathing.

"Don't worry. I have my price. What you have to decide is if it is too steep. Is it worth it?"

Chapter Twenty-Nine

At the price the mysterious man in black quoted Jay, he stumbled from the ballroom, his head spinning. He raced down the hall to the quiet morning room, the tall east-facing windows now dark. He leaned over his knees, panting, a bead of sweat running down his spine.

Though he drew in great gulps of air, he couldn't catch his breath. The price the man had proposed was too steep. Far too steep. And from his tone, there would be no negotiating. It was an all-or-nothing deal.

What was he to do? Give up Mariah and start a new life in Kansas City so that this man wouldn't go public with her late father's gambling debts in exchange for the information that would expose Hollis? Or keep Mariah and stay forever silent about Hollis' dirty deeds?

He straightened and fisted his hands to keep them from shaking. The man hadn't revealed who he was or how he had obtained the information about Hollis. Perhaps he didn't even have it. He could be bluffing.

Why Mariah? Why involve her in all of this? It could be that the man had taken a fancy to her himself and saw Jay as a rival. He held back the chuckle that pleaded to escape. Little chance of that. A man like himself stood no chance with a woman of her caliber, no matter how he longed for her.

He could stick to the original plan and get the information on Hollis himself, but that meant that Mariah would still find out about her father's past, one that had shocked Jay to the core. If it shook him that much, how much more would it disturb Mariah? It might even break her. She loved her father. No, a gate now blocked that way forward. He had to scrap the plan he and Mariah had concocted.

He made several circuits of the darkened room, only the moon illuminating the interior. "God, help me. What am I supposed to do? What is the right way in this situation? Cover up the crimes of a living man, or expose the crimes of a dead one?"

When he put it that way, the choice was clear. What Hollis was doing was wrong and could well hurt the railroad. It wouldn't be the first time a pampered son had squandered his family's wealth.

The railroad did so much good for so many. It connected towns to the outside world and brought in food, material for clothes, and other necessities. Where the lines reached, the area grew and prospered. Peshtigo, in time, might boom again now that it had a railroad nearby.

Even before, they benefited from it. If all the medicines, clothing, and tents had to be brought from Madison and Milwaukee and Chicago by wagon, it would have taken much too long. The loss of life would have been greater.

Jay pressed on his chest to cease the galloping of his heart. He may have no chance at winning Mariah as his wife, but he treasured their friendship. Losing that would be like losing a piece of himself. She understood him and accepted him.

The door opened, and light from the hallway spilled inside. "Jay? Is that you?"

He spun around. "Mr. Stanford. I'm sorry. I needed a quiet place for a few minutes."

"No need to explain. The room was getting rather too warm and uncomfortable for me as well. My days of dancing and enjoying such gatherings are long gone. This celebration is for younger folk such as yourself." He stepped farther into the room.

"I'm afraid I don't do well in crowds."

"Yes, though I did see you dancing with Miss Waldon on more than one occasion. She comes from a fine family, even if she is rather chatty."

The smile that burst forth dulled the ache for a moment. "That she is, though pleasant enough."

"That's not the woman who has captured your special attention, is it?"

"No, sir." He had always been able to be honest with Mr. Stanford. "Though I promise you, it goes no deeper than friendship, and once she and your son are married, I will, of course, sever all ties with her."

"I admire your integrity. Hollis would do well to learn from you on that subject." Mr. Stanford moved to one of the windows and drew aside the heavy drapes. "I fear we will have snow sooner rather than later. You already have it up north, from what Angelina tells me."

"May I ask you something?"

"Of course. Never hesitate to do so."

"Does integrity ever come with, well, too high of a price?"

Mr. Stanford picked up a decanter and turned to Jay. "That's an interesting question." He poured himself a drink and sipped it. "I suppose if you shy away from doing what is right out of fear of the consequences, then you have lost your integrity and have compromised it for an easier path. By definition, integrity acts despite what might happen."

Jay scrubbed his face. What Mr. Stanford said made perfect sense. Too much sense. If he didn't expose Hollis and his lying, cheating ways, he wouldn't be the man God expected him to be. He wouldn't bring glory to his heavenly Father.

Even though it would rip his heart from his chest.

"Is something troubling you, Jay?"

"I want to do what is right, what is pleasing to the Lord. Sometimes, though, it's not easy."

"The path of righteousness is a narrow one, fraught with stumbling blocks and obstacles. God never promised it would be simple or would come without pain."

Jay bowed his head. "You're right. Thank you."

"I'm sorry you are struggling against whatever it is that is bothering you. In the end, doing what is right reaps a harvest of joy."

"I'm afraid that's not possible in this situation."

"It is one of God's promises, though, so you can stand on it. Even if it is painful at the time, in the end, you will see the reward. Perhaps not until heaven, but you will see it."

"How do you maintain your integrity in the world you occupy?"

"Do you mean my business, or my wealth?"

Jay shrugged. "Both, I suppose."

"It doesn't matter, because the answer is the same either way. It's a daily choice that I make to walk with the Lord. Prayer and studying His Word help a great deal."

"Thank you, sir. Deep in my heart, I knew the answer, but this solidifies it. It doesn't make the decision easier, but I have the assurance that I craved."

"I will be praying for you."

"And I for you."

At Jay's words, Mr. Stanford stared at him for a moment then nodded and turned and left the room.

Jay would enjoy one more dance with Mariah before he went to find the mystery man and inform him of his decision.

"Has anyone seen Mr. Franklin in the past half hour or so?" Mariah inquired of the young ladies surrounding her. Or that she believed were nearby. Perhaps he had left to implement their plan, though she wasn't holding up her end of the deal and keeping Hollis distracted.

"I saw him a while ago talking with a gentleman I have yet to be acquainted with." The perfumed woman's voice was close by, so at least one person hadn't deserted Mariah.

"Yes, he was strange, wasn't he? Dressed all in black, dark hair, dark eyes. Something a bit sinister about him." This came from the giggling girl.

Mariah rose to her feet, the plate on her lap crashing to the floor. She had finished with it and hadn't known where to set it. The music continued, but the weight of a thousand stares pressed on her shoulders. "I am so sorry. How clumsy of me." Out of instinct, she bent down to pick it up, and cut her hand on a jagged piece of china. "Ouch."

"Gracious, Miss Randolph." The perfumed woman took her by the hand. "You've managed to cut yourself. Let me see what I can find to bandage you."

"I know where everything is."

Solid, steady, dependable Jay, always showing up just when she needed him most. Like he had on the night of the fire. Like he had each day she was in the hospital. "I forgot the plate was on my lap. I should never have set it down."

"Don't worry about it. Come with me, and I'll help you."

She allowed him to lead her from the ballroom, still holding her by her injured hand, and into the hallway. "Ah, here's one of the maids. Could you please fetch some iodine and some bandages? Miss Randolph has injured herself. We'll meet you upstairs outside of her chambers."

"Very good, sir."

He helped her up the steps, but they stopped before entering her room, maintaining perfect propriety the entire time, other than him touching her hand. "Let me look at it again to make sure there is no glass embedded in it."

She opened her fingers, and he probed around the wound. Each time his soft fingertips touched her palm, it sent tingles up and down her arm. "How does it appear?"

"I don't see any glass, and it isn't very deep. It could have been much worse."

"What a silly thing for me to do."

"It was a natural reaction. I'm thankful it isn't deeper. You should still be able to paint."

"How sweet of you to think of that."

"It's important to you."

Yes, it was, but Hollis wouldn't have had that in the front of his mind at a time like this. He would be more concerned about any blood on her gown or the show she made in front of the guests.

"I'm glad I have the chance to speak to you in private. I was afraid this opportunity wouldn't arise."

"First, I must ask you a question. Some of the women mentioned seeing you speaking with a man they weren't acquainted with. Who was that?"

"Precisely what I was going to tell you. He claims to have the information I've been seeking on Hollis."

"He what?"

"Yes. So it appears that I don't have to put myself at risk to get what I need to bring his deeds to light."

"That's wonderful news. You can expose him, and. . ."

"What? What were you going to say?"

She could never reveal to him that she had been about to share her excitement at them being able to be together. "Nothing. . .except that I will be free from him then, though I will miss seeing Angelina."

"Perhaps Mr. Stanford will allow the two of you to visit from time to time."

"What a nice thought. He just might, and that would be lovely. Losing her is the hardest part of all of this." Despite the pain in her hand, she managed a smile.

"The man did make me another offer in addition."

He hesitated. Was something amiss? "What kind of offer?"

"A job. In Kansas City."

"Oh." The smile slid from her face, and her hand throbbed, but the pain in her palm didn't compare to the pain in her heart. "I take it that you are of a mind to accept the position."

"I am. In fact, I was coming to claim one last dance with you before I gave him my answer."

"So you haven't committed to it?"

"Not yet, but I will."

"Please, I beg you to reconsider. You—you will be so missed. I value our friendship."

"You are the only reason I hesitated in giving my answer. However, this is an opportunity I can't pass up. This is what I have dreamed of all my life. All this tension with Hollis has wearied me, and I'm ready for a fresh start."

Oh, that it might include her. But he spoke nothing of loving her or wanting to marry her and take her to Kansas City with him. Perhaps, like Hollis, her blindness was an embarrassment to him. After all, who wanted a wife who couldn't see?

She choked back tears and fought to keep her voice as normal as possible. "I understand, and I'm so happy for you. May the Lord bless you in your new endeavor."

"Thank you. Ah, here is Daisy with the supplies."

"Go and find the man with the information. Daisy is capable of dressing my hand." She withdrew from his grip.

As she entered her bedroom with the maid, she left Jay.

Much the way he was leaving her.

Chapter Thirty

CHICAGO, ILLINOIS
MONDAY, JANUARY 1, 1872

While darkness still cloaked Chicago, Jay parted the heavy blue velvet drapes that covered the windows in his bedroom that overlooked Lake Michigan. The sun would peek its head over the water for the first time in 1872 in a little while, but for now, the sky remained a black void.

He pressed against the cold glass. A new year. Usually, despite all that had occurred in the one previous, Jay met it with a sense of hope and anticipation. A clean slate, one ready for the Lord to write His plans on, plans He had constructed in times eternal.

He whispered into the void. "I don't like these plans, Lord, not one bit. If only there was a way to get the information without having to go to Kansas City. But I can't hurt Mariah. If she learned about her father, it would ruin her, even if the matter stayed private within their family. She has faced too much loss already."

The winter's chill seeped through the panes and into his bones, so he stepped back, drew the heavy drapes again, and once more crawled under the covers to keep warm. He could start his own fire, but there was no wood or kindling in the room. This dependence on servants chafed him.

While he waited for the chambermaid, he stared at the dark ceiling, running a thousand scenarios in his mind, searching for any way out of the predicament he found himself in.

By the time he returned to the ballroom last night after helping Mariah, the man dressed in black was nowhere to be found. Jay had searched throughout the entire house without so much of a hint that the man had even been there.

Perhaps he had been nothing more than a dream or a ghost. A figment of Jay's imagination. Then again, Mariah mentioned the women she had been seated near had also seen the man, so he had been real. Jay was ready to be done with the entire sordid mess. Get the information, expose Hollis, hightail it out of Chicago. A clean break. He wouldn't return to Marinette to get what little he had left at the house. Mariah's sister could box up his few personal items and mail them to him.

Despite the crazy circles his mind ran in, he must have dozed, for when he woke, the fire had been lit and the curtains opened. The sun beamed across the icy lake and into the bedroom, landing on the blue and gold carpeting. He dressed and headed down to breakfast but stopped in the dining room doorway.

Mariah sat at the table, drinking coffee, with Angelina beside her prattling on about the ball.

While Mariah had been beautiful last night in her gown the color of the sky, her hair braided and coiled into some intricate pattern, she was even more stunning this morning. She wore a simple dark-purple gown with a little lace at the throat and sleeves. Her hair, likewise, was plain, in a bun at the nape of her neck.

But the way her dark green eyes danced when Angelina spoke was what caught his attention. They captivated him. A dimple appeared in her cheek when she laughed, and the sound of it was deeper and sweeter than the ringing of church bells.

"It's Mr. Jay." Angelina spotted him, forcing him to halt his assessment of Mariah and enter the room.

"Good morning, ladies. How is your hand, Miss Randolph?"

"Fine, thank you." She was polite and courteous, but much of the warmth her words used to hold was missing.

"I'm glad to hear it."

"Did you like the ball, Mr. Jay? It was divine."

The chuckle he worked to hold back escaped anyway. Where did a six-year-old learn such a word?

"It must have been divine to dance with all the beautiful ladies."

He laughed again. "It was divine, and Miss Mariah was the most beautiful of them all." He stole a glance at her as her cheeks warmed to pink.

"When I'm old enough to stay and dance, I will wear a divine dress and have my maid put my hair up. It will be divine."

A guffaw puffed out his cheeks, but he tamped it down. Mariah bit her lip, but her shoulders shook.

He cleared his throat to compose himself. "I'm sure it will be."

Angelina's chatter broke some of the tension in the room, and they had a pleasant breakfast. Until Hollis entered the dining room.

"Father, Father." Angelina shot from her chair and went to fling herself toward him but pulled up.

He stood scowling, his arms crossed. "Return to your chair and act with more decorum, if you will. You should be in the nursery."

"But—"

He waved his hand, and Angelina sat down and picked at her eggs.

"I didn't get a chance to speak to you much last night, Miss Randolph. I'm still in shock at the surprise you gave me."

"Angelina and I both missed you. It was only right that we be at the ball."

"Yes, well, from now on, I would appreciate. advanced notice."

Mariah opened her mouth as if she was going to give a retort, but then shut it and focused her attention on the plate in front of her.

Jay pushed back from the table, the sound echoing in the silent room. "Excuse me, please. Good day, everyone." Off he went in search of the elusive mystery man.

He hadn't made his way far down the hall before Wilson, dressed in coattails, his brown hair slicked back, stopped him. "Sir, there is a letter for you."

"Thank you." He took the paper sealed with black wax and broke it open.

I gave you time to say a proper goodbye to Miss Randolph.
I now need my answer. Meet me on the lakeshore by the
river at noon sharp. I shan't wait a moment longer.

Noon. He glanced at the grandfather clock at the end of the hall. That gave him a little more than an hour to figure out a way to get everything he wanted without giving up anything.

Life, however, rarely worked that way.

———◆◆◆———

The new nanny Hollis had hired for Angelina arrived shortly after a hasty note was sent to her, and Mariah found herself in the library, surrounded by books she had no way of reading. The fragrance of the paper and ink would have to be enough.

She had to settle her fluttery middle. What was this funny feeling? If only Mama were here to guide her and help her. What if she was misinterpreting it?

Because she took it to mean she was falling in love with Jay. Why did it take him leaving her life for good for her to understand that she desired more than friendship with him, that her life would be darker without him? Darker than it already was.

"Mariah?"

At the sound of Hollis' voice, she jumped, clutching her chest. "You startled me. I didn't hear you coming." That happened to her all too often, especially now without the aid of her eyesight.

"You appeared to be quite deep in thought."

Heat raced to her cheeks, and she was helpless to stop it. "Just mulling over a few things."

"It's just as well that I found you. I want to speak with you, and I wasn't able to with Angelina in the room."

"Why did you push her away? She was so happy to see you after such a long time. She loves you and wants to spend time with you."

"Do not tell me how to bring up my daughter. I have said it before, and I'm tired of repeating myself." His voice rose in pitch. "I'm a busy man. She has to understand that. I was afraid the journey here would be too much for her."

Mariah came to her feet. "What is going on? Why are you acting this way? I am only trying to help. I will be her stepmother, after all." But she wouldn't. Soon there would be no need for her to keep up this charade.

"A stepmother, yes, to guide her in the things a young woman should know that I have no way of teaching her. She may have gotten away with such behavior at your sister's house in the wilds of Wisconsin, but that will not be tolerated here. She must learn to be a lady, and you must behave like one."

She raised her chin, her arms akimbo. "What, exactly, does that mean? Was I not a perfect guest last night?"

"When you and I marry, you will outrank all those women, whom you associate with far too freely. We will not bring up the subject of the number of men you danced with, including Mr. Franklin, who had no right to be in attendance at all."

"I'm sorry, but I don't understand this. The last I checked, there is no peerage system in the United States. We did away with that almost one hundred years ago, so no one outranks anyone. As for Mr. Franklin, he accompanied us to Chicago and is a guest in this home. The only polite thing to do was to invite him to the festivities. How wrong it would be to exclude him, especially on New Year's Eve." The heat that had flooded her cheeks now burned in her chest.

"I will not be spoken to by anyone in such a manner, especially the woman who is to be my wife."

"Why are you even interested in me? Why did you pick me as your bride when there are all these society women falling at your feet? With your prestige and fortune, any one of them would consider herself lucky to be the new Mrs. Stanford."

"You are beautiful and talented. Intelligent, even. That's all you need to know."

"There's more to it?"

"Excuse me. I have a job I need to get to. Railroads do not build themselves." His footsteps were heavy as he left, and he slammed the door behind him.

The encounter left her shaking from head to toe, and she returned to her seat in the leather chair. If only she had her painting supplies. She would dip her brush into black paint and fill the canvas with dark, angry storm clouds.

At the beginning of their relationship, she had questioned his interest in her, and he had assured her that he loved her for the genuine person she was. Today, however, she received a much different answer.

One that left her scratching her head.

In the end, it mattered little. She would not marry Hollis. No one would ever be able to convince her to do so. Once Jay had his proof of her fiancé's dealings, she would break off their betrothal and be free of him.

She would miss Angelina, though, that bright light in the midst of her darkness. How could she leave her with a nanny she didn't know, a father who ignored her, and a grandfather who adored her but had no experience in raising precocious girls? Was that enough for her to marry Hollis and live a loveless life with a man who was dishonest and violent?

At one time, it had been, but it was no longer. Perhaps she would be allowed to write to the child, and perhaps they would be able to see each other. If the American justice system did its job and sentenced Hollis to time behind bars, she wouldn't be able to marry him anyway. Mr. Stanford might well be amenable to her remaining in Angelina's life.

More, though, she would miss Jay. He was ready to flee the destruction in Peshtigo and the chaos his revelation about Hollis would cause and start a new life far away. She couldn't fault him for wanting to be out of the line of fire. When Mr. Stanford heard about what Hollis had done and who exposed him, he would be furious.

She should follow Jay's lead and make plans to return to Marinette as soon as possible. Once she broke off the engagement, she would likely be traveling by regular coach and paying her own way.

Mariah sighed. She might as well go upstairs and pack. She left the library and headed toward the stairs. Good thing she had been in this house several times and knew the way pretty well. By following the wall, she would find the steps.

"Miss Randolph, wait." Jay called to her from what sounded like the front door.

She continued toward him. "What is it?"

Now he was near enough for her to catch a whiff of his cologne. "Noon. That's when we get what we want. Soon after that, I will make my move."

"Thank you. If I don't see you again, all the best."

"Same to you."

"Stay safe."

"I will."

Her heart broke into a thousand pieces.

Chapter Thirty-One

Jay's breath hung in the air as he paced the frozen shoreline, waiting for the man to show up with the information he needed to expose Hollis' crimes once and for all.

So why this churning in his stomach? He could have returned to Hollis' office another time and taken the pages from the ledger. Then again, if Hollis caught him in the act or if he realized the pages were missing before Jay took them to the authorities, Hollis would show him no mercy.

This time, he wouldn't escape with his life.

Not that he trusted this man more than he did Hollis, though he was privy to information about Mariah that even she didn't know, that he hadn't known himself until being informed of it last night.

Jay's fingers and toes were almost frozen by the time the stranger showed up fifteen minutes past the appointed time. "What took you so long?"

"Don't question me. Do you want the proof you've been searching for or not?"

"Are you the one who tipped us off in the first place? Who sent that note to Mariah?"

He gave a single nod.

"If you do have the proof, why don't you go to the authorities? Why involve me?"

"You ask too many questions."

"Questions you need to answer."

The man rubbed his bearded chin and stared at the pale blue sky. "Let's just say I don't have the best reputation. I took a great risk coming to the ball last night because neither of the Misters Stanford would have appreciated me being there. They accused me of stealing from the company and sent me to jail for a while, so I'm not trustworthy. I knew, though, that Hollis was in way deeper than I was."

"How do you know about Mariah or her father or that I wanted the information you have? If you do?"

"Like I said, too many questions. I have my ways, but if you must know, Mariah's father, my uncle, came to my father, begging for money to cover his debts. My father, good man that he is, turned his brother down flat. Didn't even give him a hot meal. Now, I have a warm house and a warm woman waiting for me, and I'd like to return to both as soon as possible. What will it be?"

Jay's heart battled, though his head knew what was right. He swallowed hard and drew in a deep breath. Five extra seconds before his life slipped away. "I'll take the evidence you have."

"And remember, in exchange for this, you will leave."

"Why must I go? What do you gain by making me leave Mariah?"

"You know too much. You could easily turn and rat me out to save yourself. Then my life would be in danger."

"But I won't. I promise on all that is holy, neither Hollis nor his father will ever learn how I came by the information." Mariah wouldn't say a word.

"I don't know you well enough to trust you. I've worked too hard to rebuild my life to have it ruined once again or to lose it. You agreed to this deal. If you want what I have, then you must abide by my conditions. You don't want my cousin to discover the kind of man her father truly was."

That was the period on the end of the sentence. The man's words hit their mark, where Jay was most vulnerable. Mariah. Either he knew or he guessed very well that Jay would do whatever he had to do to protect the woman he had fallen in love with so long ago.

Jay nodded. "Fine."

"I have the documents here. Everything you need to make sure Hollis pays for his crimes the way I've had to pay for mine. And a train ticket to Kansas City later tonight."

"Tonight?"

"As soon as you break the news, you need to get to the station and get out of Chicago. My brother will meet you in Kansas City and help you get established there."

"Coming from Peshtigo, I have almost nothing, not even much money."

"Don't worry about anything. I want to see Hollis brought to justice."

"To get even with him?"

"While that will be sweet, no. I've turned my life around. No more drinking, gambling, or stealing for me. Mr. Stanford was good to me, and I took advantage of him. What Hollis is doing to his father is far worse. Maybe he can change his ways. Who knows? Stranger things have happened."

Jay nodded. What more could he do? Everything the man said made sense. "Let's pray that is the case. Mr. Stanford has also treated me well over the years. I wouldn't be where I am without him."

"You mean standing on the edge of a frozen sheet of ice with no feeling left in your limbs?" The dark man from last night disappeared with his hearty chuckle.

Jay joined him in the laughter, but it didn't ease the ache in his heart at the prospect of losing everything he had.

The man handed Jay a stack of papers tied with a string then shook his hand. "Good luck. I wish you the best in Kansas City. My brother is going to let me know how you get on."

"Thank you." The papers trembled in Jay's hand. The last thing he needed to do was to drop them like he had on the street that night with Mariah.

A moment later, Jay was once again alone on the shore, the wind increasing, shooting icicles up and down his spine. Time to head back, get warm, and make his move.

The familiar *if only* mantra played in his head. If only Mariah would agree to marry him and go to Kansas City with him. Together they could start over. She would never leave her sister though. Lydia was the only family she had. Nothing would tear them apart.

And neither of them must ever find out what kind of man their father had been. Good, kind, and respectable on the outside but with many secrets on the inside. Mariah had lost too much. To also lose the good memories of her father might be more than she could bear.

As soon as Jay returned to the house, he made his way upstairs and into the privacy of his room. The maid had fixed his bed and tidied the space, so he took the packet to the small table beside the window and sat down. He untied the string and found everything to be in order. There were the papers Jay remembered from Hollis' office, both in Chicago and in Peshtigo, and a one-way ticket to Kansas City.

His heart hammered in his ears as he pulled the bell to ring for a servant. He asked the valet who answered to call both Mr. Stanfords together. By the time he left his room to make his way downstairs to the study, his mouth was so dry, he might not be able to speak at all.

Just as he passed her door, Mariah left her room and almost ran into him. He caught her by the elbow to steady her. "I'm sorry. I didn't see you coming."

"Jay?"

"Yes, it's me. I'm on my way to meet with Hollis and his father."

"I'm coming with you."

"What? No. There is no need for you to be there, to be in the middle of this. Hollis is going to be furious, and if he believes that you knew anything about this beforehand or helped me in any way whatsoever, he will ruin you."

"He wouldn't dare hurt me."

"No, I'm not suggesting physical violence. But he might say things that would ruin your reputation. There is no need for that."

"Let people believe about me what they want. Those who truly know me and care about me won't believe vicious lies."

"I insist." Why had her cousin ever dragged her into this in the first place?

"No. I insist. I've been expecting this, so my bags are packed, and I'm ready to leave at a moment's notice."

"Mariah, I am begging you to stay in your room. Please. Better even, I will ring for the coachman to take you to the train station." Best that she not be in the house at all in case Hollis spilled the secrets her father had hidden. "Won't you do that for me?"

She bit her lower lip. One that he had to hold himself back from kissing. She was far too beautiful in this moment. And far too vulnerable. "I will stand with you, Jay, the way you've stood with me these past few months."

Stubborn woman. Then again, this same stubbornness probably saved her life when she was sick after the fire. She fought so hard then.

"No. I'm sorry, but I won't allow you in the room."

She opened her mouth, but he held up his hand to ward off her protest.

"This isn't open for discussion or debate. I'll have the butler arrange for your trunk to be brought around, and then you have to leave." He leaned over and kissed her cheek. "Goodbye, Mariah." His heart shattered as he left her standing in the hallway.

After speaking to Wilson, he entered Mr. Stanford's office where he and Hollis already waited. Mr. Stanford broke off his conversation with his son. "What is this about, Jay?"

Mr. Stafford occupied the chair behind the desk, and Hollis sat in one facing him. Jay went and stood opposite his mentor, the man who was like a father to him. How this stung to cut his heart and watch him bleed. "Well, as you know, I am a bookkeeper."

Hollis harrumphed. "Please get to the point. We all know your background and how Father saved you from a life of poverty and so on. Unlike you, some of us have business to attend to."

Mr. Stanford sat back in his chair. "Don't be so dismissive, Hollis. Allow Jay to speak."

"Thank you, sir. I was referring to how my position makes me privy to information."

Hollis sat straighter. "Yes. Right before the fire, I caught him snooping in my office. On a Sunday evening. Can you believe that, Father? I should have had the good sense to sack him on the spot, but we were forced to flee for our lives."

Not quite how the story went, but Jay was not about to quibble over details. "Yes, well, I found inconsistencies in the books."

"You made an error?" Mr. Stanford rubbed his whiskered chin.

"No. I double-checked my work, and there were no mistakes."

Hollis crossed his legs then uncrossed them. Good, he was getting nervous. "Listen to how arrogant he is, bragging about his perfect math. Own up to your mistakes. That's what it means to be a man."

Jay would laugh if the situation wasn't so serious. "I am doing no such thing but am merely stating a fact."

"If you didn't make a mistake, then why were there inconsistencies?" Mr. Stanford directed the question at Jay but stared at his son.

Jay wiped one sweaty hand on his pants while holding the papers in his other. "Because of this, sir." He set the packet on the desk and pushed it in Mr. Stanford's direction.

"What's this?"

"Take a look at them."

"This is ridiculous. How do we know you haven't created these ledgers yourself?" Hollis' face went as red as blood.

"According to these papers, you have been skimming money from the company." Mr. Stanford sighed. "For a long time. And a great deal of it."

"You have no idea if these are forgeries or not." A vein in Hollis' neck throbbed.

"The pages are in your handwriting. There is no doubt about it." Mr. Stanford's shoulders slumped. "I have to admit to having had my suspicions for years, but I was too afraid to dig deeply into the accounts, afraid that I might discover the truth about my own son. My only son. My flesh and blood. Now I have."

"This is utter nonsense." Hollis stood.

Jay straightened and looked Mr. Stanford in the eye. "The night of the fire, I was in Hollis' office. I admit to that. It was there that I confirmed what I suspected. Of course, the evidence didn't survive the conflagration. I saw the same numbers in his ledgers in his office here, but I was unable to secure the papers to bring to you."

"Then you are admitting that these are forgeries." Hollis fisted and unfisted his hands.

"No. There is someone else who brought me these. I didn't question where he got them, nor did I ask his name."

"Made up. That's what they are." Hollis leaned across his father's desk. "You can't believe this. I am your son. You have to defend me."

Mr. Stanford must have aged ten years in the past ten minutes, for his face was now drawn and sunken. "Not when you're guilty."

Hollis swung around and pinned Jay against the damask-papered wall, his hands around Jay's throat. "It's your fault. Your doing. You will pay for this."

Chapter Thirty-Two

~~~~~⟩

The thump against the wall startled Mariah, who had been standing in the hall across from the office. She was not about to leave without being certain that Mr. Stanford knew the entire truth about his son. But what was going on in there?

"You will die." Hollis' voice dripped with venom.

"I... I...can't...breathe."

No. Hollis was choking Jay. She felt her way to the office door, her own breath coming in short spurts. She fumbled inside until she found the men and pulled on Hollis, judging by his thicker waist. "Stop it. Stop it now. Get off of him."

"He usurped me in my father's affections, and now he is trying to usurp my place in the company. I will not allow it."

"Hollis, let him go." Mr. Stanford's chair scraped back. "Don't do this. I love you. Don't."

Mere seconds later, the door opened, even as Mariah tugged with all her might on Hollis. "Step away, Miss Randolph." Wilson, the butler had come. What good would he do alone when Hollis was so determined?

She did Wilson's bidding and bumped into another man. He had brought reinforcements. Still, she stood to the side, trembling from head to toe. *Lord, don't let him hurt Jay. Protect him. Help him.*

A single shot rang out, echoing in Mariah's ears. She screamed. "No! No! Don't shoot! What's happening?"

"I will pull the trigger again, Hollis." Mr. Stanford's voice was calm. Too calm. "Next time, I won't point it at the ceiling. How could you do such a thing? How? Let him go, and don't make me hurt you."

"No!" The scream tore from Mariah. If Hollis was choking Jay and Mr. Stanford shot Hollis, the bullet would surely pierce Jay too. What about the butler and the other man? Where were they?

More scuffling, then came another thump. "What do you want us to do with him now?" That came from the butler. From the sound of it, they must have wrestled Hollis away from Jay.

Though she longed to go to Jay and make sure he was still breathing, there were too many people crowded in the small room. She couldn't move from her spot, and she couldn't control her trembling. "Jay?" Her question was shaky. "Jay, are you all right?"

"We'll clear out, Wilson, and leave Hollis in here alone. Guard the door, you and Virgil." Mr. Stanford's words trembled.

"I'm fine, Mariah. Shaken, but fine."

Jay. Praise the Lord.

"Come on, my dear." Mr. Stanford took her by the elbow. "Let's allow Wilson and Virgil to do their work."

"What about Jay?" She swung around as if she could see him.

"I'm right behind you."

"You can make it on your own?"

"Yes. Wilson and Virgil pulled Hollis off me just in time. A minute later, and I would have passed out. But I'm fine."

They left the library and headed in the direction of the parlor then turned into the room, from Mariah's calculations on how far they had gone.

"Jay, have a seat on the couch. Mariah, here is a chair for you. You're shaking like a leaf. Let me call for one of the maids to go for the doctor."

"No need." Already, Jay's voice was stronger. "Now that I can breathe again, I will be fine."

"Are you sure?" Such fatherly concern in Mr. Stanford's words.

"Yes. There is no need to bother with sending for one unless Miss Randolph is unwell. How are you?"

"Thankful that you're alive and well, though this feels like a nightmare."

"Let me go see to Hollis and send for the authorities." Mr. Stanford left the room.

Once he did, Mariah felt her way to the couch and sat beside Jay. "I was so frightened for you. I've never heard Hollis so angry."

"You should have seen his eyes. His grip around my throat was like a vice, cutting off almost all my air."

"How terrifying."

"It was. If not for you and Mr. Stanford in the room, I would surely be dead."

"Mr. Stanford knows everything now?"

"Yes. He's suspected Hollis for a while but was too afraid to admit it to himself. All I did was make him face reality. Still, it must be a blow to him."

"Yes, I imagine it is." She scooted closer to Jay and touched his shoulder. He responded by pulling her into an embrace, and they trembled in each other's arms. She rubbed his back, and he stroked her arm. How long they stayed like that, Mariah couldn't say, but at last, Jay released her and pulled back just a bit. He cupped her cheek, and his lips met hers.

He was kissing her. Her chest swelled. Even if he loved her only a small fraction of what she loved him, it was enough. Enough to know that she was cherished.

"What are you doing?"

Mariah broke the kiss and backed away from Jay. When had Angelina come into the room? She was supposed to be in the nursery with her nanny.

"Why were you kissing Mr. Jay, Miss Mariah? I thought you were going to marry Father."

"Come here, pumpkin." Mariah held out her arms, and Angelina came to her, allowing her to pull her onto her lap, even though she was almost too big for it anymore.

"Aren't you and Father getting married? You're supposed to be my new mother."

"I know you don't understand, and it's difficult for me to explain." Mariah squeezed Angelina. This wasn't going to be easy. How did she put what happened into words the girl could understand but in a way that wouldn't hurt her? "Your father has done some bad things. He stole money from your grandfather."

"He's not supposed to do that." She shook her head against Mariah's chest.

"No, he's not. That's wrong. You should never steal. Mr. Jay told your grandfather about it, and your father got very angry. So now the police are going to come and talk to your father."

"Is he going to jail?"

"I'm not sure." Jay's words were gentle and soft. "We don't know what is going to happen."

"But why were you kissing Miss Mariah?"

"Because I love her."

"She loves Father. Don't you, Miss Mariah?"

Goodness, what a question to have to answer. "I have known for a while what your father was doing. I don't think he loved me, and when I found out about the money he stole, I knew that I didn't love him either. That won't stop how much I love you though. Never, ever."

None of this was fair to Angelina.

"So are you going to marry Mr. Jay?"

Oh, my. The things that came out of children's mouths.

———•••———

The rosy hue in Mariah's cheeks from the kiss deepened until it was bright red after Angelina's innocent question. Like the girl, Jay waited for Mariah's answer, hardly daring to breathe.

Mariah smoothed Angelina's hair. Such a motherly gesture. "All I know right now is that I am not going to marry your father."

"But I want you to be my mother." Tears shimmered in Angelina's blue eyes.

"I would have loved nothing more. Perhaps your grandfather will allow me to visit you from time to time."

"It's not the same." Big fat tears rolled down Angelina's cheeks.

Mariah clung ever tighter to the child. "I know. I know, but this is how it has to be. Stealing is very wrong, and I can't marry someone who has stolen as much money as your father has."

"I love Father. I don't want him to go to jail."

Jay licked his lips. "No one wants that, but sometimes things happen. You don't want to get punished when you do a bad thing, but you must so that you learn your lesson. Do you understand?"

She nodded, wiping the tears from her blue eyes.

"What is important to remember is that your grandfather is going to be here to love you and take care of you."

Angelina nodded once more then buried her face against Mariah and sobbed. For a long time, the little girl wept. So much loss for one so young. The pain in his own heart from losing first his father and then, after coming to live here, his mother, was still raw and tender at times.

Angelina, too, had suffered the loss of both mother and father. With the Stanfords' connections in Chicago, Hollis may end up getting off with serving only a little time. Then again, Mr. Stanford was angry enough with his son to order the judge not to go easy on him.

Jay shifted positions on the couch, and the paper in his pocket crinkled. Oh. With the commotion after he brought Hollis' crimes to light—almost being strangled—he had forgotten.

The train ticket. Kansas City. Why had he ever kissed Mariah, knowing he had to leave? He would never be able to be anything more than the friend who had once loved her. In time, she would move on with her life, get over this ugly season, and find someone who would love her and care for her the way she deserved.

For him, there would never be another like her. There would never be another who could take her place. His heart would always belong where Mariah was.

There was no point in putting off the inevitable. He could stay another five minutes, but in the end, he had to leave to avoid inflicting further pain on Mariah. She didn't deserve that. "I must be going."

Mariah stared at him, her eyes widening. "Must you?"

"I do. We talked about this before."

"But I thought—"

He waved away the rest of her sentence then bowed over them and kissed a tearful Angelina on top of her head. "You take care, Miss Angelina. I have enjoyed getting to know you. Be good."

She straightened in Mariah's arms and gazed at him with shimmering eyes. "Where are you going?"

"To Kansas City. I have a new job there." Not one he wanted, but he wouldn't share that information with her.

"Is that very far away?"

"Yes. It is going to take me a long while to get there, so I have to leave. I don't want to miss my train."

"I don't want you to go." Angelina stopped crying.

"None of us do, sweetheart, but Mr. Jay must go to his job. We can write him letters though."

"I don't know my address." Any contact would be painful for him and potentially life-changing for Mariah. He couldn't do that to her. Wouldn't do that to her.

"But you know mine." Angelina brightened.

"That I do." He smoothed out his trousers. "Goodbye, Angelina. Goodbye, Mariah. Both of you take care." A lump grew in his throat, and he hurried from the room before he lost control. Once in the hall, he drew in several deep breaths to regain his composure then hustled up the stairs to gather his few belongings.

While the kiss might not have been the wisest move he had ever made in his life, it would be an everlasting memory, one that would carry him through the lonely days that stretched in front of him. A beautiful moment with Mariah to cherish for the rest of his life.

He should make an effort to see Mr. Stanford before he disappeared, but time was marching on, and he didn't want to take the chance of missing his train. Instead, he hurried downstairs and asked one of the footmen to hire a carriage for him.

While he waited for the ride to take him to the station, Mr. Stanford caught up to him. "Where are you going?"

"I'm off to Kansas City, where I have a new job offer. A fresh start. And please, don't try to persuade me to stay." The temptation to do so might be more than he could bear.

"I won't. Heaven knows I'll miss you and will never be able to find another bookkeeper half as diligent as you. Thank you for what you've done. That took a great deal of courage. I knew. Deep in my heart, I always knew Hollis was in trouble and taking money, but I closed my eyes to the reality and dreamed up as many other possible scenarios as I could.

"But you made me face what was happening, and I thank you for that." Mr. Stanford shook Jay's hand. "You're a good man. Drop me a line if you get a chance. You'll be in my prayers."

"Thank you, sir."

Mr. Stanford walked away, and a moment later, the footman reported that the carriage had arrived.

Jay went to turn the doorknob when Mariah called to him. "Wait. Please, don't go."

Chapter Thirty-Three

Mariah held her breath as she waited for Jay to answer her call. He had been speaking to someone a moment ago about his carriage, and the door hadn't shut, so he must still be here. Had to be here.

She couldn't allow him to leave without talking to him once more. True, it would prolong the pain, but losing her best friend, the man she loved, wasn't going to be easy either way. She might as well take each second with him she could.

"Mariah." He spoke her name with a soft sort of reverence.

She moved forward. "Thank goodness I caught you. Can we speak in private?"

"I really have to go."

If only she could witness the emotions on his face instead of just in his voice. Perhaps they would betray his heart in a way his words did not. "Just a moment, if you will."

He sighed. "I don't have much time. Let's go to the parlor."

She waited for him to come beside her and guide her toward the room. "Please, shut the door."

"I won't risk your reputation."

"People will care more about my broken engagement to a man accused of embezzling thousands of dollars from his father."

"It was far more than that."

Mariah sank to the seat behind her. "I can't even comprehend it all. But that's not what I want to speak to you about. There has to be a way you can stay, a way that you don't have to leave. Mr. Stanford will do everything he can to protect you, I'm sure of it. He isn't angry with you but with his son."

"The situation is much more complicated than you understand."

"Don't treat me as if I don't have a brain. I know much more than you believe I do."

"That's not what I meant. All I'm saying is that there is more to the story, parts that I cannot tell you, reasons why I'm leaving that I am not at liberty to divulge." His voice cracked, and he cleared his throat.

"Why can't you tell me?"

"Please, don't press me on this matter, because I won't speak further on it. I should never have kissed you earlier. It was wrong of me to give you hope when hope was not mine to give. While I will miss you a great deal, this is for the best. Please, let me go. Be happy. Live your life to the fullest. Perhaps one day I will be able to purchase one of your paintings and remember this time with fondness."

He brushed a soft kiss across her cheek. "Goodbye, dear Mariah."

Too stunned to move a muscle, her breathing the only sound, she sat in the chair until the front door clicked shut. Then the dam holding back her tears burst open, and she wept and wept until her eyes ran dry and her handkerchief was soaked. Spent at last, she rose from the chair, her legs heavy weights, and climbed the stairs.

There had been no doubt it would be a messy affair to present Mr. Stanford with irrefutable proof that his son was a criminal, but she never dreamed she would lose Jay as well. Would this nightmare ever end? The fire had taken Mama and Papa and everything she owned, even her precious dog, and now Hollis had stolen true love from her.

"I'm sorry, but you may not go outside to play. It's far too cold." The new nanny's strident voice pierced the nursery walls so that Mariah could make out her words even in the hallway.

"But I want to play," Angelina whined. "Why can't I? Why can't I do anything? Everybody is going away, and I'm stuck here with you. I don't like you."

Mariah stopped on the threshold of her bedroom. Never in the two years she had known Angelina had the child ever behaved in such a manner. Yes, she got a bit cranky when she was tired, but who didn't? In general, she was easygoing and eager to please.

Abandoning her plans to rest in her room, Mariah knocked on the nursery door, which soon opened. "May I help you?" The nanny continued with her less-than-patient tone.

"Miss Mariah." Angelina almost knocked her over. "You came for me. I knew you would. You will be my mama, won't you? Nanny Banks is mean, and I don't like her. I love you."

Mariah squatted to Angelina's level and held her hands. "I heard you talking back to Nanny Banks. That wasn't kind of you at all."

"But it's true. She doesn't let me do anything."

"This is a strange day, and everything is out of sorts. Besides, Nanny Banks is looking out for you. It's very cold and windy, and she doesn't want you to catch your death. Right now, it's best you stay inside and be obedient. Things will go back to normal soon."

"But you're going to go home and leave me here, aren't you?"

Mariah chewed the inside of her cheek. "I'm afraid so. I miss my sister, and that's where I belong."

"You belong here with Father."

"Not anymore. I'm so sorry, but I promise to come visit."

"It won't be the same."

"No, it won't."

As she had earlier, Angelina hugged Mariah's neck and sobbed her little heart out. Mariah shed quite a few tears herself. She then stood, Angelina in her arms, hoping the nanny was still in the room. "Can you point me to the rocking chair?"

"Of course." The poor young woman, her voice softer now, led her to the seat and made sure she didn't fall to the floor with Angelina in her arms.

Mariah rocked the girl as she cried and cried, and she crooned a few hymns into Angelina's ears.

What a friend we have in Jesus,
All our sins and griefs to bear!
What a privilege to carry
Everything to God in prayer!

Oh, what peace we often forfeit,
Oh, what needless pain we bear,
All because we do not carry
Everything to God in prayer!

Have we trials and temptations?
Is there trouble anywhere?
We should never be discouraged—
Take it to the Lord in prayer.
Can we find a friend so faithful,
Who will all our sorrows share?
Jesus knows our every weakness;
Take it to the Lord in prayer.

Like the dawn over the horizon, the realization hit Mariah. These past months, ever since the fire, she'd been dry and shriveled inside. Questioned why God would allow such tragedy to befall her and the entire town of Peshtigo.

But she hadn't brought her cares and sorrows to the one who understood. She hadn't sought refuge or solace within her heavenly Father's arms.

After thirty minutes or so, Angelina's breathing slowed, and her arms went limp. She had fallen asleep. When she did, Mariah closed her own eyes and prayed, releasing all the questions of the past months, all the sorrow, all the fear, and gave it to the Lord. Only with His strength would she find the strength to go on.

Lord, You promised You would never leave or forsake me. I'm trusting You to be faithful to that promise. I don't understand and may never comprehend why the fire happened and why I lost Mama and Papa or why You took my sight from me. But Your ways are perfect and right, and I choose this moment to trust in You. Help me when I falter. Be ever with me.

"Let me help you carry her to bed," the nanny whispered in Mariah's ear.

Mariah opened her eyes and rose, and together they tucked Angelina under the covers. Mariah kissed her forehead before returning to her own room.

Leaving Chicago and getting away from the situation would soothe Mariah's frayed nerves, but nothing would ease the ache in her chest from losing Jay and Angelina.

Marinette, Wisconsin
Friday, March 15, 1872

After returning from Chicago, Mariah threw herself into her painting, at least as much as she could. Before the fire, Papa had always provided her with whatever she needed. Now that the supplies Jay had brought her were running low, she had no cash to purchase more.

She sat at her easel, the sun warming her face and hands. The canvas in front of her was her last. Then what would she do? She couldn't go to Lydia and John and request help from them. They already paid for all the food she ate.

Lydia and John were likely ready to start a family soon and would need the room in their home that Mariah occupied. Then what would happen to her? Where would she go? The loss of funds from the Stanford fortune left her in a precarious position.

So she did the only thing she could. She painted and prayed that the God she trusted to never leave or forsake her would provide a buyer for her art. One who would pay handsomely for the pieces. Even so, it wouldn't be enough to sustain her indefinitely.

She swirled her brush in the paint then touched it to the canvas. In her mind's eye, she once again saw the orange glow in the sky in the days prior to the fire. If only they had realized the mortal danger they were in. If only they had known, they might have fled.

Disaster, though, rarely announces its arrival. Rather, it bursts through the door and refuses to leave until it has finished ravaging everything and everyone inside.

A heat that rivaled that of the flames scorched her chest, and she worked to transfer the scene from her mind to the canvas. Her fingers twirled the brush and twisted it upward, the flames consuming the towering evergreen trees. The memory of the scent of burning pine tickled her nose and sent her heart racing.

By the time she dipped her brush into the turpentine and sat back, she was perspiring and exhausted. And finished with all the canvases Jay had brought.

A light tap sounded at the door. "Mariah?"

"Come in, Lydia." She wiped the brush on her old petticoat.

"Did you just paint that?"

"Yes." Mariah drew out the word.

"It's the best one yet, though terribly frightening. It's the scene out our window in October. I can almost feel the heat again, not to mention that the flames almost move on their own. I've never seen anything quite like this."

"Thank you. I relived it all, felt it in my bones as I created it. Perhaps you don't understand, but I transferred the image from my mind to the canvas. At least I hope I did."

"Oh, you most certainly did. It's brilliantly executed. You've come so far." Lydia hugged Mariah's shoulder. "Well done. What is next?"

"I have to sell these to pay for more supplies and to pay you for all you and John have done for me."

"You're my sister. What else would you have me do? You will not pay us back, as we are happy to be here for you. You have been a joy and comfort to me as much as I hope I have been to you."

Mariah spun around in the chair to face her sister. "I'm so glad. We only have each other. I've lost so much that if I didn't have you, I don't know what I would do. I would be utterly alone."

Someone pulled the bell at the front door downstairs. "Oh, I'm sorry to ruin this sisterly moment, but I have to see who that is." Lydia scurried from the room.

Mariah continued her cleanup until Lydia returned. "It's a solicitor from Green Bay, and he says he would like to speak to both of us."

"Both of us? I can't imagine what he might have to say."

"I can't either, but you had better come. Let me help you with your apron." Lydia undid the tie in the back, and together they headed downstairs.

"Do you think this is good news or bad?" Mariah gripped the railing with all her might.

"Let's pray it's good."

Together, they entered the living room, and Lydia made the introductions. "Mr. West, this is my sister, Mariah."

"Very nice to meet you. Your sister has explained your circumstances to me, and you have my sympathies for all the fire cost you."

"Thank you." The odor of pipe tobacco clung to Mr. West. "I appreciate your kind words. Why don't we all have a seat." Mariah took her customary place beside the fire in the chair with a needlepoint cushion.

"I'm here because I represent your late father's estate."

"Oh." Lydia couldn't hide the surprise in her voice. "I was under the impression that everything was lost in the fire."

"This is where it becomes a bit complicated, you see." Mr. West cleared his throat. "Your father ran a successful business in Peshtigo and the one here, and he did quite well for himself. When he came to me several years ago, he wanted to ensure that both of you and your mother—my sympathies there as well—were taken care of in the event of his passing."

Mariah scooted to the edge of her chair. "So there is money remaining?" That would solve so many of her problems. Perhaps there was enough that she could set up her own household and be independent.

"Unfortunately, there is not." Mr. West clasped his hands. "I'm afraid the news gets worse. Oh dear, I so hate to bring such tidings."

Lydia too must have been jumping out of her skin. "What is it?" she asked.

Mariah had the unnerving urge to whack the man on his back so he would spit out the words.

"Throughout the course of his life, your father borrowed a great deal of money, and now the creditors are calling in the debts."

Every ounce of Mariah's blood left her head and rushed to her toes.

Chapter Thirty-Four

~⌒○

"Can—can you repeat that, sir?" Surely Mariah hadn't heard the solicitor right.

"Your father was deep in debt at the time of his passing, and his creditors are calling in those debts."

For some reason, Mariah's brain couldn't make sense of what the lawyer was saying.

"How much? And how did he accumulate all of it?" Thank goodness Lydia was managing to keep her head.

"Thousands of dollars' worth."

Mariah shuffled her feet under her skirts. Had Mr. West forgotten the second half of the question. "How did he come to owe such a great sum?"

"I'm afraid the answer will be rather shocking to you ladies." Mr. West cleared his throat once more. "He had a gambling problem, and he borrowed money from the store to pay those losses, meaning he had to take loans to purchase the goods he sold."

The world spun around Mariah, the sensation heightened because she couldn't see. She grabbed for the chair's arms and held tight. No, this couldn't be. Papa would never do such a thing. Surely, Mr. West had the wrong Mr. Randolph. The man Mariah knew and loved all her life was not one to do this. Mama would have never stood for it. Never. If she'd had even the slightest of doubts regarding his integrity, she wouldn't have married him.

"Our father was a churchgoing man, Mr. West." Lydia somehow was staying calm. "He was opposed to such establishments in Peshtigo."

"I would like to see the proof you have for this accusation." Mariah had regained her composure. Lydia was right. Papa hadn't condoned such behavior. He would never be a party to it. The lawyer's accusations made no sense.

"I have copies of everything that I can leave with you for you to examine at your convenience. Perhaps your husband, Mrs. Stuart, will help you understand what you are reading."

"I'm quite capable, sir. I did attend school, and received high marks."

Good for Lydia. She would get this mess straightened out and make this solicitor see that he had made an awful mistake.

"Of course. I meant no offense. If you do run into any questions, I am staying at the hotel tonight before I head back to Green Bay in the morning. Don't hesitate to contact me either here or there if there is anything further I can do to assist you. You should note the due date of the various loans. Many are past due, and creditors extended grace because of the fire, but they now would like to be paid."

Once Lydia had seen Mr. West to the door, she returned to the parlor. "What do you make of all this, Mariah?"

"I—I am stunned. It's unbelievable. Nothing I would have ever thought Papa capable of. It can't be right. What Mr. West said isn't true."

"I would never believe it of Papa either. Let me see if I can make sense of this."

"Don't let that solicitor plant doubts in your head. You weren't bragging when you told him you always got top marks in school."

"I don't know how complicated this might be."

Only the ticking of the mantel clock broke the silence that fell over the room, sometimes accompanied by Lydia shuffling papers. It was in such times that Mariah missed Jay the most. Not only would his bookkeeping acumen come in handy, though Lydia was capable of handling it, but also his friendship. She could speak to him about such matters, and he would understand. Would calm her down.

She needed him to tell her that this was a big mistake. That Papa wasn't that kind of man. How could he go to church and serve on the council at the same time he visited saloons and gambling halls? It was inconceivable.

No letter had arrived from Jay. Nothing at all. It was as if he'd sailed off the edge of the earth. Perhaps he truly wanted to forget about the fire and her and everything else.

Or maybe there was a way to get a letter to him. Why hadn't she thought about this earlier? She couldn't take care of it now, but she would, as soon as possible.

A tapping of papers on the coffee table told Mariah that Lydia was done with her perusal of them. "What did you discover?"

"That Mr. West was correct. Father owes thousands of dollars to his suppliers." Every bit of bubbliness that often accompanied Lydia's words had disappeared.

Mariah's stomach dropped to her toes, and she squeezed her eyes shut. *No, Papa, no. How could you do this?* Had Mama known? She couldn't have, or it would have broken her heart.

Ever since she was small, Mariah had tagged along with Papa to the store. He allowed her to sweep the floors, which she believed to be great fun at the time. At the end of each day, he paid her with a piece of penny candy.

All the while, he wasn't the man she and the rest of the world believed him to be. "How could he have done this to us? To Mama?" Mariah's voice rose in pitch with each word. "Did he even think about how this would affect her if she ever discovered what he was doing? The precarious financial situation he put us in?"

Lydia sighed. "I don't know." Her voice was tinged with tears. "I don't know about any of this. I can't make my heart believe what my eyes showed me to be the truth."

And then another terrible thought struck, and Mariah went icy cold. "Can the next of kin be held responsible for those debts if the one who incurred them died penniless? There is no money in Papa's estate. Not a dime. It all burned in the fire."

"He did have a bank account in Green Bay, apparently, but what was in there has already been given to satisfy some of the loans. I don't know about the rest."

"I have no money to contribute. The only way I'm able to keep body and soul together is because of you and your generosity."

"And Mr. Stanford's."

"Yes, he did help as well, but that means of support is now over. You and John can't be expected to repay all of Papa's loans, can you?"

"I don't know. I suppose that is one question I do have for Mr. West. Would you care to accompany me to his hotel while I pay a call on him?"

"I don't know." She longed to curl up in her bed in their house in Peshtigo, fall asleep, and wake up to find this nightmare finally at an end. Or at the very least, to shut the door to her room here and weep for all she lost, including her most precious memories.

Then again, she needed to understand precisely what was going on and how they would repay Papa's loans. If they could. If they were even responsible. "Okay. I'll go with you."

Mariah shrugged on her winter coat and slid her hands into a pair of soft kid gloves that Mr. Stanford had included in the clothes he had purchased for her. She clung to Lydia's elbow as they made their way down the street to the hotel.

Mariah shivered, though her coat was plenty warm. "These past few months have been so unimaginable, this cannot be my life."

"I understand, at least a little. Papa, of all people, gambling. It's a good thing Mama isn't here to find this out. She would have had an apoplectic fit."

"Yes, it would have been enough to put her in her grave."

Lydia stopped, and Mariah with her. A team of horses jangled by. "Are you disappointed in Papa? Has this news made you think less of him?"

Mariah shook her head. "I don't know. It's all so new, I haven't had time to properly digest it. Those are questions you'll have to ask me again in a few days or weeks. Right now, I'm barely managing to keep from falling apart."

"My thoughts are a jumbled mess. I can't make heads nor tails of them. One minute, I'm furious with him. Another, I think this can't be true."

"I understand. I'm so grateful to have you. Where would I be without you?"

"Let's hope you never have to find out."

"I know I have to lean on God and trust Him, but it's so hard. Now I've even lost my good memories of Papa."

Lydia stood still. "At times, with everything that has happened, I wonder. Both Mama and Papa dying, you going blind. It has to be so much worse for you."

"I'm lonely and frightened. I miss Mama and Papa. I miss seeing my paintings and Jay and Angelina. And I miss the Lord. Since I can't read my Bible, it's hard."

Lydia squeezed her hand. "I'm so sorry. I should never have had you come with me. You don't need another worry."

"No, I would rather find out and know what to expect than to have it hit me when I'm not anticipating it."

They arrived at the hotel, and the man at the front desk gave them Mr. West's room number. With Lydia once again in the lead, they climbed the stairs and knocked.

"Oh, ladies. I didn't know I would have the pleasure of seeing you so soon. Is there something I can help you with?"

"Yes, there is." Lydia continued taking control of the matter. "Perhaps we can find a quiet corner downstairs to have our conversation?"

"Of course. Let me grab my suit coat, and I will be right down."

Lydia secured them a spot that she said was as private as could be while in a public room, and Mr. West soon joined them. She filled him in on what she had gathered from the papers and also their question.

"My apologies for not explaining that fully. Because you were not cosigners on the debts and you are not the spouse but the children, you are not legally responsible for the loans your father incurred."

Mariah blew out her breath. "What a relief." At least that was one thing that had worked out well. "So if we don't owe the money, why did you travel all the way here to tell us about the debts?"

"The creditors, of course, may come looking to be paid, and I wanted you to be informed, to know ahead of time what might happen. I didn't mean to leave you thinking that you had to come up with that money. Those were your father's legal obligations, not yours."

They concluded their meeting, and Mr. West returned to his room, but Mariah stopped Lydia before they left the hotel. "There is another person staying here I would like to speak to, if you don't mind."

"Of course." Lydia took them to the front desk.

"May I help you again?"

"Yes." Mariah used her most polite, cheerful tone to soothe the man's shortness. "All I need to know is which room is Shawn Atkinson's. I appreciate the help."

The man provided them the information, and Mariah blew out a breath. For all she knew, Shawn may have found new accommodations in

Peshtigo. Now that the winter snows were melting, from what John had told her, new buildings were springing up like hyacinths. Lydia led the way. "Why do you want to see him? Wasn't he a friend of Jay's?"

"You answered your own question there, dear sister. I haven't had so much as a letter from Jay. If he has been in contact with anyone, though, it will be Shawn." She knocked on the door.

"Miss Randolph. What a nice surprise to see you. How are you doing?"

"I'm well, Mr. Atkinson, thank you for asking. I hate to take up your time, but I was wondering if you had heard from Mr. Franklin or if you had an address for him."

"Of course. Let me get it for you."

In short order, Lydia and Mariah left the hotel with Jay's address. "Why did you want that?"

"When we get home, I want you to help me write a letter to Jay."

"Oh, Mariah. You do love him, don't you?"

"I do. Very much." Her heart pounded as she made the admission. "I allowed Hollis to blind me with his offer to get my paintings in galleries and museums around the world. In the end, that wasn't what was important. I almost traded my soul for fame. Why? What would it have gained me but misery?"

"Jay is a wonderful man."

"He calls himself a bumbling fool, but he is the furthest thing from that. He is intelligent and wise and caring. Compare how he interacted with Angelina to the way her own father treated her." She swallowed away the growing lump in her throat, but she couldn't rid herself of the ache in her heart. She needed him, especially now.

"He was very good with her, and she adored him. I'm happy to help you with the letter."

"Thank you." Mariah might not be able to pour her heart out the way she would prefer, but she would at least be able to tell him she loved him and missed him. That would have to be enough.

They got to work as soon as they arrived home.

Dear Jay,

How I miss you. Life isn't the same without you around. The house is empty and quiet most of the time, and I can't look forward to you coming home from work and telling me about your day, about the world outside of my darkness.

I hope Kansas City is treating you well. I have never been there or heard much about it, so please write and tell me. Do you like your new job and the place where you are living?

I have painted on all the canvases you brought me. You should be here to give your opinion of them. Lydia likes them, but she's my sister, so she has to say that. You would tell me the truth. I always appreciated that about you.

Lydia is writing this letter for me, and so I had better close. I already said I miss you, but I truly do. It would be so lovely to have you here. Your leaving has left a void in my life that only you can fill.

With much love and great affection,
Mariah

Chapter Thirty-Five

CHICAGO, ILLINOIS
WEDNESDAY, JUNE 19, 1872

After a long, hot, dusty trip, Jay stepped off the train in Chicago. It was a far cry from the last time he had traveled in such luxury and comfort in Mr. Stanford's private cars. Because he had come to testify at Hollis' trial, there could be no whiff of favoritism on Mr. Stanford's part, no chance that it might appear Mr. Stanford was attempting to buy Jay's testimony.

When he had left Chicago, he hadn't dreamed of returning here, but since he had been subpoenaed, he had no choice. Thankfully, because of his job in Kansas City, he had the means to pay for his ticket and hotel.

What if Mariah had also received a summons? Would their meeting be awkward? Would she hate him for leaving her, for never answering the several letters she sent? He had passed along his greetings through Shawn. Nothing else that might give her a glimmer of hope of rekindling their relationship.

The city was rising from the ashes. All around, there was construction, the debris swept into Lake Michigan, expanding the size of Chicago, the buildings even taller now than they had been before. Soon it would be difficult to tell where the fire had scoured the place.

What did Peshtigo look like? Was there the same kind of progress being made on rebuilding the town? Had any of the businesses reopened? Were its remaining citizens moving into new homes, finally with roofs over their heads? Had they planted crops?

Perhaps in time it would be restored, maybe even rebuilt better with more stone buildings rather than ones constructed of flammable wood. Over the course of the years, the forest would regrow and maybe the lumber industry would boom again.

Funny how he lived in a large city with all the luxuries and conveniences it afforded but longed for a rough lumber town secluded in far northeast Wisconsin. Or maybe it wasn't the town he missed but some of its residents.

One in particular.

It would be awkward to see Mariah, to gaze on her beautiful face.

He had done something though. Something a little brash and daring. He had written to her sister via Shawn and asked a favor of her. That was why, as he settled into the carriage that was to take him to his hotel, he held on to the brown-paper-wrapped package. One of Mariah's paintings that Lydia had sent him.

He instructed the carriage driver that, before dropping him at his hotel, he should take him to the same gallery he had visited just after the fire. Soon they pulled up to the establishment, an imposing brick building with the gallery's name painted on the front window in gold lettering.

As he entered, a little bell chimed on the door, and a small man with a round face and rather befitting round glasses came from the back. "Good afternoon, sir. I am Mr. Horlick. How may I help you?"

"I would like to show you something, if you don't mind." Jay didn't give the proprietor time to answer but instead bent down and unwrapped the painting then held it up for Mr. Horlick to inspect.

The gallery owner gasped. "Oh, my. Did you paint that yourself?"

"No, I did not. If you have a moment, I would like to speak to you about this painting's creator, her other pieces, and where we go from here."

"Very good, sir. May I interest you in a glass of port or scotch while we discuss this?"

"No, thank you. If you don't mind, I would like to get down to business."

"A man who doesn't beat around the bush. I rather admire that. Come to my office in the back where we can be more comfortable."

Jay followed Mr. Horlick to the room on the right. Paintings sat in various places along the walls, and papers littered the top of his desk. Despite his neat appearance—his hair slicked back, his clothing immaculate and pressed—Mr. Horlick was none too tidy when it came to his workspace.

"Please excuse the mess and have a seat. Are you sure you wouldn't like a drink? Even a cup of coffee?"

"No, thank you."

"Tell me about the artist. He has a unique style."

"Actually, the artist is a woman, and she has a different style for a reason."

Mr. Horlick clasped his hands behind his head and leaned backward, but as soon as Jay launched into his story about Mariah, he sat up, his focus solely on Jay.

When he finished describing Mariah, Mr. Horlick shook his head. "I truly don't know what to say. This is quite remarkable. And you can attest that this is all true?"

"I know her personally and have for quite some time. As I said, I was with her the night of the fire, and I stayed at her sister's house following that, though I am now located out of state."

"Well, Mr. Franklin, here is what we can do."

"Excuse me, Miss Randolph?"

She glanced at the spot where the train conductor's deep voice came from. "Yes?"

"We are at the station. Let me take your handbag for you, and I will show you to the hotel's carriage. It's waiting just outside."

As she rose to her feet, she trembled, much as she had for the entire trip, from the time she left her bed very early this morning. She and Lydia and John had planned each aspect of this journey from beginning to end, ensuring that she would have the help she required at every step. So far, so good. She had managed to make it to Chicago in one piece.

Traveling alone was not what she considered fun. Not in the least. It was necessary though. She had been called to testify in Hollis' case, and there wasn't money for her and Lydia to come together. And if she arrived in Mr. Stanford's private rail car, that would be sure to raise eyebrows.

So here she was, holding on to a stranger, being led through the fire-damaged Great Central Station and to the carriage that was supposed to take her to the hotel. She had to put so much faith and trust into the hands of people she didn't know and couldn't see.

No. That wasn't true. She had to put her faith and trust in God. How easy to say. How difficult to do.

Perhaps He had taken her sight away for a reason, to teach her to rely on Him more than on herself or any of her senses or in man. When her life lay in ruins around her feet, though, it was difficult.

But she had done it. Almost. Her final destination lay a short distance away. The conductor handed her into the carriage, and she settled herself on the leather seat. "Take care now, ma'am, and you have a pleasant stay."

"Thank you, sir. You have been very kind."

He shut the door and, a moment later, the carriage jolted forward. They wound their way down the streets she couldn't see. Did they travel through the area destroyed by the fire that had ravaged this city? How were their recovery efforts coming?

When she had sat in John's wagon that morning on the way to the train station, they had gone through Peshtigo. The odor of freshly cut pine almost made her forget that anything had happened. Of course, that smell came from the boards brought in from mills in unaffected areas, lumber that was being used to rebuild the town.

Unlike Peshtigo, her life was at a standstill. She should have thought to bring some of her paintings along with her on this trip to show to different galleries around the city if she had time. That way, she could have made enough money to at least pay for the journey.

She was a burden to John and Lydia, and that had to change.

The carriage pulled to a stop, and soon the door opened. "Good afternoon, Miss Randolph. Welcome to our hotel. We have been expecting you. Allow me to help you down." The man's words were careful and cultured. Why had John and Lydia chosen this hotel? Could they truly afford this?

With his help, she alighted, and once on the ground, she had to reach up quite a distance to take his elbow. He must be rather tall. He led her inside, got her checked in, and took her to her room. The maid came inside with her, unpacked her trunk, and helped her get familiar with her surroundings.

Now all she had to do was sit in the chair in the room's far corner.

She had nothing else going on until her court appearance the next day. Thankfully, the evening was wearing on, so she didn't have too much time on her hands.

Because she hadn't eaten much on the train, she should put a bit of food in her stomach at least. The bell pull was next to the chair, so she rang it, and the same maid as before answered then showed her to the dining room.

The music of conversations floated around her as she waited to be served, but she sat at her table alone. Was this to be her life? Was it to be like this forever? Always a burden to her sister and brother-in-law, always alone because a man could never love a blind woman?

Of all things to take from me, Lord, why did it have to be my sight? I'm trying to trust You, but it is so difficult. So very, very hard. Help me to rely on You and You alone for all things. And please, ease my fears and my loneliness.

The clinking of silverware against china entertained her for a while, and the fragrance of roast beef and mashed potatoes had her mouth watering.

Someone bumped the table. "Excuse me. Is this seat taken?"

She almost fell off her chair. "Jay, is that you?"

"Yes, it is. How are you, Mariah?"

"Please, sit down." Her heart constricted as a long moment of silence passed.

"For a short time. You look well."

"I am. And yourself? I was worried when you didn't answer my letter."

"I'm fine. My job is occupying my days and sometimes my evenings."

Why was he so stiff and formal? Had time and distance cooled his feelings for her that much? "I imagine it must. Have you settled in well?"

"I have. Kansas City is a nice town."

The waiter brought her order and filled her coffee cup. She bowed her head to say grace then turned her attention to her meal. "Have you eaten?"

"I have, thank you."

After two bites, she set down her fork and dabbed her mouth with the corner of her napkin. "What's wrong?"

"What do you mean?"

"I sense a hesitation on your part, almost like you don't want to be here with me. Did I do something wrong? Have circumstances changed? I imagine you must have met a lovely young woman who has fallen madly in love with you."

"No, I haven't." He sighed. "It's like I said, I truly am very busy. Now that I'm the financial head of the company, it takes a great deal of my time."

"You had the chance to write a letter to Shawn."

"Just a note, really. Nothing much."

So she was unworthy of even a line? "I see." She returned to her meal, the meat tough and the potatoes lumpy. All of it sat and soured her stomach. "Please, don't let me keep you."

"Mariah." Now a bit of warmth infused that single word. "If you only knew."

"Knew what?"

In a snap, his tone changed once again. "Nothing at all. I should be going. If you'll excuse me, I suppose I will see you in court tomorrow."

"Have a good evening, Mr. Franklin."

Chapter Thirty-Six

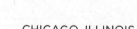

CHICAGO, ILLINOIS
THURSDAY, JUNE 20, 1872

Even though Mariah couldn't see Hollis sitting at the defense table in the just-constructed courtroom, his stare weighed heavy on her shoulders as she took the witness stand. She swore on the Bible to tell the truth then sat in the chair.

"Good morning, Miss Randolph." The prosecutor had a rather high-pitched voice for a man. "Can you tell the court your relationship to the defendant?"

"I was his fiancée."

"And now?"

"I broke off the betrothal on the first of January of this year when I learned of his embezzling."

"Have you had any contact with him since then?"

"No."

"How did you meet him?"

"He came into my late father's dry goods store, and they struck up a conversation and got along well. My father introduced us." At her words, her thoughts caught. Hollis and Papa hadn't met at the store. At least, that's not where they got to know each other well.

They had both accrued great gambling debts. They must have met at the saloon.

What other secrets had Papa hidden?

"Miss Randolph? Are you all right?"

"Quite, thank you."

"Shall I repeat the question?"

"Yes, please." Heat rose to her cheeks, and her hands shook, even though she clasped them in her lap.

"What was Mr. Hollis Stanford's financial situation?"

"I was not privy to his records, so I have no idea."

"Did he buy you jewelry and other trinkets?"

"Yes."

"Did he provide for you after the fire that devastated Peshtigo?"

"Yes."

The line of questions continued in the same vein for quite some time. She answered each to the best of her ability, just as the prosecutor had instructed her to do. At last, he finished, and she breathed out a sigh.

But the ordeal was not over yet. It was the defense lawyer's turn. As he stepped close to question her, the stomach-churning odor of cigars reached her. Not anything she cared to smell before the noon hour. Her mouth went dry, and she fought to keep down the small breakfast she had consumed.

"Good morning, Miss Randolph. I am attorney Bruce Abel. How do you do?" He spoke with a nasal tone and a strange accent. Perhaps he was from out east. It would figure, because Hollis was sure to hire the best lawyer in the country that money could buy.

"I am well, thank you."

"Let's pick up where the prosecutor left off, shall we?"

She nodded.

"Very good. Were you ever present when Mr. Stanford was gambling?"

"No."

"Did you ever see money exchange hands between him and a known gambler?"

Had she ever witnessed her father and Hollis handling cash? She bit the inside of her lip but didn't come up with anything. "No." That was her truthful answer.

"Did he spend lavishly?"

"He bought me expensive gifts, and after the fire, he and his father provided me with a new wardrobe, but I believed that was normal with someone who was born into a railroad-owning family."

"Is that what attracted you to the defendant? His wealth? All the things he could give you that you wouldn't get as the daughter of a humble shopkeeper in a backwater town?" The lawyer managed to keep his high-brow tone even while peppering her with questions.

"No, absolutely not."

"Perhaps it was his influence that you admired? He could make connections for you and get your artwork displayed in Chicago and New York and beyond."

"No. I cared about him as a person. He was engaging and attentive and intelligent. That all changed, however, when I lost my sight after the fire."

"How so?"

"He didn't visit me or his daughter. In fact, he left her in my care."

"You did testify that he purchased you a new wardrobe, correct? Did he provide for his daughter also?"

"Yes, but—"

"Just answer the question I asked, please, Miss Randolph, and nothing else. Were you to become the girl's new mother?"

"Yes." She bit off the rest of the answer to avoid another reprimand.

"Then didn't it make sense for her to remain in your care while he saw to his business both in Chicago and in Wisconsin?"

"Yes."

"Isn't it true that you fell in love with another man around that time?"

She swallowed hard and clasped her hands even harder. She had sworn on the Holy Bible to tell the truth. Admitting it in open court meant that Mr. Stanford would hear it, and it would break his heart. "Yes." She whispered her answer.

"I'm sorry, but I don't believe the entire court heard what you said. Did you fall in love with another man?"

"Yes, I did."

"Is that man in the courtroom today?"

"You forget, sir, that I am blind. I cannot see who is here and who is not here."

"Excuse me. Who is it you had a romantic relationship with?"

"We did not have a relationship."

"Did you declare your love for each other?"

"No."

"Did you ever express your love to him in another way? Say, in kissing?"

"Yes."

"Who was the man?"

"Mr. Jay Franklin."

"That same man that the court will find out later is the one who said he had proof of Mr. Stanford's embezzlement?"

"Yes."

"Yet you didn't break off the engagement until Mr. Franklin made public his accusations against Mr. Stanford."

"No."

"Why not?"

"Mr. Franklin shared with me his suspicions about Mr. Stanford, and I thought that by remaining close to Mr. Stanford, I might get him to admit the truth."

"It had nothing to do with your painting?"

"By that time, the fire had already occurred, and all my paintings were lost. I have created new ones, but I never told Mr. Stanford."

"A blind artist?" The attorney came close to snorting.

"Yes, I do manage to paint. I have developed a technique that allows me to do so."

"Have you had any contact with Mr. Hollis Stanford since the evening of January first of this year?"

"No."

"That is all."

The prosecutor had no follow-up questions, so she was allowed to leave the stand, drained of all energy. It took every bit of her strength to lean on the arm of one of the bailiffs and exit the courtroom. In this case, not seeing was a blessing.

She wouldn't see the venom in Hollis' eyes, nor the disappointment in Mr. Stanford's.

———◆◆◆———

Mariah sat on a bench outside of the courtroom, the seat hard, the wall she leaned against even harder.

She had done it. Testified to what she knew and remembered about Hollis. The man he had portrayed himself to be but who he likely never was.

So why had he been interested in her? The answer he gave to that question whenever he shared it was too pat. It wasn't the truth, like much of what came from Hollis' mouth.

Jay was on the stand now. From what she could hear of his testimony, he was going through the financial details—dry facts that she didn't understand and that bored her. Still, she sent up a prayer that his words would be effective and clear, that the jury would understand those facts and figures, and that justice would be served.

How simple life had been less than a year ago. Hollis was the man she had dreamed of marrying all her life. Her painting was going well, and she was anticipating gaining an exhibit in a prestigious gallery. She was about to become a stepmother to a sweet, precocious little girl. Mama and Papa were still alive, and Papa was everything a father should be.

How had one fire—one night—changed so much? There were entire families wiped out. Like Lucy and Henry, they were simply gone without a trace. Nothing marked that they had ever trod this earth.

If the fire had never happened, she would still have one of her best friends. Perhaps by this time, they would both be expecting children. How much fun that would have been, to raise them like siblings.

If the fire had never happened, her art career might have soared and she might be on her way to being famous.

Too many *ifs*. The trouble was the fire did happen, and it had robbed her of almost all the good in her life.

Only Lydia, John, Jay, and Angelina remained. The only points of light in her world of darkness.

No, that wasn't true. Through everything, God had remained faithful, even in the losses. She had clothes on her back and a roof over her head. People who loved her. Not all those who had loved her before the fire, but some of them.

Even if He would have stripped away everyone and everything from her, she would still have Him.

And that was enough.

She was so lost in thought that the opening of the door beside her startled her. It took a moment for her heart rate to return to normal.

"Are you all right, Mariah?" Jay was beside her.

"Yes. Why do you ask?"

With his finger, he wiped away moisture from her cheek. "You're crying."

She touched her face and found it was damp. "I didn't even realize it."

"What has you so upset?"

"I was thinking about what life was like a year ago and how much it has changed since then. I've lost my home, my career, and my parents. I've even lost my unsullied memories of my father."

"Yes, all of that has been difficult." She heard him gasp. "What do you mean, you've lost your unsullied memories of your father?"

She shook her head. "Not here. Can we perhaps go to dinner and talk? Really talk as friends?"

At her request, he stiffened. "I suppose that would be fine."

"Thank you."

He helped her to her feet, and together they left the courthouse. It was a short walk to a nearby restaurant, and soon they were seated at a table not too far from the door. That was what she deduced from the air that blew across the back of her neck from time to time.

Jay assisted her in choosing her meal, and he ordered for both of them. "It's good to see you. Are you here on your own?"

"I am. Mama would have a fit knowing I traveled by myself, but there was no one else. It was too expensive for Lydia or John to accompany me, so I had no other choice. Every part of my travel was well planned, and we telegraphed ahead so that there was someone at each step of the journey to take care of me."

"Good. I am glad to hear that."

"How is your job?"

"There's nothing wrong with it, though there is a great deal of pressure with it. I'm not used to operating all the finances of a company."

"I have no doubt you are brilliant at what you do. You are missed in Wisconsin."

"I miss it there as well."

The waiter brought their plates, and the salty sweet fragrance of broiled chicken wafted to her. Jay said grace, and she tucked into her meal.

"Will you now tell me what you meant about your father?"

She sipped her water and wiped her fingers on the napkin in her lap. She had worked so hard to learn to do such small acts without her sight. "It is awful, Jay, just awful. When I found out about Papa, I wished so much you were there to be a friend and to help me make sense of it all." Her throat burned.

"What did you discover, Mariah?"

The way he asked the question, the emphasis on the word *did*, was strange. Like he knew about it. "Is there something you need to tell me?"

"Who told you?"

"You knew? You knew and didn't let me know? How could you do it?" Her breathing was ragged. "Why, Jay, why? I thought you were one of my very best friends, the one person who wouldn't lie to me."

"I didn't lie. I only found out about it right before I left for Kansas City. In fact, it's why I left."

"Are you a gambler as well?"

"What?" The question came out an octave higher than his usual pitch. "Of course not."

"Then how did you find out?"

"Your cousin had the information I needed to expose Hollis. He's the one who sent you the note at the very beginning. I begged him to take the proof to the authorities himself, but he refused. The only way he would give it to me was if I left town and you. If I didn't, he threatened to tell you about your father. I wanted to protect you. This was all about keeping you from finding out. From being hurt and losing your good opinion of your father."

"How did my cousin know?"

"He said your father had come to his father asking for money to cover his debts."

Now her tears fell in earnest, and she dabbed them away with her napkin. "What else is there that I don't know?"

Chapter Thirty-Seven

~~~~~~~

Mariah sat beside Jay inside the courtroom, which, judging by the general din and the heat, was packed. The jury had reached a verdict, and every muscle in Mariah's body was tense.

"All rise."

The judge was entering, and so Mariah came to her feet.

"You may be seated."

Again, she did as instructed. Half a lifetime might have passed before the judge received the verdict from the jury foreman and read it.

Hollis was guilty.

She slumped in her seat. Guilty. What should have brought her joy did not. Poor Angelina. She had never known her mother, and now her father would be ripped away from her as well, through his own actions. Not only would Hollis be sentenced because of his crimes, Angelina would be too.

Once the jury was dismissed, so was the rest of the courtroom. Jay guided her into the bustling hallway, voices ringing off the walls of the brand-new courthouse resurrected from the rubble.

"Miss Randolph, Mr. Franklin, please wait." Mr. Stanford called to them from down the hall.

They stopped. In her mind, she imagined him snaking his way through the crowd to them. What must he be going through? If he was angry, would he take it out on Jay? He wasn't that sort of man, but she had once thought Papa incapable of what he had done.

"I'm so glad I didn't miss you." Mr. Stanford was out of breath.

"My condolences for what you must be going through." Mariah shook her head. "I wish it didn't have to be like this. How is Angelina holding up?"

"We told her, of course, that her father might go to jail for taking money that didn't belong to him. Now I have to return home and inform her that her father will be imprisoned for some time."

"Please, give her my love."

"Stop over tomorrow and say hello to her in person. She asks about you all the time, and she will especially need you right now."

"I will. I couldn't visit the city without seeing her."

"And Jay." Mr. Stanford thumped him on the back. "What you did wasn't easy, but it was right. I admire your courage in standing on your moral principles. While I may not have done right by Hollis, you are a fine young man. I would like to think I had a little to do with that."

"You did, sir, you did. I never meant for you to get hurt in the process."

"After my wife died, I went into deep mourning and ignored my son when he needed me the most. Then, to make up for it, I spoiled him. Gave him anything and everything he wanted. He grew used to that, and when I made him work for it, he turned to gambling and then to stealing when that wasn't lucrative enough."

Mariah touched Mr. Stanford's arm. "You did the best you could. No one could ask for more than that."

"Thank you, my dear. I do appreciate your kind words. Rest well tonight. I hope to see you both in the morning." Mr. Stanford kissed her on the cheek then left them.

"I hope you don't mind. . ." Jay guided her through the less-crowded hallway. "Before I take you back to the hotel, I have one stop to make."

"If it's easier, I can hire a carriage to deliver me."

"I worry too much about you traversing the streets of the city alone."

"And sightless."

"No, you have proven yourself quite capable in that regard. I will be more at ease if you are with me."

She shrugged. "I have nothing else to do today except arrange for my train ticket home and send a telegram to John and Lydia so they know when to expect me."

"I can help you with that as well. Let me get a carriage, and we can be off."

In short order, they were in the conveyance and on their way to. . . ? "Where are we going?"

"I just have a bit of business to attend to. It won't take me long."

"Can you describe the city for me? What does it look like now, all these months after the fire?"

"It's a city that is rediscovering itself and reimagining itself. All the rubble is gone, and there are new buildings everywhere. Some are reaching many stories into the sky. In the end, I imagine it will be even more imposing than before the fire."

"That's quite something. They are far ahead of Peshtigo, from my understanding. Lydia gave me a description of the village as we drove through there earlier this week."

"Ah, here we are." The carriage pulled to a stop. "Come on."

"Oh, you didn't want me to wait here for you?"

"No, I would like it if you came in. Do you mind?"

"Where are we?"

"It's something of a surprise I have for you."

"For me?"

"Yes. If you don't mind."

She slid across the seat, and Jay helped her down. He led her up a walk and into a building, a bell jingling overhead as she entered.

There were no bustling crowds, no odors strong enough for her to identify. All was quiet.

"Ah, Mr. Franklin. How pleasant to see you again. And this must be Miss Randolph."

She glanced at Jay and raised an eyebrow, not wanting to ask aloud where they were and what was going on.

"Miss Randolph, may I introduce you to Mr. Horlick, owner of the Horlick Art Gallery."

Though a thousand questions swirled in her head, she smiled and shook the man's hand. "I'm pleased to meet you."

"Not as much as I am to make your acquaintance. Ever since Mr.

Franklin told me about the blind artist who painted such a brilliant piece, I couldn't wait to be introduced to you."

"You have seen my work? I don't understand." She huffed out a small breath.

Jay squeezed her hand. "Lydia helped me pick out one of your paintings, and she sent it to me. I brought it with me and showed it to Mr. Horlick. He was very impressed by your work."

"So impressed that I would like to feature you in our gallery. We will plan a grand opening reception that is sure to be the talk of the city. Your piece is remarkable."

"All of them? How do you know what they are like?"

Jay answered this question. "What you don't know is that Lydia shipped the rest of your paintings on the train with you and had them sent here just in case Mr. Horlick liked what he saw in the one I brought with me. So he has had them for a few days and has had a chance to peruse all of them."

"May I say: they are stunning. No one will believe that a blind painter created them. That is why they will cause such a stir, and I have no doubt we will sell them in short order."

"Oh, Jay, what can I say?" For the second time that day, her tears threatened to flow. "This is amazing."

"You didn't need Hollis in the end. You did this on your own."

"With your help."

"I merely walked into the gallery. Nothing I said made a difference."

"He is correct. You, young lady, have a rare talent that speaks for itself. All I needed to see was that one painting, and I knew I had to feature you. What do you say?"

"Yes. Of course I say yes. This is tremendous. Thank you." Happy butterflies danced in her stomach. Was it really true? Was it happening to her? It might be a dream she would wake from, but she would enjoy every minute of it while she could.

They spent the next hour or so going over some of the details and drawing up a contract that stipulated how she and Mr. Horlick and the gallery would split the proceeds of the art show. When he quoted prices on some of the pieces, her mouth fell open, and she was rendered speechless.

"Believe in yourself, Mariah," Jay said. "I always have."

If she could have leaned over and kissed Jay in that moment, she would have.

———— •• ————

Jay couldn't keep the smile from his face. The art gallery surprise for Mariah had gone better than he had dared to hope. Now they sat together in the carriage, headed toward his next surprise, fingers intertwined.

God bless the solicitor who had broken the news to Mariah about her father. Yes, it had hurt her, and for that, he was sorry. Jay had fled to Kansas City to spare her that pain. But the lawyer had, unknowingly, done Jay the biggest favor of all.

He had cleared all obstacles remaining between him and Mariah and their future together. No more threats. No more blackmail. Just skies as clear as the Chicago summer day that was hastening toward twilight.

"Do you know that you have made me the happiest woman in the world?"

"Have I, Mariah?"

"You have. For a while, when my sight didn't return after the fire, my life might as well have come to an end. I questioned why God allowed me to live. But you, in more than one way, have given it back to me. I can paint, and now I am to have a gallery exhibition. Horlick Gallery is one of the best known and most respected in all the city."

"Really? I didn't know that. God led me to the right place at the right time, didn't He?"

"Yes, He truly did. I will forever be grateful to you for making my dream come true."

Jay prayed that he would be able to make more than one dream come true.

The carriage wound its way through the city streets, vying for space on the road with other conveyances—buggies, horses, and wagons—as well as pedestrians. All around, life went on as it always did, a testament to the resilience of the human spirit and the goodness of the Almighty.

He turned to Mariah, her profile soft against the early evening light. Her hair was done up in a simple style, and she was more beautiful than ever. It suited her. Soft pink colored her cheeks and her lips. How was it that he dared to love such a gorgeous woman? Even more perplexing was that she loved him too.

The carriage driver pulled to the side of the road, and Jay assisted Mariah in alighting. "Do you know where we are?"

She stood still for a moment and lifted her face. "I hear seagulls calling to each other and waves lapping at the shore, so my guess is that we are at the lake."

"You are correct. Very good detective skills, Miss Randolph."

"Thank you. The question that remains in my mind is why are we here?"

"I have another surprise for you."

"Another one? How many can I take in one day? So far, all of them have been good. Hollis was convicted, and I am getting my own art show. Is this one as nice as those?"

"It's even better."

"That's impossible."

"Wait a few minutes, and then you can tell me what you think." He led her onto the sand, the ground soft beneath his leather shoes. Here and there, families were scattered, children running to and fro in an attempt to get their kites in the sky. Couples sat on blankets and stared over the glistening water.

She laughed. "There is so much joy in this place it's almost palpable."

Yes, there was. He aimed to make it even more joyful. He held her by the hand and turned toward her. "Do you know how happy you have made me? That you care for such a bumbling, fumbling fool is amazing. I am so blessed to know you and to love you."

"I feel the same way. When I think about how close I came to ending up in a loveless, faithless marriage, I shudder. You are the opposite of Hollis in every way, and you are certainly not a bumbling or fumbling fool, or any kind of fool for that matter. I love you with all my heart."

He cleared his throat. Hopefully she didn't notice how much his hand sweat as he held hers. "A week ago, I couldn't see a way in which we would ever be able to be together. Now, God has worked out His perfect plan, and it is amazing. I promise to spend the rest of my life making you as happy as I can and loving you with all that I have if you will agree to be my wife."

"I am the most blessed woman in the world to be loved by such a wonderful man, one who stands by me no matter what. You saved my life that horrific October night. You gave me back the gift of painting. You even tried to protect me from finding out about Father." Her smile outshone the sun.

"Is that the answer to my previous question?"

"It is. Yes, I will marry you."

Right there, on the beach, he claimed a kiss from her.

Chapter Thirty-Eight

CHICAGO, ILLINOIS
SATURDAY, JUNE 22, 1872

The carriage bumped over the streets as it made its way to the Stanford mansion. Inside, Mariah sat beside Jay. She had yet to return to earth from the clouds after becoming engaged to this wonderful, wonderful man.

He leaned over as if to kiss her, and she pushed back against him. "What are you doing?"

"I am trying to kiss the woman I am going to marry."

"Someone might see us."

"People saw us yesterday on the beach. Besides, we are in a carriage."

"No more until our wedding."

"Oh, Miss Randolph, then it had better be a very short engagement."

She smiled at him and crossed her arms over her chest. "I think that could be arranged."

He leaned in for another attempt at stealing a kiss but, just then, they pulled up to the Italianate mansion. "Saved by our arrival."

Jay pecked her on the cheek then moved to assist her in alighting.

"You, Mr. Franklin, are a thief."

"Then make an honest man of me."

They were still laughing when Wilson opened the door and showed them to the parlor. "It's good to have both of you back."

"Thank you, Wilson." Mariah settled on the couch, the feel of the room familiar.

Just a moment later, Angelina burst through the door. "Miss Mariah, Mr. Jay, you came to see me." She ran to them, the heavy footsteps of the nanny coming after her. Angelina wriggled to position herself between them.

"Hello, sweetheart." Mariah hugged her. "How are you doing?"

She sagged against Mariah. "I'm very sad about Father. By the time he gets out of jail, I will almost be grown up. And you and Mr. Jay are going to leave too."

"Before we do"—she squeezed Jay's hand and got a squeeze in return—"we have some very exciting news for you."

"You're going to move to Chicago. Am I right?" Angelina bounced on the couch.

"No, I'm afraid not."

"Then it's not very good news."

Jay chuckled at this but covered it up with a cough. "Miss Mariah and I are going to get married."

"You are?" Angelina squealed.

"Yes." Mariah nodded. "Maybe your grandfather will bring you to Wisconsin for the wedding."

"Ah." Mr. Stanford's voice came from behind them. "There is to be a wedding?"

Mariah nodded.

"Then I would be happy to escort my granddaughter to the ceremony. I'm so pleased for both of you. You have my most sincere congratulations."

"Thank you, sir." Jay rose and shook the older man's hand.

"Where will you live? Kansas City?"

"If you wouldn't mind, sir, I would like to come back and work for the railroad. I miss my job, and of course, the most amazing woman is in Wisconsin."

"I would be delighted to have you return to my employment. We can talk about a new position and a pay raise for you, but all in good time. Nanny Banks, would you please take Angelina outside for a little fresh air?"

"I want to stay with Miss Mariah. Can't she come with me?"

"Later, darling. Please do as I have asked you and go with your nanny for a while. We won't be long."

Angelina shuffled her feet but did leave the room with the nanny. Mr. Stanford shut the doors behind them and then came and sat in front of Mariah and Jay. "The news of your engagement is the best word I've had in a long while, and it solidified an idea I've had in my mind for a time, in the eventuality that Hollis would be convicted."

Mariah smoothed her skirt. "I'm relieved that you aren't upset with me."

"How could I be? You are as dear to me as a daughter, and your happiness is my happiness. Of course, I would have loved to have had you for a daughter-in-law, but it would have been a terrible match. I'm afraid you wouldn't have been happy with Hollis."

Though she hadn't seen it at the time, Mr. Stanford was correct. She may have had material wealth, but she would have been miserable. Jay did well enough, though he possessed nowhere near the income of the Stanfords; but it was their love that would make them rich. How many dollars they had made no difference.

"Anyway." Mr. Stanford slapped his knees. "Without father or mother, Angelina is left here with an old man and a nanny. Neither of us can keep up. There is no one left on her mother's side either, poor tyke. So I have a proposal for you, made possible because of your upcoming nuptials. I would like for you to take Angelina and raise her."

Mariah's mouth fell open, and she blinked several times. "I'm sure I didn't hear you right. You want us to raise Angelina?"

"You heard just fine, my dear. I have watched you over this past year as you have interacted with my granddaughter. She adores you, and I would say the feeling is mutual."

"Of course it is. I love her like she is my own." Mariah's voice caught on the last word.

"And Jay?"

He cleared his throat. "She is an amazing little girl."

"And active and a handful and too precocious for her own good." Mr. Stanford chuckled. "Take some time and think about it. Let me know when you've come to a decision." He leaned forward to rise.

"Sir, please don't leave." Jay rubbed his thumb over the back of her hand. "What do you think, Mariah?" Though she couldn't make out his features, she didn't need to in order to know what he was asking her. She nodded.

Jay returned his attention to Mr. Stanford. "My fiancée and I have discussed it, and we would be happy and honored to raise Angelina. Would you expect us to live in Chicago?"

"I won't dictate your lives, though I would like for you to be in charge of my operation in Northeast Wisconsin."

"That would suit me just fine."

"I do hope, however, that you will allow me to be a frequent guest in your home and that you will travel to Chicago as often as possible so that I may see my granddaughter. I don't want her to forget about me."

"Of course." Mariah's heart swelled. "You will always be important to us."

◆◆

Monday, June 24, 1872

Angelina skipped toward the train car as she clasped one of Mariah's hands and one of Jay's. "I can't believe you are going to be my new mother and father and that I get to live with you in Wisconsin."

"We have to get married first." Mariah worked to temper Angelina's enthusiasm, though she and Jay had agreed that they would wed as soon as they could make the arrangements and find suitable accommodations.

"But then you will be my mother and father, and I will be the happiest person on earth."

They came to the private train car that Mr. Stanford had arranged for them, Johnson waiting to welcome them on board. Before they climbed the steps, Angelina tugged on Mariah's hand and pulled her to a stop. "Can I give Grandfather one more hug?"

Mariah was about to become the mother of a truly wonderful little girl. "I think he would like that very much."

Angelina turned to Mr. Stanford. "Goodbye, Grandfather. I'm going to miss you. I wish you could come with us."

"I will miss you very much, but you are going to have such a happy life with Miss Mariah and Mr. Jay." His voice was deep with emotion. "May I come and visit you sometimes?"

"Yes, yes! That will be the best. And I can visit you too, can't I?"

"Of course you may. So then, this isn't goodbye. Until we meet again, my sweet Angelina."

"Until we meet again. I like that better than goodbye."

"One more hug, and then it will be time for you to get on that train. You don't want it to leave the station without you."

"That would be the worst."

Angelina released her grip on Mariah for a moment before grasping her hand again and climbing aboard.

They entered the car and got comfortable on the plush seats. As the train chugged from the station, Jay reached over and took Mariah by the hand. "Are you ready for the rest of your life, my dear?"

"Very much so. When the fire burned away everything I treasured, I never imagined God would restore my life and then some." She was a very loved and blessed woman.

And just this once, she allowed Jay to kiss her.

Author's Notes

When the Sky Burned is a book I've wanted to write for a long time. In fact, I did write it back in 2003. Trust me, you don't want to see that version of it. When Barbour Publishing put out a call for books about historical American disasters, I knew what I had to send them. From that, *When the Sky Burned*, a revamped version of my 2003 novel, was born.

While every student who has ever gone through fourth grade in Wisconsin knows this story (Wisconsin history is mandatory in that grade, and the Peshtigo Fire is part of that curriculum), not many outside the Badger State's borders know about it.

The summer of 1871—and, in fact, the winter and spring prior—was very dry in the Upper Midwest. Little rain had fallen, the last decent shower occurring in July. The railroad was coming through to Peshtigo and beyond to Marinette and to Menominee, Michigan. When the workers cut the timber for the line, they simply piled up the trees on the side. The virgin woods were dense, making clearing the woods difficult for farmers eking out an existence from the sandy soil, so they resorted to burning the trees on their property. All of this led to fires that burned that fall throughout Northeast Wisconsin.

Peshtigo was threatened on several occasions, including Sunday, September 24, 1871. Just at the end of Pastor Beach's fire-and-brimstone service at the Congregational Church, the whistle blew. The men battled all afternoon to keep the blaze from overtaking the town, and only a wind shift spared Peshtigo that day.

The town of Peshtigo, with an estimated 1,700 residents in 1871, was a booming lumber and woodenware village, and that growth was expected to continue when the rail line reached it. Lumberjacks and immigrants came and went on a regular basis. Despite having four churches, the town boasted a number of saloons that were frequented by the jacks on the weekends. Because of the almost-constant operation of the sawmills, Peshtigo was littered with sawdust that covered the streets and walkways. Piles of lumber were stacked outside the sawmill, and barrels, bowls, and other woodenware items sat outside the woodenware factory.

All this combined was a disaster waiting to happen.

And disaster did strike on the evening of October 8, 1871, at approximately the same time as the Great Chicago Fire. Many survivors reported a great rumbling like that of a train as fire rolled into town. The wind was enough to lift homes from their foundations and toss them in the air, where they burst into flames. A strong cold front was passing through the area at the time, so it is possible that the fire was carried along by a tornado. It's also possible that the fire created its own weather phenomenon that resembled a tornado.

Whatever the case, the safest place that night would be the river, though many died there from hypothermia or from breathing the noxious fumes. Unfortunately, many didn't make it that far and were burned alive. The firsthand accounts are gruesome. For somewhere between five and six hours, the people in the river continued to dunk themselves under the water in an effort to keep from bursting into flames. Slowly they emerged, only to find the entire town and surrounding countryside reduced to ash.

The injured were taken to various places. Some went to Green Bay, while others were taken to locations in Marinette, including Dunlap House. What I describe is a later version of the building and not what would have been there at the time of the fire. Other than the description that there was a large ballroom on the second floor, there is no other account of what the building looked like in 1871, so I used my artistic license to create it.

Though Marinette was in the direct path of the fire, God spared the town that night. Many of its residents took the precaution of fleeing to a boat, the *Union*, which was moored on Green Bay at the edge of town, and spent the night there. Some of the outskirts of the town were burned, but the majority of Marinette escaped unscathed.

While the Great Chicago Fire was horrific enough in itself, it didn't compare to the losses sustained in Peshtigo and the outlying Bush. About three hundred perished in Chicago; anywhere between 1,200 and 2,400 died in Peshtigo. The true toll will never be known because the fire reduced some bodies to nothing but a thimble full of ash.

I do reference the rumor of Mrs. O'Leary's cow kicking over the lamp and starting the fire in Chicago. It was a rumor that started immediately after the fire, but there is no truth in it, though the fire does appear to have started in the vicinity of the O'Leary residence.

Father Pernin was a real person, and much of what I recorded about the time before, during, and after the fire comes from his account. He did dig a hole to preserve the items used in the mass, but his shovel was very small. He did carry a number of people to the river as they stood in shock on the riverbank, and he dunked them underwater to save their lives. He tried early on to leave the water but burst into flames. Thankfully, he wasn't seriously injured, though his eyes did swell, leaving him blind for a few days. He was greatly affected by the fire and left Peshtigo soon afterward.

Mr. Stanford was based on William Ogden, an actual railroad baron of the time. He was also the first mayor of Chicago and the richest man in the city. All the other characters in the book are products of my imagination.

It is true that William Odgen was anxious that the fire in Peshtigo not set back his plans to extend the railroad line. Despite losing his house in Chicago the same night, he pushed forward with the building of the railroad. Because they didn't have to clear the timber, the building went quickly, and the line reached Marinette by Christmas. After losing his home, he returned to New York and died there a few years later.

The fire halted the booming of Peshtigo. Today, it is a small village in Northeast Wisconsin with just over 4,000 residents. It is known, as you would guess, mostly for the fire. In fact, there is a museum there and monuments in several cemeteries honoring the dead.

Acknowledgments

I am so grateful to Becky Germany, Shalyn Sattler, and the entire team at Barbour Publishing for allowing me to write this book after wanting to for twenty years. Hopeful authors, don't throw away those early manuscripts. You never know when they might come in handy.

Thank you, as always, to my fabulous editor, Ellen Tarver. It is such a joy to work with you. Thank you for your quick and thorough work on this. It has come a long way because of you.

Tamela Hancock Murray, you are the best agent a girl could want. Twenty years ago, you were my critique partner on this book. Look how far I've come. I hope I've done you proud.

To Jenny, my current critique partner, thank you for looking this over and catching so much of what I missed. You spur me to be better. I couldn't have done it without you.

I owe a great deal to the people at the Peshtigo Fire Museum. Though I was there many, many years ago to research this book, I do appreciate all you did for me in helping me get the details right. Thank you for preserving what you have and for allowing the outside world to know what happened in your corner of Wisconsin that day more than 150 years ago.

To Doug, Brian, and Alyssa, my amazing family. Thanks for interrupting our vacation all those years ago so that I could spend time learning everything I could about the fire. And thanks for putting up with me telling you all about it when you hit fourth grade! Alyssa, I'm not sure you even remember our stop there, but you were a trouper.

And as always, all praise, honor, and glory to the Lord, without whom none of this would be possible. We may not always understand His ways, but we can rest in the knowledge that He has a perfect plan for each of our lives.

Soli Deo Gloria.

Liz Tolsma is the author of several WWII novels, romantic suspense novels, prairie romance novellas, and an Amish romance. She is a popular speaker and an editor and resides next to a Wisconsin farm field with her husband and their youngest daughter. Her son is a US Marine, and her oldest daughter is a college student. Liz enjoys reading, walking, working in her large perennial garden, kayaking, and camping. Please visit her website at www.liztolsma.com and follow her on Facebook, Twitter (@LizTolsma), Instagram, YouTube, and Pinterest. She is also the host of the Christian Historical Fiction Talk podcast.